Praise for *The Fairest of Them All*

"Intricate, inventive, and charged with magic. Carolyn Turgeon masterfully clears the mists of fairy tale and legend to reveal the complex humanity that lies beneath the stories of Rapunzel and Snow White."

—Eleanor Brown, *New York Times* bestselling author
of *The Weird Sisters*

"Magical, mythical, and totally original, Turgeon's haunting story of Rapunzel and Snow White unfolds like a waking dream, with prose that shimmers like cut diamonds. About love, longing, and loss, it turns the fairy tale into something as provocative as it is profound."

—Caroline Leavitt, *New York Times* bestselling author
of *Pictures of You* and *Is This Tomorrow*

"Forget everything you know about fairy tales filled with glamorous princesses and happy endings. In Carolyn Turgeon's skilled hands, characters that have long been the bedrock of literature come to life, revealing their all-too-human desires and a mesmerizing, hidden darkness. Her body of work is already substantial and growing, which is good news for readers everywhere. *The Fairest of Them All* will move her into a larger sphere, worldwide. I loved this book from start to finish."

—Jo-Ann Mapson, author of *Solomon's Oak* and *Finding Casey*

"Turgeon reimagines two fairy tales to produce a lush, dark yarn. Her steadfast vision reveals the shadow and light battling in each of the characters' hearts."

—Margaret Dilloway, author of *How to Be an American Housewife*

"There are fairy-tale princesses like Rapunzel, who are lovely and compassionate and kind. And there are fairy-tale villainesses like Snow White's stepmother, who are ambitious and clever and wicked. In Carolyn Turgeon's brilliant retelling, however, good and evil are combined to create a fairy tale anti-heroine who could break your heart—and then eat it."

—Alisa Kwitney, author of *Token*, *Flirting in Cars*, and *Moonburn* (as Alisa Sheckley)

"*The Fairest of Them All* possesses the spirit of all great fairy tales—filled with brave hearts, twists of fate, and incredible transformations. Carolyn Turgeon honors the traditional stories of Rapunzel and Snow White, yet intertwines their lives in a way that gives the tales, as well as both women, new dimensions. The dark, sensual magic at work in this book will allure readers right to the shocking, beautiful end."

—Ronlyn Domingue, author of *The Mercy of Thin Air*

"To call Carolyn Turgeon's *The Fairest of Them All* a retelling doesn't seem quite accurate. This story of Rapunzel and Snow White may feel as familiar as it is thoroughly innovative, but it reads like an original—like the *real* story. Turgeon has managed to peel back centuries of dressing and sweetness and lace that have been heaped upon these characters. She has plucked them from their perfumed clouds and returned them to their primal form, to the unique women they were once, before their fairy tales diluted them. In gratitude, they sing from the pages, all full of suffering and longing and ferocious intellect. This is the Rapunzel I have always wanted to know."

—Jeanine Cummins, author of *A Rip in Heaven*

"How very lucky we grown-ups are to have Carolyn Turgeon's fairy tale to captivate us. What a joy to be delighted again by witches, princesses and kings—now all fleshed out and psychologically complex and compelling. Under Turgeon's deft hand, Rapunzel's and Snow White's tale is as beautiful as it terrifying. Enter into this enchanted forest and be enthralled!"

—M.J. Rose, author of *The Reincarnationist*

ALSO BY CAROLYN TURGEON

The Next Full Moon

Mermaid: A Twist on the Classic Tale

Godmother: The Secret Cinderella Story

Rain Village

THE FAIREST OF THEM ALL

CAROLYN TURGEON

A TOUCHSTONE BOOK
PUBLISHED BY SIMON & SCHUSTER
NEW YORK   LONDON   TORONTO   SYDNEY   NEW DELHI

Touchstone
A Division of Simon & Schuster, Inc.
1230 Avenue of the Americas
New York, NY 10020

First Touchstone trade paperback edition August 2013

TOUCHSTONE and colophon are registered trademarks of Simon & Schuster, Inc.

For information about special discounts for bulk purchases, please contact Simon & Schuster Special Sales at 1-866-506-1949 or business@simonandschuster.com.

The Simon & Schuster Speakers Bureau can bring authors to your live event. For more information or to book an event, contact the Simon & Schuster Speakers Bureau at 1-866-248-3049 or visit our website at www.simonspeakers.com.

Designed by Akasha Archer

Manufactured in the United States of America

10 9 8 7 6 5 4 3 2 1

Library of Congress Cataloging-in-Publication Data
Turgeon, Carolyn.
    The fairest of them all / Carolyn Turgeon.—First Touchstone trade paperback edition
        pages cm
    I. Title.
PS3620.U75F35 2013
813'.6—dc23
                                2013005232

ISBN 978-1-4516-8378-3
ISBN 978-1-4516-8379-0 (ebook)

To my mother, father, and sister

THE
FAIREST
OF
THEM ALL

PROLOGUE

I was the girl with the long long hair, trapped in the tower. You have no doubt heard of me. As a young woman I was very famous for those tresses, even though I lived in the middle of the woods and had never even been to court, not for a feast or a wedding or a matter of law.

My hair was like threads of gold flowing down my back and past the floor. If I didn't tie it up, it would sweep across the stone and collect dust like a broom. I could lean out my tower window and it would fall out like an avalanche, gleaming like the sun hitting the water. It was as bright as sunflowers or daisies, softer than fur, stronger than an iron chain.

Every night I took horsetail and aloe from the garden, spoke words over them, and boiled them and mashed them into a thin pulp, which I then combed through my locks to make them strong and healthy and almost impossible to break. I would sing, and inhale the rich scent, to make the work go faster. To this day I love that feeling, of fingers running through my hair, the weight of it as it falls on my back.

Poets and troubadours sang of my beauty then.

It was sorcery, that hair. Sometimes now I wonder if things would have been different, had I been plain.

It is a hard thing, not being that girl any longer. Even as I sit here, I cannot help but turn toward the mirror and ask the question I have asked a thousand times before:

"Who is the fairest of them all?"

The mirror shifts. The glass moves back and forth, like water. And then my image disappears, until a voice, like a memory, or something from my bones and skin, gives me the same answer it always does now:

She is.

I turn back to the parchment in front of me and try to ignore the ache inside. The apple waits on the table next to me, gleaming with poison. All that's left to do is write it down, everything that happened, so that there will still be some record in this world.

1

I was seventeen when I first saw him. I was drying herbs by the fireplace in the main house, as I sometimes did back then, enjoying the scent of the burning pinecones and wood, when I heard a knock at the front door. Loup, our cat, was curled up on the couch next to me, and our falcon, Brune, was perched on the mantel. Mathena was out back, tending the garden that grew behind the crumbling tower I lived in. The tower was a space of my own, and I loved sitting in the window, from which I could see the whole forest and even, on clear days, the king's palace in the distance, while I brushed my hair and sang to the sparrows that gathered in the trees around me. But on those late summer afternoons, when the air was just starting to chill, I found myself in the main house, stealing time by the fire.

Without even thinking, I got up and opened the door, assuming it was another lovelorn client come to tell Mathena and me her woes and get a spell to fix them. Instead I found myself looking into the eyes of the most handsome man I'd ever seen, dressed in rich clothes that were unfamiliar to me: a velvet tunic, a neat cap, an intricate sword stuck through his belt. His mouth was full and curved into a smile. He had sparkling eyes, grayish blue, the kind I'd only ever seen in cats, and there was a mischievous joy about him that made me like him instantly. No one had ever looked at me like that, either, like he wanted to devour me, and in that instant my whole body changed into something new.

When I say he was the most handsome man I'd ever seen, I have to admit: at that time, I'd barely seen any men at all.

You see, I'd grown up hearing about the dangers of the male portion of our race. Mathena had disavowed men altogether, and was quite convincing in her reasoning. "Men will ruin you," she'd say. "They'll drive a woman mad more surely than the plague. Just look at what's happened to Hannah Stout." I'd shudder, thinking of our once-beautiful client, nearly bald now from having ripped out her own hair, hair that had been lush and shining before her new husband ran off with his stepdaughter. Mathena had cures for love, like yarrow root, which could halt infatuations when added to bathwater, or elderberry bark, which could numb a heartache when boiled down and pressed against that most fickle organ. You could tell sometimes when a woman was suffering from love, from the cord twisting around her neck, from which the bark performed its duty.

Most of my experience with men came from the stories Mathena and I heard every day, from the women who sought out our cures. Men themselves did not consult us for ailments of the heart, especially as it was considered women's work to have a heart at all. Day in and day out, I heard tales of men seducing ladies, abandoning wives, abusing daughters. I'd sit and help Mathena dispense salves and teas and potions and think how strange it was that so many women succumbed to foolish notions, as if one man could make them feel full and complete, even when he was married to someone else. But I knew so little then. I had barely set eyes upon a man in all my seventeen years, other than the occasional troubadour or marksman—or group of hunters, sometimes accompanying the king—who dashed by, through the woods.

It was only the daughters for whom I felt real sympathy, back then. If it hadn't been for Mathena, I would have ended up like one of the bruised, tear-stained girls who showed up at our door. Once upon a time, Mathena had lived in a cottage next door to my mother and father, in the center of the kingdom. She kept a wonderful garden with a brilliant patch of rapunzel that my mother, who was with child and could see the garden from her bedroom window, longed for so much that she refused to eat anything else. She began wasting away, Mathena told me, until one day my father climbed over the wall into Mathena's garden to steal the rapunzel, trampling over all her carrots and cabbages in the process. He came back and back. Even after I was born, my mother cared only for the plant, which was never enough for her, and she'd take out all that need and frustration on me. When I was seven, Mathena rescued me from my parents and brought me to the forest and made a potion for me so that I'd forget everything that had happened before, all that I'd suffered at my real parents' hands. For that, I thought I'd be forever loyal to her.

Then there he was, this beautiful richly dressed man at my door, so close I could count his eyelashes, and I understood for the first time what all those spells and salves and magic teas and baths and candles were for.

I dropped the hollyhock in my hands. Immediately I was conscious of my unwashed face and ragged clothes, the cloth wrapped around my hair, which Mathena let me unloose only in the tower, so as not to attract too much attention from birds as we worked . . . the fire crackling in the background, which made me smell like smoke. I felt like a savage next to this man's clean velvet shirt and gleaming sword. I could feel my face grow red, and the heat seemed to come right from the center of my body.

"Good afternoon," he said, refusing to turn away despite how visibly embarrassed I must have looked. He took off his cap and bowed, though he watched me the whole time, that same impish smile playing about his lips.

"Good afternoon," I stammered. "May I . . . help you?"

Just then Brune flew from the mantel and to my shoulder, where she perched herself menacingly. The man looked from the bird to me and back again, and seemed more delighted than perturbed.

"Well, I feel a little awkward," he said. "But I was on a hunt a fortnight ago and I heard a young lady singing, and I was wondering. Well, I was hoping to find her." He paused, clearing his throat, looking down shyly and then back up at me. "I have not been able to forget that voice. That song."

I could feel my face flushing, as I remembered the hunting party passing, the way I'd sung out to them. I'd called him to me, I realized. I'd wanted to know who they were, where they were going; I'd been excited by the violence of the hunt. And here this man was, at my doorstep. My heart raced.

It did not occur to me that he might be feigning his own nervousness in order to woo me.

"Oh, yes," I said, finally. "I saw the banners, but I couldn't see your faces. I heard shouts and cries." I remembered, too, the song I'd been singing when I heard the pounding of the horses' hooves on the forest floor, how I'd aimed my song at them. Something I'd made up about the sparrows feeding their young. *Their hungry mouths, their hungry hearts, the glowing worms they rip apart.*

"It was you, wasn't it? Singing up in that tower? With that glorious hair hanging down?"

The way he said it made me feel as if he'd come upon me bathing naked in the lake. "Yes," I whispered, touching the cloth covering my hair now.

"Ah, I thought so the moment you opened the door, though you have hidden that hair away. Do you live here alone?"

The flirtatious, almost predatory note in his voice made me remember the stories and the warnings. My body tensed, and for a moment I wondered if he was going to push past me, into the house. Then he smiled, and I realized: *I want him to come inside.* It was a feeling I'd seen but never experienced, the feeling in those grieving women: *I want to be broken.*

"No," I said. "I live here with my mother."

"She's a witch, isn't she?"

"No!" I said. "Of course not." I knew enough to know that *witch* was a bad word, a dangerous one, especially with those who came from the kingdom. "At court, a woman can get killed for a word like that," Mathena had said.

"I didn't mean to offend," he said. "I heard stories, when I was inquiring about you."

"We only heal here, sir, we do not practice bewitching."

"I might have to argue with that," he said, raising his eyebrow.

I could not help but laugh at the funny expression on his face. "What is your name?"

"Rapunzel."

"Isn't that a type of . . . lettuce?"

"Yes," I said. "Though I've never seen it myself."

Just then, the back door opened and Mathena stepped into the room, her hands dirt-covered from the gardening, her dark hair damp with sweat. The sight of the man visibly upset her; I watched shock, then fear, pass over her face.

"Your Highness!" she said, falling into a curtsy. Brune left my shoulder for hers, her wings spanning out in warning.

I looked from Mathena to the man and back again, confused by her reaction.

Mathena rushed forward, causing Brune to fuss, and put her arm around my waist. "Excuse her, sire, she is just a country girl and does not know the royal manners."

"Oh, I am not yet a king, madame," he said, causing a blush to rise from Mathena's chest to her cheeks. "I am still subject to the rule of my father, as we all are."

I breathed in with surprise, and attempted to curtsy as Mathena had done.

"Of course," Mathena said, stepping in front of me. "It has been so long since I've been at court, I forget the proper addresses." She curtsied again. "I am Madame Mathena Gothel, and this is my daughter Rapunzel."

He bowed to us both. "Enchanted," he said. "And I am Prince Josef. You have a fine falcon, I see."

"Thank you," she said. She reached out her hand behind her, as if to make sure I was still there. To keep me there.

"My father is quite a passionate falconer," he said.

"Yes," she said, and now her voice was hard, cold, "and a very fine one at that."

I began to feel dizzy. Not only because of Mathena's behavior and the fact that there was a handsome prince standing before us, but because I had called him to me, using my own magic. I was sure of it.

"This is a charming house," he continued. "I sometimes wonder what other kind of life I might have had, in a place like this, for instance."

"I assure you it is much less exciting than your life in the palace. You would be quite bored here in the forest."

I watched this exchange with fascination. I'd never seen Mathena speak the way she was speaking now, or stand the way she was standing, with her spine straight, her shoulders back, her chin lifted. She seemed years younger, suddenly. I knew that she'd spent time at court as a young woman and was versed in the royal decorum, but she seemed more defensive than courtly. Her body had become a fortress holding me back, as if her arms had grown and were stretching out from wall to wall. She was doing everything she could to make me disappear behind her, much as I was trying to stay in his line of vision, and keep him in mine. Who knew when I would next see a man this close, let alone a prince?

"Perhaps," he said, ignoring her clipped tone, "if I did not have such delightful company. But if the lovely Rapunzel has not been to court, maybe it's time to bring her? The harvest ball will be taking place on the night of the equinox. I do hope she would like to attend."

I was equal parts astonished and delighted. A ball! Visions flashed before my eyes. Men and women twirling across a marble floor. And a palace—a place full of sunlight and diamonds and a richness I couldn't quite visualize but knew I craved. A blurred, bright idea, like a child's image of heaven.

"That is a generous offer," Mathena said, yet it was clear from her voice that she did not find it kind at all. She was usually not so rude, and I bristled with embarrassment. Of course, she was not usually addressing princes. Brune didn't help matters, jutting her beak forward and staring at him threateningly from Mathena's shoulder.

"Yes, thank you," I said. I craned my neck around Mathena and tried to look my most alluring. I reached up nonchalantly to move the cloth back so that he could see a swath of golden hair.

"You're both invited," he said. "And I hope you will each do me the honor of saving a dance."

"We'll try to attend," Mathena said, "though the harvest here promises to be very demanding."

He took Mathena's hand to kiss it, and then somehow managed to angle past her and take mine, which I extended to him. The moment he touched me, I felt it through my whole body, shooting out as if he had fire burning in his palms.

"I look forward to seeing you again," he said, looking straight into my eyes before turning back to Mathena. "It will be my pleasure."

"You're very kind," Mathena said, with the same sharp edge in her voice. He took a step back. I wanted to pinch her, force her to invite him in for tea.

"Well, thank you," he said. "I am pleased to have made your acquaintance."

He bowed to us, put his cap back on, and turned. I watched

him walk to a black horse draped in a velvet and silver harness, tied to a tree. Within seconds he was gone.

For a moment, I was not sure if it had even happened at all, or if I'd dreamed it. The woods sounded just the same as always: the birds in the trees, the leaves rustling, dropping to the ground.

And yet, everything was different. Just minutes ago, the room had seemed so calm, with its crackling fire and dirt, its rug-covered floors, the simple tapestries on the walls. Now, suddenly, it felt like the loneliest place on earth.

I turned to Mathena. She was trembling—with rage, or fear, or sorrow, I could not tell. Brune was leaning into her, as if to offer comfort.

"You cannot go, Rapunzel," she said, before I could speak.

"What?"

"You must forget this ever happened."

I stared at her. "But . . . why?"

With a small flick of her wrist, she returned Brune to her mantel. The bird stared down at us disapprovingly, then turned away. Mathena took my hands in hers and led me to where Loup was still sleeping on the couch. "Sit, and listen to me," she said. She reached up and pulled the cloth back down to my forehead. "You must forget that the prince ever came here. I cannot let you go to court, Rapunzel, not yet. The palace will ruin you."

What she didn't see was that I was already ruined.

"But he is a prince," I said, clutching at the words. They floated in front of me, like pieces of a shipwreck. "He . . . invited me. How can I not go?" I imagined running to the stable and untying our own horse, and following after him. But I was not yet that brave, and so I burst into tears instead. "He came here looking for me. It was like something out of a fairy story!"

"Only the kind where the maiden's hands get chopped off."

I had rarely seen her so upset, and she flashed and sparked with it, her brown eyes glittering. She stood and stalked over to the fireplace, stoking it with a branch. I watched her as she stabbed at the flames. Her hair whirled about her face, hung down in curls along her cheeks.

"It's not fair," I said. "I've been cooped up in the forest for so long. Why can't I see what life is like at court?"

She turned to me. "Someday, Rapunzel, you will have the life you long for. But not yet."

"Why not yet? He came here looking for me! I've been invited to a ball!"

"Because he is promised to someone else."

"I don't believe you," I said. A terrible burst of pride moved through me. I was young and beautiful. I had hair like sunlight. I had heard passing minstrels composing songs to my beauty, at the tower window as I sang. "You just want to keep me here," I said. "I will go to the ball and make him forget anyone else."

"No," she said. "I forbid you to go."

I stared at her in shock. We had never argued before, and she had never forbidden me something I wanted.

But I'd never wanted this.

"You can't do that," I said.

"I already have."

She stood over me, looking right into me. I looked away, but could still feel her eyes burning through me. Already I could feel myself waffling, my heart softening. Mathena *was* a witch—I had lied before, to him, when I said she was not, to protect the both of us—and for the first time she was turning her powers against me.

I leapt up. "You cannot control me," I cried. "You can't forbid me to go!"

I strode to the door, then turned back to her. She was so beautiful and majestic, even when I hated her.

For a moment we just eyed each other. I knew that something was changing between us then, and was tempted to go back and throw my arms around her.

Instead, like the child I was, I slammed the door behind me.

I stormed to the tower, stomped up the many curving stairs to my room. Until the year before, I'd lived with Mathena in the main house, but on my sixteenth birthday she'd let me move into my own little room in the crumbling tower with vines climbing up the side. She'd helped me make a colorful quilt for the bed, and given me one of her tapestries to hang on the wall, next to the old, oval-shaped mirror that hung by the hearth. I'd always loved that tower, where I spent many happy hours playing, sticking my head out of the window and letting my hair hang to the ground as if I were a girl in a storybook.

Little did I know then that it would become my prison.

I lay on my bed and stared at the stone walls, the tapestry with its images of peacocks and castles, the light that poured in through the one window and illuminated the late summer air. Outside, branches laced over each other like fingers. I caught a glimpse of my face in the looking glass and realized I was crying.

I thought back to all the ladies who'd sat in front of Mathena over the years, sobbing as they relayed their heartbreaks, and me watching them, fetching teas and dried herbs for Mathena while despising the women for their weakness. The peasant woman who was having an affair with her lord, the lady who was certain her husband no longer loved her, the rejected and weak and aching. I had not known any better. I was beginning to understand, now, the passions that had moved them.

I would go to the prince's ball, I decided, no matter what Mathena said. I would take the horse and go. All I needed was a gown. I marked the equinox on the stone wall, with the bit of rock lying on the trunk beside me: I had fourteen days. I would steal into Mathena's room and find something to wear. After she took me from my parents, she had packed everything she owned into trunks. These were my first memories: the two of us coming together to the forest and finding the old tower, the crumbling remains of a castle, her moving the trunks into her room, remnants from her other lives, her past selves. I'd sifted through her things—the fine gowns, the corsets and ribbons—with fascination. *She* had been at court once, and yet now, like mothers and would-be mothers everywhere, wanted to protect me from her own mistakes.

It was not fair.

All I knew was *this,* this stone cottage and this crumbling tower. My memory began in the forest: the call of birds, the howling of wolves, the way the wind rustled through the trees. The forgetting potion had erased all memory of what came before, the life I'd had in the kingdom. I remember how we came upon the ruins of the castle, the magical stone tower thrusting through the forest canopy.

How I raced up the crumbling stairs and into the round room at the top, twirling around with delight. There'd been a girl in the room with me, with hair like sunlight, and I'd moved toward her, moved away, delighted by this fantastical creature who mimicked my own movements in the piece of glass propped up on the floor. It was Mathena who first showed me how a mirror worked, and who hung it from the wall like a painting.

Now I watched the sun dropping in the sky, dusk filtering through the forest. In the distance, the spires of the palace glittered. The world was so alive and open. I was meant to be out in that world, beyond the woods. Otherwise, why would I have been made the way I was, with hair like the sun?

Sleep was impossible. Once the sky was dark, and the moon and stars bathed the forest in silver, I stole out and gathered fresh thyme, lavender, and rue from the garden, along with a pile of soil from where his horse had stood, then returned to the tower. I lit a fire in the small hearth and carefully scattered the mixture in a half circle around me. I pressed my palms into it, sifted it through my fingers. The earth remembered him, kept something of him in itself. I just had to let it work its magic.

I stood and stared at myself in the mirror, flame shadows playing against my face. My eyes were huge, blue, like pools of water. My cheeks flushed. I let my hair stream down like a river along the floor behind me. I *looked* different, I was certain of it. My body felt lush and soft, touchable. Womanly. I was ready for a man like this.

"Love me," I whispered. I used my fingertip to draw the words into the mixture. "Love me."

Outside, I could hear the sounds of the forest: the wolves

and owls, the wind moving through the branches and leaves, the rush of river, the sound of the moon scraping across the sky.

I slipped off my shift, and imagined him in the room beside me, that my hands were his hands, traveling the length of my body.

The half circle glittered in the moonlight, from the stone floor. The mirror moved in and out, watching.

Love me.

The next morning I gathered the mixture from the stone floor and filled a sachet with it that I wore around my neck, against my heart. It was basic magic, using the land around us, the energy of growing, living things, the mystery of plant and earth, to link one soul to another.

I acted as if everything were normal, dressed in a high-necked gown to cover the talisman I wore, and joined Mathena in the garden. I could feel her watching me as I knelt down, but I did not look up. There was work to do, as we prepared for autumn. The air was just beginning to crisp, and though it was still summer, the trees were already changing color.

"Are you all right, Rapunzel?" she asked finally, leaning back on her haunches.

"Yes," I said. "I'm fine."

"You know I only want to protect you."

"Yes."

Tears stung my eyes and I turned away. We worked quietly together after that, the way we'd done forever, our hands in the soil. I'd always loved these moments with her, surrounded by vegetables and fruits and flowers, being able to feel a plant's roots moving into the earth, knowing from a touch what it needed to thrive.

Mathena's hands were defter than mine would ever be, as she packed the soil with bark.

While I worked, I imagined him at the ball, watching for me, waiting for me. I touched my dress, feeling for the sachet underneath, filled with the earth and herbs that connected me to him. I kept him around my neck. I did not want to take any chances.

A few days later I stole into Mathena's room, when she was out hunting with Brune. I dragged her trunks from below her bed, and opened them until I found the one I was looking for. Inside were gowns in rich colors, corsets, and gems. I breathed out a sigh of relief. She'd cut up many of her old clothes to make curtains and blankets, which decorated the house in fine fabrics—swaths of night-blue damask, crimson taffeta, gold brocade on purple silk—but there were several gowns still stored away. They were covered in dust, but they were finery nonetheless, clothes I could wear to a palace ball. I sifted through until I found a red silk dress that I knew would suit me, with its jewel tone and simple, striking design. Carefully, I spread it on Mathena's bed and returned the trunks to their places. I draped the gown over my arm and rushed to the tower, terrified that Mathena would discover what I was doing.

Breathless, I slipped on the gown. It clung to my body perfectly, though now Mathena was rounder and thicker than I. I imagined what she might have been like twenty years before, when she was my age now. Even as a woman nearing forty she was stunning. How slender she would have been before, how striking her dark hair must have been against this deep red. And I let down my own hair, and turned to face myself in the mirror. The color made my skin look like the whitest cream, my hair shine like spun gold. If I stood on my toes, I could see the way it swept down to the floor. I trembled as I watched myself, afraid that the image would vanish.

The morning of the ball, I woke up full of excitement. I planned to work with Mathena all morning as usual, and then grab my bow and arrow and pretend I was going off to hunt on horseback. Instead, I would ride to the palace, and let Brune help guide me.

I raced down the stairs that twisted the length of the tower, and pushed against the great wooden door to get out.

It did not budge.

I pushed again.

At first I thought it was stuck, and I used all my weight to press against it.

And then to my right, against the wall, I saw wine, bread, and water, enough for several days.

I screamed with rage. My scream echoed against the walls in the tower, blasted up to my room, into the sky through the only window. Never in my life had I felt the kind of fury I did then.

She had locked me in.

⤞⤞⤞

I pounded on the door, kicked at it, sobbing with frustration. After some time passed, I called out to Mathena, begging her to let me out, but she did not answer. I tried spells to open the door, tried to fashion a key from air as I knew she could, but my magic was no match for hers. Finally, I gave up and sulked back up the stairs. I paced furiously around the small room, stood at the window, and stared at the glittering spires, as if I could will myself to them. The hours slipped past. Throughout the day I called out to her, but she did not appear. When evening came, I could feel the king's palace filling with wine and candles and diamonds, lords and ladies whirling about, all that life pressed in together; it was torture.

For hours I seethed and cried and called to her. Finally, I slept. When I woke the next day, I had a new resolve.

One thing I knew, from all my years of working with Mathena: it was in the focusing, and the wanting, the fashioning one's desire into a point of light, that the magic took place. I'd called him to me before, hadn't I? Now, for the first time, I took everything I had learned and felt and I pressed it together inside me, filled it with my own longing and need until I could *see* it, feel it like a blade, and turned it into that light.

"Come back," I whispered, clutching the sachet around my neck.

She thought she could keep me away from him by locking me in a tower. But I could bring him to me. He was already tied to me, through magic, through the earth, and now I would make him return.

I looked at myself in the mirror the way he would look at me. I could hear his heartbeat, his breath, in and out, and I slipped into his mind and heart as if my whole body, my very being now, had turned to spirit.

After that, I waited. I used the water she'd left me sparingly, to keep myself washed for him, and I dressed carefully in front of the mirror, and brushed and brushed my hair, using the bit of potion I had left. To make it strong.

It would need to be. When he came, it wouldn't matter that I was locked in a tower.

I had my hair.

The next day, I watched her working in the garden, chopping tree trunks and carrying firewood into the house, heading out into the forest to collect mushrooms and wild raspberries. I watched women come and go, into the house. I watched the candles flare up as evening came, watched the lights flame out when she was going to bed.

She called up to me a few times, but I did not answer her.

And then the next day, when she was out hunting with Brune—as I had willed her to be, when the time was right—I heard the horse's hooves, and I knew he had returned.

I went to the window and let down my hair, let it fall from my head and out of the window, where it stretched down and tapped the ground, like a flag waving from the mast of a ship.

He rode into view just as the sun caught my hair and turned it to fire. He looked up at me, a dazed expression on his face. Never in my life had I felt the kind of power I felt right then. I was young and beautiful. I had all the magic of the forest at my fingertips. I was foolish, too; I understand this now, after so many years have passed, how I confused infatuation for true love, the power of beauty for real power in the world.

"You came back," I said. I whispered the words, and let the wind carry them to him. "I've been waiting for you."

"You were not at the ball."

"She locked me in this tower, to keep me away."

He left his horse, walked toward the tower.

"You have to climb up here," I said.

"What?"

He looked around, and then headed for the great wooden door. I could hear him struggling, just out of my vision. A moment later, he was standing again under the window.

"I'm locked in," I said.

"I'll get the key from her."

"No. She is not here. Climb."

He tilted his head, not understanding. "There's no rope or ladder."

"Climb my hair."

"How . . . ?"

"You won't hurt me," I said.

Tentatively, he reached out and touched my hair, grasped it in his fist. I could feel that touch. My hair was as alive as skin, as blood. I reeled back from the force of the feeling that spread through me. I could feel him. I *knew* him.

"Climb," I said again, holding on to the windowsill and bracing myself for the pain in my scalp. But no pain came. Instead, images flashed through my mind: a bed covered in furs, a heavy manuscript scattered across a desk, bright colors blotted across stone. They were all images from his life, I realized with surprise, flowing from him to me. I'd never felt anything like it before. Of course, outside the tower Mathena always made me keep my hair tied back, hidden under cloth. Was this why? Did she know what it could do?

He hoisted himself up and I could feel his full weight, as I braced myself against the window.

"Are you all right?" he called up.

"Yes," I said, through gritted teeth. "Just climb!"

His anxiety moved from him to me. He was afraid to hurt me, pictured me flying sideways out the window like a golden bird, my body smashing into the ground.

But my hair was strong, stronger than iron. It could hold him ten times over, and I anchored myself against the tower.

After a moment of hesitation, he stretched one hand up over the other and twisted his thighs around my hair. He began to climb. I could feel his fear dissipating, his excitement to see me pulsing through every strand.

I closed my eyes, as everything he'd ever thought or felt or dreamed passed into me, like water seeping into the soil. I could feel the way he'd ridden through the forest to come find me, stopping at an inn at the edge of the woods, for the night. Hear the songs he'd sung to himself as he rode. I could barely breathe, as it poured through me, unfurling, moving further back in time. I could feel his worry over his mother the queen, the way he'd begged her, as a child, to see him when she was busy talking to ghosts, his loneliness and hurt when she looked past him, his love for poems and stories that filled him, that populated his world, his anger at his father the king, all of it combined with a deep love for them both, a love for me . . .

It was overwhelming, feeling that I knew every part of him, feeling I was seeing all the secret parts of his heart that should have remained hidden.

Finally, he grabbed on to the stone windowsill. His face was right next to mine and he pulled himself into the room. He moved gracefully, like an acrobat.

And then he was standing before me, several inches taller than me, still clutching my hair in his hands. I looked up at him. His face was sweet and glowing. I had to look away, embarrassed to see him as nakedly as I did.

"I could live in this hair," he said, pressing his face into it. I felt his breath, his lips, through the strands.

"Give that back to me," I said, grateful for his silliness. I pulled it from him and yanked more of it in from the window until it reached the floor, then reined in the next batch.

He turned to help me, gathering my hair into the tower, letting it brush against his face as he did. A thousand more images sparked in front of me: painted letters on a page, banquet tables covered with gold plates and sparkling glasses, childhood afternoons on horseback chasing falcons, stretched-out canvases and the feel of a brush dipped in paint, artists and dancers and musicians . . . Infusing all of it, a deep love for art and beauty, a desire to fill the world with wonderful things. I could feel my own heart expanding as I took him inside me, and everything became possible for me, the way it was for him. More than anything else, there was joy. I had never felt the kind of joy that he did. Even at his most hurt, his most lonely, he contained this wonder inside him, a passion for the world and all its beauty. People loved him for that, I realized.

I could love him for that.

"This must be what heaven is like," he said, interrupting the flow of emotions.

"Pulling my hair in through a window?"

"Yes," he said.

I was giddy with happiness. "You don't seem very much like a prince," I said.

"And what is a prince supposed to be like?"

"I thought princes were dignified."

"You don't find me dignified?" He made a face at me, twisting his features into a ridiculous expression.

"Well, you are the most dignified prince I've ever seen, though it's true I've only seen one."

"You might have better luck if you didn't get yourself locked inside of towers."

I laughed, as he reached out and ran his palm along my cheek. I leaned into it. And then we fell silent, just watching each other.

"You're here," I said, finally. "I can't believe it."

"Did you not call me to you?"

I was so moved, I found it difficult to speak. I *had* called to him, and he had felt it.

"Yes," I said softly.

"I waited for you at the ball," he said, his voice curling into my ear, vibrating along every strand of my hair. "I was afraid that bandits had attacked you, that you weren't safe; I know the dangers of the forest and the dark forces at work here. I came as soon as I could. When you called to me . . . it was as if you were inside me. I hadn't slept that night and at first thought I was imagining things. But your voice was so clear."

He stepped closer to me, and took me into his arms. As he

held me, I could feel myself transforming, as if under a spell. My body changed into liquid, into points of light. His body became an anchor as I felt myself melting, disappearing into him. I couldn't get close enough to him.

I knew it was too fast. I knew it was foolish, and wrong, but I'd brought him to me, the flow of feeling was overwhelming, and he was—I knew it, with absolute certainty—my fate.

The sun spilled into the room. His hands were on my waist, my neck, pulling off my dress. I let him press against every bit of my body, ensuring that I was still there, that I hadn't dissolved into light, too. I pulled off his shirt, slid my palms down his chest onto his smooth belly. And then we were on the bed and I looked up, saw my own face in the mirror—was it only mine? I was sure I saw a rippling, another face appear beside it—for one moment before he pulled me down beneath him. And then it was only his thoughts, the press of his skin under my hands, the feel of him entering my body.

After, we lay tangled together on the bed, as the sun dropped in the sky. My hair cocooned us, humming with a contentment that moved from him to me, and back again. And then I felt, underneath it, something else. As he pulled himself up, a panic swept over me. I knew he was going to leave, that something was wrong. Why hadn't I sensed it before?

"I must return to the palace," he said, as I sat up next to him. "Though I'd like to stay here with you. Can you let your hair down for me again? I'll send soldiers back here to release you. I'll have her punished for what she's done."

The room came into relief. My body was a solid mass. "No, don't send anyone," I said.

"But she has done wrong to you," he said.

"No! Please, don't punish her. She just wanted to protect me. That's all."

"From what?"

"From you."

He stared at me.

"She didn't want me to go to the ball," I continued. "She said . . . that you wouldn't love me. That you were promised to someone else."

He did not answer. He didn't need to.

"It's not my decision, Rapunzel," he said, finally.

I pushed him away, forced him to look at me directly. "Who are you promised to?"

"I'm to marry the princess from the East."

"When?"

"In two months."

The room had gone cold. His heart had shifted, clouded over with guilt and pain and regret. I could feel every bit of that shift, pulsing up from him to me through my wretched hair.

Tears pricked at my eyes. He was still bewitched, I could see the glaze in his eyes, feel the strength of his desire. But it didn't matter now. He was marrying someone else.

He buried his face in my neck, ran his hands up and down my spine.

"I'll try to return to you," he said.

"Marry me," I said. "Marry me instead."

"I do not have that freedom."

He kissed me again, shoved his hands and arms into my hair, which made me feel his grief more intensely. He didn't want to leave me, but would anyway. I had misunderstood the way things worked, overestimated my power. He pulled my body into his, and I kissed him back even though tears streamed down my face. And then within what seemed like seconds I once again lowered my hair out of the window, and he climbed down. His own sorrow streamed up to me but it didn't matter, there was nothing at all I could do to change what had happened, what I'd given him.

He was gone.

2

When Mathena returned that day, just as the sun was dropping in the sky and melting over the mountains, she could sense immediately that something had happened. Brune got to me first, landing on my shoulder and nuzzling me with her beak. I was sitting cross-legged on the floor in a pool of hair and my own tears, sobbing with grief. Moments later, I heard the great door creaking open, and Mathena's footsteps as she raced up the stairs to me. What she'd tried to protect me from had happened despite her efforts, and now her sole concern was to see that I was all right.

I was not.

"My child," she said simply, over and over, stroking my hair back from my face. "Shhhh."

Even in my sorry state, I noticed that her touch had no effect on me, and that I could not feel anything of her in it the way I had with the prince. It only made me feel more bereft. She seemed so distant after the kind of closeness I'd felt with him. Only his touch, it seemed, could awaken all the magic within me.

She led me out of the tower and to our little house, where she sat me in front of the fire and served me tea and stew. She heated water on the fire and washed me, rinsed the tears and dirt out of my hair, the imprint of his lips, and slipped a clean dress over my head. She wrapped up my hair and covered it with cloth. I sat, silent. Neither of us spoke about what had happened. Her magic sometimes was a convenient thing; she already knew.

In the following days, we found out all the details from the women who visited us: that Josef was marrying a princess from the East to strengthen a still-shaky alliance his father had made the year before, and that his bride was a pale, dark-haired beauty with eyes like the sea. She was named Teresa, after the saint. She would not only ensure peace between our kingdom and the East, but bring us all closer to God. This was what we heard, over and over: that the new queen would bring happiness, peace, and God's favor to the kingdom, which had been ravaged by failing crops, illness, hunger, the threat of war.

I listened bitterly. All those spells I had watched Mathena cast for women over the years, she cast for me then, because I had forgotten them. All those teas and baths and potions, she made for me. "Bite down on this," she said, handing me a stick of wood she'd boiled with hemlock root. "Close your eyes," she said, handing me a steaming bowl, "imagine him, and drink this all at once, to flush him from your body." She put elderberry bark around my neck, so that it hung next to my heart. She rummaged through my room and when she found the sachet I'd made, she burned it, then swept every bit of earth and herb from my hearth, down the stairs, and onto the forest floor. But I was committed to my suffering and nothing worked to rid me of it.

It was the first rule of witchery, at least the kind she practiced on me then. One had to be open to it. Changing hearts was something else altogether.

Still, I could not wallow for long, even as the prince's wedding approached. The days grew shorter, leaves began to cover the ground, and we had much work to do to prepare for the long winter, which would not wait for any human grief. We had a root cellar to fill with vegetables and meats, a garden to harvest and cover before the snow came, firewood and wild herbs to gather, birds and animals to hunt and butcher. It seemed fitting, the earth dying, the plants going to seed, all the leaves gathering on the ground and rotting there. I liked stalking through the dead forest with my bow and arrow, searching for prey. In a perverse way, I delighted in it. If my heart was going to be broken, the earth might as well be, too, and there we were, scavenging from it before it retreated under ice and snow.

So, slowly, we filled the root cellar with beets and carrots and turnips and onions and garlic, and prepared the soil to turn back into itself.

At the same time, I began to eat. More than I ever had. I craved meat and attacked the store of it in the root cellar, to the point that Mathena began to worry about having enough food for the winter, despite the abundance of our garden and the heaping bags we carried down each day. I promised her I would continue to hunt, that I did not care about the cold or the snow. We would be fine. At the very least, we would survive. In the meantime, I took hunks of venison and pheasant to the tower, gnawed them down to bone.

And then the swelling came, and the sickness in the mornings, and the strange shiftings in mood that left me in fits of giggles one hour, and wailing the next, as we worked. Through all of it she watched me, and brewed me special teas that, considering what happened, I'm not sure were for my benefit. But that is something I do not like to think about.

Josef's wedding day came on one of those last days of autumn, after the leaves had all fallen and our garden had been harvested and covered for winter. For us, it was a regular day, or so we pretended, and we did not speak of the royal marriage. We sat by the fire, repairing some clothes. It was good for me, watching clothes mend under my hands, seeing how broken things can be fixed, that with each pull of thread the world kept moving, healing itself, becoming something new.

Brune walked back and forth across the mantel while Loup slept in Mathena's lap. Outside, the wind rattled through the trees, carrying the faint scent of rot.

"Rapunzel," Mathena said.

I looked up.

"I know you've been feeling strange lately, have you not?"

I shrugged. "It's the season," I said.

"No." She shook her head. Her face was pained, which was unusual for her. "It's because you are with child."

"What?" I dropped the shift in my hands. I looked down at my belly, under the thick wool shift I was wearing. The slight swelling there I had attributed to my recent appetite, which I was sure derived from grief. "How do you know?"

"I've been watching you," she said. "You have all the signs of it, and your cycle has not come, has it?"

"No," I admitted. I had not given much mind to that, either.

I did not expect my body to function the same way it had before, after all that had happened.

"Have you lain with anyone besides the prince?"

"Of course not!" I said. My face reddened with embarrassment. We had never spoken about my lying with Josef in the tower, and how foolish I'd felt afterward.

"I just wanted to make sure," she said. "There are some ardent poets around these parts at times."

"Mathena!" I said, blushing. "Don't be horrible." I felt my belly again, the swelling that seemed to have doubled in the last few minutes, and looked up at her. "Do you really think I'm pregnant?"

"Yes," she said. "Can you not feel it yourself?"

Even as she answered, this new knowledge was moving through me, taking up residency in my blood and bones. The idea that a child could be growing inside me . . . in the midst of all that sadness and loss, autumn and death. It was unthinkable. A miracle.

A gift.

"So we will have to do something, then," she said, matter-of-fact, as if we were talking about a bad harvest.

I narrowed my eyes. "Do something, how?"

"What we have done countless times, Rapunzel, for the women who come to us," she said. "Do you want to have the child of a man who belongs to another?"

The fire sputtered and crackled. Outside, the wind swept about the house, bending the trees.

"No," I said. "I *want* this baby." And the moment I said it, I knew it to be true. I wanted this child, born of him and me.

"There are ways to remedy this. It will be as if it never

happened at all, you know that, and then you can be pure for the man that you will marry."

"No," I said. "I want this child!"

For the first time in weeks, something like joy entered me, and it started to sink into me, the miracle happening just below my skin. There was a *child* inside of me. Already I loved it. I knew it was a boy. I could see his gold hair, his bright eyes.

I looked up at her and laughed, and it was a laugh that came from pure happiness. The way I sometimes felt watching the flowers and plants come back to life every spring, when it had seemed impossible only days before, when the world was covered in snow and ice and frost. The natural world was full of miracles. This body of mine was a miracle.

She watched me, worried, as I leapt up from my seat and spun around, right there in the little room, in front of the fire, with our sewing strewn around us and batches of dried sage hanging from every window and doorway.

"A child, Mathena!" I said.

I imagined myself happy, glowing, my son against my breast, swathed in my hair. It was the warmest image I could conjure, perhaps because my own mother was lost to me. This would be a child born of love. It did not matter that his father was, that very day, wedding another. I would love our child enough for both of us.

I danced over to Mathena, grabbed her hand, and pulled her to her feet. Brune and Loup just watched suspiciously, most likely wondering if I'd gone mad. "Be happy for me!" I said. "Think how beautiful a child it will be. How much life he'll bring to this house."

Perhaps it was in my mind or perhaps the child reached to

me, in that moment, unfurling his fist like a flower, uncoiling himself, pressing himself into my heart and making me whole again.

"Please," I said, gripping her hands in mine, "help me bring this child into the world. Help me be a good mother to him, as you have been to me." I looked into her dark eyes, inhaled the comforting scent of spices and bark that clung to her all the time.

She did not answer me, not then, but when she took me into her arms and passed her hand over my face, stroking my cheek, I thought it was her way of saying yes. That she loved me and would love my child, no matter what.

And for the first time in weeks, I felt entirely at peace.

It changed everything, knowing that I would be a mother. My whole life seemed to shift into focus. Even when reports came of the extravagant royal wedding, how beautiful the bride was, how happy the couple seemed, I thought only of my child. My body suddenly was an alien, wonderful thing, and now that the garden was ready for winter, I spent hours up in my tower alone, my hair strewn around me, watching my shape in the mirror, looking for every little change. I rubbed oil on my belly to help prepare it for what was coming. I asked Mathena to teach me every spell she could, to make my child strong, handsome, a warrior. A king.

I asked her, too, about what life had been like, for her, at court, now that I was carrying the child of a prince.

"What did you do there?" I asked one evening, as we drank tea together next to the fire. "What is it like to live in a great palace?"

"I spent much time with the queen," she said. The flames threw shadows across her face. Outside, the air was crisp and clear, the world bracing itself for the first snow.

"You mean . . . his mother?" I was surprised she had not mentioned such a thing before.

"Yes," she said. "Queen Anne."

"I didn't know you were so important!"

She laughed at my enthusiasm. "I gave her advice. Spells. Like what we do now for the women who come see us, I did that for her then. She was a great believer in the stars. I expect she still is."

"You read the stars for her?"

Our work suddenly had a glamour to it that hadn't been there before. I imagined myself, sitting beside the queen—I pictured a stunning woman draped in jewels—reading her cards, her stars, her tea leaves.

"She wouldn't do anything without checking the sky. People used to be like that then."

"At court? I thought magic wasn't allowed there. That's why we can't call ourselves witches."

She looked at me sharply. "Don't ever use that word, Rapunzel. Not even here. Do you understand? People can be hanged for that now."

I sat back, reprimanded, but her words were hard to understand when such terrors seemed so far away. I set my tea down on the floor.

"Things were different then," she said, leaning back on the couch. "It wasn't a bad thing to be known as . . . an *enchantress*." She smiled at the word. "People believed in magic. They still do, obviously, but things changed in the palace before I left. A new priest came. The king reformed, and it became a crime to talk openly about such things."

I nodded, but I was already far away, imagining Mathena and the queen sitting side by side, the queen's jewel-covered hand upturned on a table between them.

I wanted a life like that. I wanted to have more in my life than this cottage in the forest.

"Here," Mathena said, setting down her tea and grabbing my wrist, "let's go outside." She dropped the branch she'd been holding. In front of us, the fire leapt up as if to grab it.

We walked outside, the sky black and clear above us, scattered with thousands of stars. The garden squatted down next to us. Above us, the tower seemed to stretch indefinitely.

She sat, cross-legged, on the grass, gathering her long skirt into her lap. I sat next to her, despite the cold. Breathing in, I smelled smoke and rotting leaves.

"I spent a lot of time at court just staring at the sky," she said.

I stared up with her, wondering at the mysteries embedded with it. Already I could make out the characters in the great stories she'd told me. Pegasus. Orion, Artemis's lover, with his bright sword. Scorpio, who killed him, stretching his tail across the sky.

"Can you see anything about my son?" I asked.

She hesitated. "I think he will be born in Cancer," she said. "Do you see it up there, the crab?"

I followed her finger to the faint spots in the northern sky, the line of stars splitting into thin claws. "Yes! Hercules kicked the crab into the sky, right, after Hera sent it to him? While he was battling the Hydra?"

She smiled. "You remember. It's been years since I told you those stories."

"I remember all of them," I said.

"He will be strong and gifted," she said. "Like his mother."

We lay back, side by side, watching the stories in the sky. I imagined my own body being placed in the heavens, outlined by diamonds.

I felt a rumbling through the earth before I heard it. I sat up, instinctively placing my palms over my belly. It sounded as if a whole army were heading toward us, with hundreds of horses storming over the ground, their massive hooves shod with iron.

Mathena sat up and put her hand on my shoulder, keeping me seated. "It's all right," she said. "Stay where you are."

The hooves got louder. Leaves shook on the trees around us, rattling together, and then I saw several figures—five, I counted—men with sacks raised up in their arms, knives and crossbows strapped to their sides, approaching through the woods. In the dark, their bodies were hulking shadows and it was impossible to tell where man and horse divided, so that it seemed as if great mythic beasts were bearing down on us.

Bandits.

My heart hammered in my chest. They came right toward us. I ignored Mathena and scraped at the ground, trying to move out of their way, but I felt as if my own feet were covered in iron. The sound deafened me, the earth shook beneath me. All the while, Mathena sat calmly watching.

And then they were upon us, we were right in their path and there was no way to move. I bunched myself into a ball, tears streaming down my face, waiting to be run down.

The sound, the smell of horse and man passed over me. The horses ran right through me as if I were not even there. I twisted my neck and watched their shadows disappearing into the woods on the other side of us.

For a moment, I wasn't sure what had just happened. If it weren't for the taste of dirt in my mouth, the overturned earth all around us, I might have thought I'd imagined it.

I looked over at Mathena, who was steadily watching me.

"What . . . ?" I began, not sure what to say.

"You're safe," she said.

"Those were bandits, weren't they?" I'd heard stories about them for as long as I could remember—how they lived in a house by the river, outside the kingdom's rule, preying on those who entered the forest.

She nodded. "Yes, but they cannot hurt us. Not here."

I looked at her, amazed, this woman who'd read the stars for a queen.

It was the first time I had seen one of Mathena's protection spells at work.

That night I slept in the tower and was plagued by strange dreams, in which my son was alive and whole, come to see me. His blue eyes stared up at me, his fists unfolded and became massive. Antlers rose from his skull, twisting like branches into the air, puncturing the clouds.

I woke up with my palms under my belly, cradling him, on my side on the stone floor, clutching my stomach. I was so ravenous I couldn't make it to the house and the cupboards there. I wrapped myself in furs and flew down the winding stairs and out into the winter frost and I dropped onto the ground, shoving leaves and dirt into my mouth. My child wailed inside me. I could hear him, blending in with the wind that whipped my hair into a storm around and above me. I wished I had two mouths, three mouths, to take it all in, to eat the earth, the leaves and grass, the acorns that tasted as marvelous as cream.

After, I hauled myself back up the stairs, shaking from the cold, crawling on my hands and knees up the stone.

I dropped the fur from my shoulders and looked in the mirror, and what I saw seared itself into my memory: I was reflected in the mad light of the roaring fire, half in shadows and smeared in dirt. My slight, rounded belly. My hair like a wild robe hanging to the floor and swirling on the stone, scattered through with leaves and bark and frost. My breasts, too, were becoming rounder, and my nipples were black with dirt. Earth pushing through my body, tangling around my stomach, entering my womb.

Outside the wind howled. The moon cast its eye on everything. The fire crackled, devouring the wood. Inside me, he was screaming, and the world turned feral.

The mirror seemed to ripple, like water, as I peered into it.

This is who I am, I thought.

The woman in the glass. Wild and broken.

I thought of the stories Mathena had told me of my real mother, who craved rapunzel and wasted away without it, because she could not stand to eat anything else. She could not grow it in her own garden, apparently, which was as barren as

Mathena's was lush and full. I imagined my mother standing at the window, growing thin from hunger, longing, that inexpressible need for something just beyond her reach to fill the dark space inside, even after she'd birthed me. And me, wailing beside her until she was forced to make me stop.

Something blasted up inside me, a memory or not-memory, a banshee cry, a feeling that there was a dark force nearby wanting to harm me and that I would fight and die to protect myself, my child, from it. And then it seemed that this darkness was inside of me. Passed down from my mother to me.

Winter came quickly and buried us in snow, and we sewed, mended, embroidered, ate the food and burned the wood we had gathered during the vibrant summer months and the bountiful fall. Mathena made me teas to keep me strong and healthy. The occasional woman came and went, the more desperate ones willing to march through drifts that came up to their thighs to see us—sometimes they complained of love, sometimes of hunger and bare pantries, not enough food to last through the winter. I knew these women's desperation now, and became a better practitioner for it.

Occasionally, we heard word from court, usually half rumors and gossip that came to us third- or fourth-hand. I was always eager to hear of it. Of him, his wife, the palace.

One day a young woman came to our door, an already small girl thinning from disease. I was stirring a stew over the stove. Mathena was spreading salve on the girl's back when the girl told us the news.

"The new princess is pregnant," she said. "People say it's a good sign, that things will be better for us now."

I dropped the spoon I was holding. "The wife of Prince Josef is with child?"

"What wonderful news," Mathena said quickly. "That we will have an heir."

"Yes," the girl said, her feverish face shining with hope. "They say the princess has already taken to her bed. She doesn't want to take any chances."

"It is a good sign indeed," Mathena said, placing her hand on the girl's shoulder. When the girl bent over in pain a moment later, Mathena looked over at me worriedly. Worried more for me than the girl, I realized.

I stood there in stunned silence. I don't know why I was so surprised by the news, but I was. Teresa was his wife, her main purpose was to bear him heirs. Yet somehow it had felt like what had happened in that tower was special, mine alone. Maybe she could have him, but only I could have his child.

Mathena focused back on the girl. "Breathe this in," she said, holding a packet of lemon balm and lavender to the girl's face, "until it passes."

The girl breathed in. She sat back up, clearly exhausted.

With shaking hands, I wrapped various treatments for the girl to take with her—salves and teas, special incense and potion—as Mathena helped the girl back into her dress. My shock shifted to anger, sorrow. Teresa's child would be born in the palace, become a prince or princess, have everything in the world laid out for it, while my own son would have nothing at all.

Mathena wove protection spells for the girl as she left, to protect her from bandits if not from the disease.

"Do you really believe what you said?" I asked, after the girl disappeared from sight. "That it is a good sign?" My voice was hurt, accusing.

"No," she said, giving me a surprised look. "Of course not."

I nodded, blinking back tears.

"Rapunzel," Mathena said, sitting next to me. "You must forget him. For now."

The way she was watching me scared me. I could feel myself weaken, feel her magic at work. She was trying to make me tired and relaxed enough that I might not care what she did, or might find it easier to listen to her than to my own heart. I blinked, to stop it.

"I *have* forgotten," I lied.

She sighed, not even bothering to acknowledge my statement. "It is the duty of his wife, to bear him children." She hesitated, put her hand on my arm soothingly. "Not yours. It's still not too late to be rid of it."

"Of what?"

She gestured to my belly. "It's more difficult now, but possible."

"No," I said, gaping at her. How could she suggest such a thing?

"You are destined for great things, Rapunzel," she said. "You've become a powerful practitioner, and your beauty is a gift. A great gift that gives you strength and increases your magic. You'll have many more gifts in this world. A child will only hinder you."

"Mathena! You're speaking about my son."

"In the world, he'll be a bastard. The queen's child will have everything your own son will be denied. Don't you want those things?"

She continued to watch me in that same intent way.

Her words confused me. "Yes, but . . . what can I do? I cannot have those things. It's too late."

"Be patient," she said. "Haven't I taught you that the world can change in an instant?"

3

Over the rest of that winter, darkness seemed to envelop us, so thick it was like a physical thing. The rush of women who came to us slowed down to a faint trickle of the truly desperate. The daylight, when it came, was ghostly, pale. All that mattered was keeping the fire lit, keeping food in our stomachs, making sure the child inside me survived. We spent most of our days with dried herbs spread around us, making potions and poultices for every kind of ailment, ripping pieces of cloth to wrap around particularly potent mixtures.

My hunger did not abate. I wanted to eat everything, to lock myself in the cellar and devour every herb, every vegetable, every dried piece of meat. No matter how much we carried up and roasted in the hearth, it never seemed to be enough to fill me. Mathena even began locking the cellar at night, so that I would not run down in my half sleep and gorge myself.

The days passed slowly. To distract me, Mathena told me stories of the old goddesses—Artemis turning Daphne slowly into a tree, limb by limb, Aphrodite rising from foam and sea, Hera ruling over all of them at the side of her brother Zeus, who was also her husband—and of the days when the queen consulted her on everything from what to eat for breakfast to which of her husband's advisors would betray him. I loved her stories. Sometimes I would get so lost in them that I'd look down at the cloth and stalks and seeds in my hands and forget what they were, why I was holding them.

At times, when I was restless and burning, I would take to the woods in the pure light of the afternoon with a fur wrap, often just with a bow and arrow, to hunt.

Which was how I found myself outside one afternoon, stalking through the forest with Brune flying above me and my bow at my side, several arrows sticking out of the quiver on my back. I scanned the trees, the ground, but I was distracted, consumed as always by thoughts of what would happen, once I had brought his child into the world.

What I would do then.

And so I didn't hear the swishing of branches, the light step of hooves, the way I might have normally, and did not sense the stag until it was right there in front of me.

It stood in my path. I stopped, astonished. It stared back at me, and was unlike any deer I'd ever seen. It looked as bewildered as I did, and for a moment we both stood there in the snow, frozen. Antlers twisted from its skull like tree branches, a crown. Its eyes were big and black and round, soft. Beautiful.

I was mesmerized.

And then everything came into focus. I remembered why I was there, and could not believe my good fortune. Hunting was difficult in the winter, even when I was not with child, and at best I would return home with several squirrels or rabbits.

I lifted my bow and aimed.

"Stay," I whispered.

My heart pounded. I kept my fingers perfectly still.

I released my hand and let the arrow loose. It flew through the air, and those moments seemed to stretch out and become hours, days, until the arrow landed, right in the animal's throat. I could feel the arrow entering. I heard the wet, hard sound of it breaking the skin, entering blood and bone.

The stag's eyes never left mine.

It staggered, blinking, and let out a terrible bleat.

And then it turned and ran, and I took off after it, my fur-lined shoes pounding over earth and snow. I raced through the trees, Brune following in the sky, the scent of blood and death and dying all around me.

I was surprised at how much life the animal still had in it, and I was forced to slow down, my body more lumbering than usual. But I was fleet and strong still, a daughter of Artemis, intent on my prey. Already I could taste the meat roasted over the fire.

I ran through leaves and over tree trunks, past the great oak that had been split in a storm, along the river, following the animal's tracks and blood, the sounds of it stumbling through the wood.

And then I heard it falling, and I raced forward, toward the sound. I pushed through a cluster of trees, and found myself stepping into a small clearing.

The tree branches swayed overhead. Brune landed in one of them, waiting for her reward.

The wounded creature lay there, twisted in the snow, the arrow jutting from its neck straight into the air. I pulled my knife from my boot, ready to slit its throat, and moved forward. The stag shifted its head and looked up at me. I could see its anguish, hear its ragged breath, and then something pulled me up short.

At first I thought I was seeing things. There was a glow around the animal's body, the way it began to shimmer and shift. The antlers seemed to twist down, melt, just as everything on its body was transforming, like a tree throwing off ice and snow and sprouting green leaves. Its body was shrinking, its fur disappearing, until all that was left was pale skin.

Human skin.

I blinked, disoriented, wondering if I was imagining what was in front of me.

There was a young man lying there now. Naked, wounded, blood streaming from his mouth, my arrow in his neck.

For a moment I stood frozen, and then I ran to his side and collapsed on the ground next to him.

His eyes were now a deep dark green, the color of leaves in summer. I placed my palms on his skin, half expecting him to disappear and for my hands to move right through him. But he was real, solid flesh, still warm. I moved my hands away.

I knew there was magic in the forest, but I had never seen anything like this. His torso and legs were bare and muscled, his sex dangling down between his strong thighs. The only other man I'd seen naked—or even this close—was the prince, and I'd barely looked at his body, not like this, not in the sunlight, stretched out before me.

The man's face moved in pain, and I was disgusted with myself for caring about his nakedness.

"I'm sorry," I said, conquering my initial fears and taking his hand in mine. Liquid ran down his skin and I realized it was my tears. "You were . . . were you not a stag, just before? I did not know . . ." The words felt ridiculous, even as I said them.

He was trying to speak, and I bent my head down to hear

him. I noticed how his face was starting to line, his hair beginning to gray. He was becoming a middle-aged man before my
eyes.

"Cursed," he breathed.

"Cursed?" I couldn't be quite sure what he was saying. "What
curse?"

He struggled to form the word. "Mathena . . ."

"Mathena?" I tilted my head.

But I could not stop to think; he was dying, the arrow lodged
in his throat, the blood spilling out of him. Desperately, I tried to
remember my craft, the spellwork I'd done. I called to the four
winds, raising my hands, and tried to channel their power into
him. "Help him!"

I focused all my desire and need into him, to restoring him,
and yet I knew there was no way to save him, not with that
wound, not even with all the magic I'd learned. Mathena could
have saved him, but not me. Still, I focused my heart and mind
on him, clasping his hands in my own.

"Mathena Gothel," he said, so faintly I might have imagined it.

"She . . . did this?"

He watched me. His mouth forming over words. I remained
close, to hear.

"Tell me," I said.

He was struggling to breathe now and I strained to hear his
words. But then he stopped moving, and I was positive I saw
his spirit slipping from him. A shimmering sliver of light that
moved up into the forest canopy, toward the sun. And the whole
time a feeling of love—what else could it have been? A warmth,
magic, desire, and need—cascaded through me, moving from
me to him.

The snow hit my face as I squinted to the sky, watching his spirit drift away. I turned to him, and he was silent, still.

At that moment, Brune left the tree and came down to me, landing on my shoulder. To comfort me.

Irrationally, I thought how cold the man must be. Bare, in the snow! His skin was already blue from it.

I took down my hair, let it unspool all around me, like a golden blanket. Brune flitted from my shoulder as my hair cascaded around her, and landed on the ground next to me. I covered his body with my hair and lay down, curling beside him.

At first I couldn't tell if it was the strange mood of the forest right then, the pale light, the remnants of the magic that had just taken place . . . But my hair came alive the way it had before, with the prince, and I could feel something coming from the man's body to me. Sparkling, faint images, an old, old sorrow as soft as the feel of air on skin. I could see the man, a crowd of people, a woman screaming into the air, enacting an ancient spell, and when she turned I saw it was Mathena, but years younger, her black curls tumbling around her face.

As quickly as the images came, they went away, and then a great calm came over me, and I knew it was the feeling of dying. I looked up, and his spirit was gone now.

"I'm so sorry," I whispered again, stretching my hand over his chest.

I don't know how long I lay there in the snow, curled up next to him, holding on to him, with Brune as witness, but it was only the fading light and the shivering that overtook me, as the air grew more and more cold, that warned me to head home.

If I could have, I would have carried him. If I had not had a child inside me, I might have stayed there with him indefinitely, letting my grief cover us both. But something lifted me from the ground, made me pull the arrow from his neck and cover him in leaves and snow. The ground was too frozen to bury him properly.

I let my hair drag behind me. Clutching the arrow in my hand, I marked my way by the sun, and headed home. Brune did her best to guide me, moving from tree to tree to show me the way. I stumbled through the snow. Images rose up to me from the ground, of forest animals, travelers, bandits, but I just let them pass over me, numb to everything. The arrows rattled as they clicked against each other in my quiver.

I felt like I'd walked for days in the dark, though it could not have been more than a few hours. I walked along the river, whispering protection spells in the air. All around me, I heard the sounds of forest animals and thought I saw shapes hiding behind the trees, watching me. The trees had eyes, the branches were arms reaching out for me. I thought of the bandits on their great horses, preying on unsuspecting travelers, tales of the house on the other side of the river where they lived together. Were my own spells strong enough to hide me? Could they see me now? Were they out roaming through the forest? Dark eyes shone out at me. The cold bit through my furs, to my skin.

I had killed a man. Perhaps I deserved to have the bandits find me.

By the time I arrived at the cottage, I could barely feel any part of my body. My hands were numb as I pushed through the front door.

The fire was crackling, meat cooking on top of it, and I collapsed on the couch. Brune flew inside and found her way to the mantel, squawking a warning.

Mathena rushed into the main room, carrying a basket of dried rose petals. Her face registered her shock as soon as she saw me. She dropped the basket, and the petals scattered on the dirt floor beneath her.

"My god, what has happened? You're covered in blood! Your hair!"

I looked down. I hadn't even realized that I was soiled. My hair trailed out behind me, full of the forest. The arrow in my hand was still bloody.

She ran over to me, moving around me to grab my hair in bundles so she could shut the door.

"Your hair is stained with blood," she said. I could hear the terror in her voice. "Are you hurt? The baby . . . ? You know better than to wander through the woods at night!"

"There was a man," I said, "in the forest. I killed him."

"You what?"

I knelt on the floor and let my body give way to sobs. She was next to me then, on the floor, carefully taking the arrow from my hand and placing it on the table.

"He was . . . a stag. I hit it with my arrow, I followed it, and when he fell . . . he was a man. I saw it. I saw him change."

"Oh," she said, leaning back on her heels. She looked at me sharply. The fire flared up in front of us. Outside, the snow drifted down like tiny feathers. She nodded to my hair, the arrow. "This is his blood, not yours?"

I nodded. "I had no idea I was killing a man. I saw the stag, his antlers, and my arrow hit him in the throat. I killed him. Mathena, I watched him die!"

I was consumed by my own pain and guilt, but I could feel the room change. Something in her change.

She stood and lifted me by the shoulders. And then I was on the couch, and she heated the kettle and started carefully washing the blood off of me with a wet cloth.

"Did he say anything?" she asked, after a while. Her voice was uncharacteristically quiet.

I lifted my head. I couldn't believe I'd forgotten to tell her. "Your name," I said. "He said your name as he was dying."

She stopped, the cloth wet on my forearm, under her hand. Something new flashed in her eyes, a pain I hadn't seen before.

"Do you know who he was?" I asked.

"Yes," she said.

I waited for her to tell me, but she stayed silent and did not move. I glanced up, saw Brune perched on the mantel now, watching me.

"Did you . . . curse him?" I asked.

Slowly, she nodded. "It was not a curse, or at least I did not intend it to be. But I changed him, yes," she said. "A long time ago."

"Who was he?" I asked.

"Someone I loved once," she said. To my surprise, she started crying. She was not making a sound. The tears ran down her cheeks, and she wiped them with the back of her hand. I had never in my life seen her cry.

I watched her in horror, knowing I'd caused her this grief. That it was my fault. I was a terrible, hateful person, I thought then. There was a reason my real parents had neglected and beaten me, let another woman come in and take me away. Even as a child I'd been all wrong. It was a thought that had come to me before, but always as a tiny fear, a sense of hollow dread. Never as a full-blown truth, the way it came now.

"I'm so sorry, Mathena," I said. "I didn't know."

"It's not your fault, Rapunzel," she said, looking up at me with wet eyes. "Please don't think it's your fault. I didn't realize he was so close by, or I would have warned you. You didn't know it was a man."

Loup appeared and curled into my lap, purring. I stroked her behind her ears, cupped her face in my hand.

"Who was he?" I whispered.

Slowly, she picked up the arrow and began turning it around and around in her fingers. "When I lived at court, he was a knight in the king's army. His name was Marcus. He was a powerful magician. I was in love with him, and he taught me many things."

"Why did you change him?" I asked.

She looked down at her hands, and the arrow she was gripping between them. Her hands were wrinkled, run through with veins. I hadn't noticed how old she'd become.

"He was condemned to die," she said. "I changed him so that he could escape. I thought I'd be able to change him back. I tried every spell I could find, but I couldn't change him. I've never stopped trying." She sighed. "Perhaps you gave him the relief I couldn't."

"I'm so sorry," I said again.

Her grief overwhelmed me, and I could not bring myself to say anything else. We sat in silence. She traced the arrow's tip with her fingertips, and then tossed the weapon into the fire.

Sparks flickered from the flames for several moments before the fire calmed down again.

"When the snow melts," she said, finally, "we will go back and bury him."

✦

But the snow would not melt for many weeks yet. The trees stretched blackly into the sky, which we could barely see for the snow that kept falling, covering everything, hiding every sin except for those I was forced to remember. Whether I slept or lay awake at night staring at the dark room, the man I'd killed haunted me, his green eyes looking up at me, full of pain and surprise. Those few moments when he became a man again, his skin pink, alive, naked, beautiful, the fleeting joy he must have felt as he returned to his own body though he was already dying, me standing over him with my bow in my hands. I was possessed by the idea that I might have saved him, had I had more knowledge.

I wanted to learn everything, the spells that could change the order of things. Not just the salves or teas that could mend hearts or make a man desire you or ease the ache of a sore shoulder. Not just the bewitching that had made a prince come to me in the tower, or the spells that could make a garden flourish. I wanted to alter lives, and history. With knowledge like that, I might one day have the power to change a man into a stag, a stag into a man, a child into a king.

A murderess back into a woman who could win the love of a prince.

One day I asked Mathena to scry my future, the way she sometimes did, scattering the tea leaves and seeing what stories they shaped themselves into. As she did, her brows furrowed and I could see that something was wrong.

"What is it?" I asked.

She passed her hand over the leaves, gathering them up, and

tossed them into the fire. They hissed slightly, and glittered as the flames consumed them.

"What did you see?"

"There will be great changes," she said, watching me with a strange mix of sadness and something else, something I could not pinpoint. "Things are happening now . . . that were not destined to happen before."

"Is that good?" I asked.

"You have changed your future."

"How?"

"By killing the stag and breaking the spell. There was powerful magic at work. Interfering with it always comes with some cost, but I can't tell yet if it will benefit or harm you. Either way, you need to be ready."

"For what?"

Mathena did not answer. She brought out an old book of spells, which I'd seen her consult for as long as I could remember. An ancient, crumbling thing she'd inherited from the line of women who had preceded her. I had never before wanted to read it myself. I'd never thought I needed to.

"Take this," she said.

And I did, with trembling fingers. The grief emanating from the book almost suffocated me. Not only Mathena's, but that of all the women who'd consulted it, their longings, their pain and anger and sorrow, their dark, bitter hearts.

A few days later we had news from the kingdom. We were resting, having tea by the fire, when a woman told us that the king, Josef's father, had died unexpectedly and that Josef had ascended to the throne.

"So he is king now," I said. "And she is queen."

"People think King Louis might have been poisoned," the woman told us, leaning in to whisper.

"I would not doubt it," Mathena said. The sharp tone in her voice surprised me. She had known this king, of course. I sensed that she had not liked him. "Though whenever a king dies before his time, people talk of murder."

"He was fine when he went to sleep," the woman said, "and the next morning, he was gone. People say that King Louis and his son never took to each other much." The woman crossed herself. "God rest his soul."

"He was a difficult man," Mathena said.

She did not say any more, but I knew he had changed during his reign, when the new priest came, and that people no longer spoke openly about magic afterward. I knew that her lover couldn't have been sentenced to die without this king's approval. It made sense that news of his death did not come hard to her.

Over the coming days, we heard all the stories and gossip, and I saw a bitterness in Mathena that I had not seen before, as she listened. But she did not say any more about it.

I did not press. My main thought, which I kept to myself, was of my child, and I ran my palms over my swollen belly. It was a thrilling idea: that I was carrying the child not of a prince now, but of a king.

4

Spring finally came, as it always did, and the forest awakened slowly. The snow melted into little rivers. By then, I was heavy with child, and I was soothed by the notion that I could redeem myself through this new life. My own parents had mistreated me, given me away, and now I would bear an infant I would love in a way my parents had never loved me. It filled something broken and black inside me, and this was not something I could explain, especially to Mathena. We went back to the garden, to tend the soil, loosen it for the planting. The flowers burst open around the house and along the edges of our garden, long before they would anywhere else, in the forest or kingdom.

We waited for the soil to warm, and then one morning we went back to the clearing to bury what was left of the man I'd killed.

We measured our movements by the sun. Brune flew along-side us. The forest felt like a graveyard, despite the life every-where, which seemed only to be paying homage to the dead.

"Was he the reason you left the kingdom?" I asked.

"I left for you," she said. "To save you."

"But why did you have to leave and come to the forest? Was it Marcus? The king?"

"I've told you, Rapunzel. We came to the forest so you would be safe."

She strode in front of me, though I had not told her where we were going. Her black hair was a mass of curls behind her. She stepped quickly over brush and branches, as if she knew exactly where each one was located. The forest floor was a map of roots, veins, bones, and all of it seemed to speak of my own grief. We passed the split oak tree, moved along the riverbank. I moved awkwardly compared to her—and now even more so—though I was a daughter of the forest, too.

Eventually, the clearing opened up before us. I braced myself for what we'd find there.

The light poured down through the tree branches, illuminating the massive, dark green plant that was growing there, its zigzag edges. It was the length of a man, with leaves spilling in all directions, like hundreds of flailing limbs.

Mathena gasped next to me. "Rapunzel," she said.

I turned to her. "What is it?"

"Rapunzel," she repeated. "The plant I used to grow, that your father stole from my garden. The plant you're named after."

"This?" I leaned in. She'd told me it would not grow in the forest, and I looked up at her, waiting for an explanation.

The scent wafted over to me then. Sweet, slightly spicy. I breathed in and a series of images passed before my eyes, making me dizzy. A girl running through the forest, a knife flashing in the moonlight.

I blinked.

Mathena stepped forward. The breeze fluttered through her hair, her dress, as she walked to the plant and knelt down next to it. I moved to her side, and sat on the grass next to her, inhaling the scent of the plant. All kinds of words pressed against my tongue, questions, but I stayed silent and waited.

I watched her inhale the scent, which I swear came off the rapunzel in whiffs of glittering smoke. I saw it, and then it disappeared. I looked up overhead, just as Brune passed over us. A nest of birds twittered from one of the tree branches.

I reached for a leaf, shining and green.

"Don't," she said, snatching my hand back.

I stared at the leaf in my hand, shocked. I had been about to eat it. I tossed it back onto the plant, nearly gagging. "This is him, isn't it?" I asked. "This . . . plant?"

She nodded. Gently, she ran her fingers across the rapunzel, the leaves shooting out in every direction, a bright red flower bursting from its center. I hadn't seen it at first, that blooming scarlet thing, right where his heart would be. As I watched, she reached in and—to my horror—she plucked it out, in one quick movement.

Mathena whispered words into the leaves and then stood up, holding the flower out in front of her, clasped between her hands like a wedding bouquet.

"We will tend this place," she said. "And plant fennel all around it for protection."

She tore the flower in half and handed one of the pieces to me. I grabbed it, opened my palm. The petals fanned out, an intense red against my pale skin.

"Now," she said, looking at me directly, her expression purposeful. "Eat it."

"Why?" I looked up at her.

"To honor him."

"I don't understand."

"He was a powerful man. Though you didn't mean to, you took his life, and now you must honor him, take his strength into you. We both must."

I looked down, feeling suddenly faint. I stuffed the flower into my mouth. Its tang extended out like fingers, making me shiver with pleasure. I felt something drip from my lips, and without thinking wiped my chin with the back of my hand.

A strange, woozy feeling went through me, as I stood in the liquid sunlight and saw Mathena cupping the flower in her palms and drinking it in. For a moment I was sure we were underwater, that the birds passing overhead were fish, the trees' spears reaching for the surface.

I looked down, and my hands were stained red.

We walked to the river, and bent down to wash our hands and arms in it, splash the water on our faces. Every water droplet like a diamond, suspended in the air and on our skin.

I don't know if it was because of the flower we ate or not, but I felt better that spring. I was filled with the pleasure of moving my fists into the earth, burying seeds within it, knowing that those seeds would grow into the lush fruits and herbs the summer would bring. It was arduous work, especially with my expanding belly, but I reveled in the exhaustion that blotted out everything else. We planted the seeds we'd gathered the autumn before, and we saved scraps of food to turn back into the earth. Mathena bent over the garden, thinning the vegetables, while I did less taxing work in the kitchen, cooking our meals and brewing teas for the garden with the skins of onions, cucumbers, and quince, the ends of carrots and cabbage and wild celery, feathers and bones that I'd burnt down to ash. The earth was thirsty, starving it seemed. Every afternoon I'd tromp through the garden, pour in the compost tea, and add in the droppings of our horse, piles of leaves, anything we could find, while overhead the sun beat down and the world came to life all around us.

Our garden grew more bountifully than it ever had. We ate great piles of spinach topped with vinegar, oil, and salt, and I boiled delicious stews of potherbs and meat while bread baked in the oven. It was far too much bounty for two women, even with a child growing inside me, and so we gave out food by the basketful to the ladies who came to see us, often in the evening hours, when their own work was done.

One morning I woke and found spots of blood on my nightgown and the sheets under me. I dressed and carried the linens to the river, let the blood wash out in the clear water.

Over the course of the morning, I realized that my baby seemed unusually still. Mathena was off hunting with Brune, and so I sent up a quick prayer to Artemis and kept at my tasks. At midafternoon I was standing over the fire, inhaling the scent of boiling beets and porrettes, when the cramping came, so strongly that the room began to spin around me. I dropped the spoon I was using, which clattered on the hard floor.

Something was horribly wrong.

I crumpled to the floor, doubling over and holding my belly. "Mathena!" I cried.

As the cramping began to subside, I reached under my skirts, to the center of my body. When I pulled my hand away, it was covered in blood.

I forced myself up, and reached for a cloth to wad up and press between my legs.

Another wave of pain moved through me and I bent over again, grasping the back of the couch. Sweat poured down my face as I slumped back to the floor, twisted to my side, and pressed my face into the cool dirt.

I don't know how long I stayed there, moaning and crying as the pain assaulted me and retreated, and then came back again.

I could feel him leaving me, this child I loved too much already, and it might as well have been my heart slipping from my chest. My body was coming apart, my insides wrenching themselves. I was like bread dipped in water, unloosening. It was so real to me that I am sure, even now, that there was a whole child there, screaming and flailing and looking up at me, something deeply wrong with it, it was all wrong, though I know it was my own being screaming like that as the makings of my child fell from me and left me scraped out and bare.

When Mathena found me, the blood and tissue had seeped through my gown, staining it bright red.

I had dreamt him, I knew his face, his bright eyes.

I was on the floor, balled up, my legs knotted together around that ruined dress drenched in blood. Too exhausted to speak.

She lifted me into her arms, carried me outside, into the fresh air, onto the grass.

I was sobbing, talking gibberish, and Mathena just sang and soothed me and cleaned me the best she could, and finally, when I had exhausted myself, she pulled the dress from my body, and took it away.

"Shhhh," she said, moving her hand along my forehead, smoothing back my hair.

She washed me gently as if I myself were a child—and I suppose I was—cleaning me and putting me back together, the way she'd always done, as far back as I could remember.

Later, much later, she would tell me that it was a boy, as I'd known it would be. "It is better that he slipped away," she would say then, "rather than live the life it would have lived. He was not . . . shaped the way children should be shaped."

The day my son died, Mathena took my soiled dress, along with all that was wrapped inside it, and placed it on the fire. As it burned, she whispered spells, prayers, and sprinkled the fire with potions and oils. I was not conscious enough to know what was happening, but I could feel it, smell the scent of the burning, the anguish of what was left of my son disappearing from this earth.

She buried his ashes at the edge of the garden.

For several days, I slipped in and out of a dream state, and in my dreams my son came to life. I could hold him and smell his milky scent, I could walk up the steps of the palace and present the child to the king. And in my dreams, the court recognized him and took him to soft beds, to places where he'd never be cold, where he'd grow strong and ferocious and never die. Imagine! Being able to move through time as if it were water, and change the course of things, prevent the coming of grief. I dreamed of Josef standing over him, saying, "My son."

"My son."

Sometimes I'd dream that I was holding him in my arms,

his soft soft skin folding into mine, the smell of him infusing everything, entering me, my whole body, every cell of it filled with love and relief and a crazy new happiness, and then I would wake up, the whole world going flat when I remembered he was dead.

And then one by one I'd see the stone walls of our cottage, the fire dying in the hearth, Mathena curled up next to me for warmth, my hair blanketing us both.

I'm surprised it didn't choke us to death.

When I finally rose from the bed and rejoined the waking world, I begged Mathena to give me that ancient potion that would make me forget: forget my lost child, forget the prince who was now king, forget his wife the queen and the child who would be born when my own child had died. I longed to go back to the time when all I knew was the woods around us.

"You gave it to me once," I said. "The forgetting potion. Please do it again. Let me start over the way I did before."

But she refused. "Better things await you," she said, as we opened the shutters and stared out at the melting world. Because finally, too late, the world began to warm. "You need only to be patient."

I stared at her blankly. The word had no meaning to me when my anguish swallowed me whole, when all I could see was grief unfurling in front of me.

I began to think that if she wouldn't perform the spell, I could find it and do it myself. I started poring over the book she had given me. It was slow going. I knew how to read, of course, Mathena had taught me that, but I had not done very much book learning before then. Now I welcomed the relief the words offered me, the opportunity they gave me to disappear, at least a little, the promise they gave me of forgetting everything altogether.

I came upon spells I had not encountered before in our practice. Spells to change the color of one's eyes, to call forth a storm, to enter someone's dreams, to transform a stone into gold, a leaf into a feather, a rose into a bird. There were endless spells, and the more they meddled with the substance of a thing, or sought to change a human fate or heart, the more difficult they were to decipher. Warnings abounded, scribbled throughout. *Do not cast this spell during the full moon, or while the crops are being harvested. Do not cast this spell with a black heart.* I came, too, upon new spells for things I had seen plenty of times before: spells to seduce, to call a love to you, to end a pregnancy or help create one.

It was something I saw in one of those spells that first made me suspicious of Mathena, and the teas she had fed me while I was pregnant. When women came to see us desperate to end their pregnancy, we'd always given them pennyroyal and mugwort, with their distinctive, sharp scents. In the book, I saw herbs like tansy, parsley, cotton root bark, and had a visceral memory, the spice of parsley on my tongue. She would have been very careful, wouldn't she? Feeding me herbs I did not know, in small amounts. Would she have done that to me? I knew I had had parsley, and the more I read about tansy and cotton root bark, the more I suspected that these were the herbs I'd been given. I stole into the root cellar and sifted carefully through the baskets of dried herbs we kept there. But I did not find what I was looking for.

When I confronted her, she denied it.

"Why would I want to harm you, Rapunzel?" she asked, looking at me. "When I have given up my whole life for you?"

I remained silent after that.

❧

As spring shifted to summer, our garden became more and more lush, filled with vegetables and fruits so large and bright they were almost obscene. We kept the garden watered and fed and were able to start harvesting, filling baskets with bright vegetables and storing them for colder months.

And every day I visited my baby's grave. Soon enough, a twisting, green-leafed plant grew from that spot, with beautiful crimson flowers bursting from it, like hearts. I stroked its leaves and petals, whispered into its roots, watered it with my tears.

In the fine weather, women started appearing at the house regularly again. We were constantly working to tend to them as well as the garden, which everyone who came to us whispered had to be the work of pure magic. No one could imagine vegetables like that growing from the earth on their own.

I threw myself into my work. What else was there for me to do? I knew now the grief of those women, with their unrequited loves, their fatherless children, their falls in fortune, their barren gardens and fields.

It occurred to me one day to take down a lock of my hair and brush it along the arm of a woman sitting in front of us, her sick child on her lap. I moved my hair from her to her child, and it happened just as it had happened with the prince and the man in the forest: I could feel them. The woman, who until that moment had been like any other woman from one of the kingdom's villages, now had a life and soul to her as vivid as Mathena's or my own. I could see her memories, the years she'd spent caring for her sick mother, her sick children, her husband who'd gone into the king's army and never come home. I could feel their hot, wet foreheads under her palms, under *my* palms. I could feel the illness that even now was wending its way through her boy's body, draining him of the little strength he had left.

Without even thinking I told her what to do. "Wash him with vinegar and rosewater," I said, momentarily possessed. "And burn rosemary as an incense around his bed. Also, you must roast eggshells and grind them into a powder. Add the powder and chopped rosehips into a pot of ale, warm the mixture, and let the child drink it."

"I will get you the rosewater, incense, and flowers," Mathena said, her face registering her deep shock, and she quickly left the room.

"Could you get some angelica as well?" I called out after her. I turned back to the woman. "You will weave the leaves into necklaces, for protection. Let everyone in your household wear one."

She nodded. The boy moaned and shifted in her arms.

"You will be well again," I said softly, taking her hand, as Mathena had so often taken mine.

When the woman and child left, I was exhausted. Her sadness had latched onto my own.

Mathena was uncharacteristically quiet as we ate our stew and prepared for bed that night.

"Your hair is a great gift," she said, finally. "I didn't realize how great. You can be more powerful than me, or any of my teachers."

"You believe that?" I asked, taken aback.

"Yes."

"Did you always know what it could do?"

"I suspected," she said. "When you were . . . a child, I saw the way feelings came to you, through your hair. You were so sensitive. I thought it was safer for you to keep it up."

"Have you hidden yourself from it?" I asked. "I cannot feel anything when you touch me, the way I can with others."

"Yes," she said softly.

"I thought Josef was special," I said. "I thought it was only him I could feel that way. But I suppose it is most everyone, isn't it?"

"Yes," she said. "I'm sorry I did not warn you. You might have seen him differently."

I nodded, and remained quiet.

Over the next day, and all the days to follow, I focused on this gift that I'd been given, and took solace in it. If I couldn't have Josef or my baby or any other happiness in the world, then through my gift and through my own suffering, I could help others. If I couldn't redeem myself by giving my son a beautiful life, loving him more than any child had ever been loved before, I could do this.

Between the garden and the ladies who came to see us, and the work that was so much more exhausting for me now, we were so busy that I almost managed to forget the king and queen. I even began to imagine that I would be all right living my whole life in the forest, taking over for Mathena one day, spending all my days helping those who needed help, healing, relief.

And then came more news from the palace. "Isn't it

wonderful?" a peasant woman asked. She had come to us because her family's crop was failing and her children were starving. I was packing a basket of vegetables and meat for her to take home when her voice shifted, the way everyone's did when there was news like this to share. "About the new princess?"

"The new what?" I stopped, my hand clasped around a cucumber.

"The queen has had a child. A perfect pale baby with a tuft of black hair. The very image of her mother."

"Wonderful," I said. My knees nearly buckled under me. "Yes."

In all my own grief, I'd forgotten about this other child.

"What's her name?" I asked, my heart twisting in my chest.

"They call the child Snow White."

We were told that the infant's christening was a great event. Queen Teresa's father and mother—the king and queen of the East—came with their entire court to celebrate the result of the union of kingdoms, and there were celebrations for days.

As woman after woman told us about the festivities, I listened without saying a word.

They told us how beautiful the infant was, with jet-black hair, skin as white as snow, lips as red as cherries in the height of summer.

Sometimes, in those moments, I was sure it was my own child in the palace, that there was some mistake.

And as soon as I could, I'd hurry up the tower stairs and stand looking out over the trees to the distant palace, imagining my son there in a golden crib, surrounded by adoring courtiers, swathed in expensive silks. They were dangerous thoughts but when they came, less and less often through the next years, I found them comforting. Imagining that somewhere, he lived still.

And so the years passed. Our garden flourished and died and then flourished again. Women came to see us complaining of broken hearts and unfaithful husbands and lovers, and later their daughters came to us with the same troubles. We heard news, eventually, that the queen mother died, and reports that the princess Snow White was growing into an uncommonly intelligent child. Crimson flowers bloomed on my child's grave every spring, vanished again every autumn. The seasons passed and the world did not stop the way, sometimes, I was sure my own heart had.

The king never came to see me, though I often thought of him, and sometimes tried to call him to me the way I had once. By all accounts, my beauty only grew greater with each passing day, but it did me little good. I would avoid the tower for weeks on end and then find myself gripped by passion, nostalgia, running up those stone stairs to the room where our child had been made. There, sometimes, in the mirror, I found him. I'd look at my own reflection and see the prince—now king—sitting behind me on the bed, holding our child on his lap.

"You're really here," I'd say, the way I had before. "Aren't you?"

But he never answered, though every year he grew more distinguished, and every year my child grew bigger, with bright blond hair like his mother's. I'd see them in flashes, behind my face in the glass, but whenever I'd turn to them, my heart swelling, my eyes burning with tears and hope, the vision would vanish and the real world, with its constant needs and ever-present hunger—of the earth, the body, and the heart—asserted itself once again.

5

Seven winters had come and buried us in snow when one afternoon an unusual woman came to see us.

It was nearly dark outside, despite the time of day. Mathena and I were indoors by a massive growling fire, mixing batches of herbs into poultices. It was easy, soothing work that allowed each of us to only be half there—until a knock on the door yanked us into the present.

"I'll get it," I said.

Outside, a figure stood hunched over, the wind whipping around her, furs pulled tightly against her body. Behind her, the trees swayed, shaking snow into the air.

"Come in," I said, stepping back to give her room.

She looked up at me and I was struck by how lovely her eyes were, wide and gray. "My horse," she said weakly.

"I'll take him to the stable and make sure he is tended," Mathena said, grabbing her own skins and moving outside.

I looked at the girl more closely, and was surprised to see that her face was marked with tears, which had frozen on her skin in tiny crystals. What a beautiful effect, I thought—it was as if her skin were covered in jewels. She stepped inside, shivering.

Underneath her furs, which I helped her take off and then hung by the fire to dry, she was dressed richly, in silk and velvet.

"Come and sit," I said. I led her to the far side of the couch, next to the fire, where she could warm herself, and put the kettle to heat with herbs for a nice tea. I watched, transfixed, as her tears melted and ran down her face.

Mathena returned a few minutes later, her face red from the cold.

"How far did you travel?" I asked.

"I came from the palace," the girl said, her voice cracking, and I looked at her in surprise.

Aside from the prince, no one from the court itself had ever come to us, in all this time.

The fire crackled, kicking up shadows over her face. She had a small red heart-shaped mouth, auburn hair twisted in braids around her face. And on her face, a faint black marking, next to her right eye.

"My name is Clareta," she said.

I handed her the cup and her hands trembled as she took it. As I did, a few loose strands of my hair must have brushed her skin, because I could feel, suddenly, her guilt and longing, as if they'd smacked me. A moment later, I knew what she'd done. I could see it.

"Do you serve the queen?" Mathena asked, sitting next to her on the couch.

"Yes," she said. "No one must know I have come here."

"Of course." Mathena glanced up at me, watched me as I sat in a chair across from them.

"I am her favorite lady-in-waiting," she whispered. "I have heard that you can be trusted, and that you know how to heal . . . how to do things. That you know magic."

"Where do you hear this?"

"The queen mother," she whispered, "before she died last year."

Mathena nodded. "She was a good friend to me once. Do not worry. You can trust us. I know it's a crime for you to come here."

"Thank you," Clareta said. "I love my lady truly, but of late I have been . . ." Her eyes welled up, and she was having difficulty speaking.

"Been what?" I asked, impatient. The fire roared, thunderous. Above it, Brune stretched her wings.

"I have done wrong by her."

"You have lain with the king," I heard myself saying.

The girl gasped, looking at me. Tears streamed down her face. "How do you know that?"

"I can see it," I said. And I could: see his arms encircling her, that hair of hers unbraided, dropping down her back, into his palms.

Half of me wanted to soothe her, the other half wanted to smack her wet face. How could she think he would ever love her, if he wasn't able to love *me*? I knew, suddenly, that he had been with many women. He was a king, after all. I must have been one of countless lovers. The knowledge leaked through me like a poison.

"What happened?" Mathena asked, making her voice soothing and low. She shot me a warning look and I leaned back, but did not take my focus off Clareta.

"I lay with him," she said. "I knew I was doing wrong, and

yet he called me to him and I . . . I went with him. I don't know why I did it, but I didn't feel like I had a choice, when it happened."

"And now?"

"And now he does not look at me."

Mathena held the girl's hand. "I know how painful that must be."

"Yes," she said. "And the way she looks at me, I'm afraid that she knows. My heart is broken already, but I do not want to break hers, too."

"Why not?" I asked, leaning in. "Why do you love her so much?"

"She is kind," she said, "and beautiful. She is a good woman, too, and is always saying her devotions. My family was starving and she took me in, made me one of her ladies. I don't know if you know how hard it is now, in the kingdom, for those not favored by the court. My family has nothing. If she finds out, if I lose my position, they will starve. And she and the king, together—it is what we all long for. The way the king looks at her! For one day he looked at me like that and I couldn't resist it. I know it was not my place, I'm not a princess or a queen, I'm not his, and yet . . ."

Mathena put her hand on my shoulder, and I brushed it off.

"For a moment," she said, "I felt like I was her. Someone like her."

"You liked lying with the king?" I asked softly, letting my voice wash over her, like a soothing hand.

"I liked the person I became when I was with him. I am someone who is never happy."

I tilted my head, watching her. "Does he love his wife?"

She nodded.

"You want him to love you, the way he loves her?"

"I did, yes."

"You want to be sure that she never knows what you've done," Mathena said.

She nodded. "Please help me."

"Rapunzel," Mathena said, "can you get some arrowroot and dandelion from the cellar?"

I looked sharply at her, then realized that I was shaking, barely breathing. I stood and went down to the root cellar, where we kept the dried herbs and potions along with our food. The scent of earth overwhelmed me, as always. It was like being buried alive.

Mathena was right to give me a moment alone, I realized. I leaned against the wall, crouched down onto the dirt floor.

Everything came back to me. The wounds so fresh it seemed as if no time had passed at all. I wanted to scream with frustration. What good was our craft if I could end up like this, mourning a moment that had long passed? Surely Mathena's powers extended past this. Surely mine did.

I felt something land on my shoulder, shocking me back to the present. Brune had flown downstairs and was rubbing her beak against my face. I laughed, cooed to her. It was odd behavior for such a ferocious predator, but I was used to it. I'd watched Brune rip apart animals limb to limb, and had turned away so I wouldn't retch. I'd watched her race through the air more quickly than one of my own arrows, right to her target.

"Let's go," I said, quickly gathering the dandelion and arrowroot. As an afterthought, I grabbed some dragon's root and stuffed it in my pocket.

When I returned, Clareta was at the kitchen table, eating a bowl of stew Mathena had set before her.

I spread out the arrowroot and dandelion on the counter, and began to mix them together into a piece of cloth. As I did, Mathena stood and left the room. I watched her step down to the root cellar.

"Thank you," Clareta said, pausing from her meal and looking up at me. Of course, she must have been famished, unused to such hard travel. "Thank you for helping me."

I did not respond, but focused on my work. I added in the bit of dragon's root, too, infusing it with intent. There was no harm in making her more unappealing to the king. *More ugly than a snake,* I mouthed.

When I held the bundle under her face, finally, and asked her to breathe in, I could feel the pain easing in her. The whole house became lighter, instantly. Even the fire seemed to shift color, becoming more brilliant.

I could not help but think how weak she was. The magic worked on her so quickly.

"Now that is better, isn't it?" I asked softly.

Mathena reappeared and walked over slowly, a strange look on her face. She handed Clareta a small, cloth-wrapped package.

"Here is something else," she said, "because I've taken pity on you."

"What is it?" Clareta asked.

I looked at Mathena, trying to catch her eye. I'd never seen her do anything like this before. Her face was bright, alive. Only I would have seen how carefully she was watching the girl. The package bulged and I thought I saw a faint glimmer come from inside of it. I blinked and shook my head.

"I've gathered some special charms for you," Mathena said. "Brew this into a tea for your queen. It will ensure that she will never know what you have done. No one else should drink it. Only her."

Clareta took the package and clutched it in her hands, as if Mathena had handed her a bag of jewels. Her eyes were wet with pain, with gratitude.

After, I led her to the tower. She was still exhausted from her travel, and from the magic working to calm her. There was no way she could return home tonight.

We crunched over snow. The torch in my hands flickered in the night air. I was thinking only about the packages she was holding.

"How strange that there is a tower, in the forest," she said dreamily. The moon shone down, making the snow sparkle. The tower loomed up in front of us. I was so used to it, I could forget how it looked to strangers, the way it reached up into the stars as if it were stabbing them.

"There was a castle here once, is all," I said. "Our house is built from the ruins. They're all around." I pointed to the piles of stones sticking out of the snow, the top of an old wall just past the garden, still visible.

"I feel like I'm going to be locked up," she said, laughing nervously.

I looked up at the window, imagined myself leaning out of it, my hair stretching down to where we stood now.

"Don't be silly," I said, more harshly than I intended.

I pushed open the heavy door, and began walking up the

winding stairs, holding the torch in front of me. She followed closely behind and I had the wicked thought that I could kick my foot back, drop her down the stairs.

I pushed such thoughts away and led her up to my room. What had happened was not her fault.

"I will light you a fire," I said, throwing new wood and leaves into the hearth and carefully lighting them with the torch.

In the mirror, I watched her set the packages on the bed. She moved about the room, touching the walls with her palms.

I had a sudden flash of anger. My eyes shifted to my own face, and I was the same woman the troubadours sang about. Could he have loved this girl, with the marking on her face? Could he love his wife, more than me? Had I not been the most beautiful, of the three of us? Was I not still?

I walked over to the window and looked out into the snowy night.

"Is that the palace?" she asked, appearing next to me, her voice full of wonder. In the distance, the palace glittered in the dark.

"Yes," I replied.

For a moment we stood next to each other, staring out over the forest to the palace. I imagined how we looked from the ground, our two pale faces in the moonlight. She was my height, my stature. So close to me I could hear her breathing, feel the slight warmth from her body.

I turned to her, studied her auburn hair and delicate features, her moony, sad eyes gazing out at the world she'd left behind.

"It must be so peaceful out here," she said, sighing.

I thought of the wild howling, myself in the mirror feral and strewn through with leaves and dirt, Brune ripping apart everything in her path. The bandits racing in the dark woods. Plants in the root cellar that could make a woman lose her mind, her heart, her child.

I thought of the world she was comparing it to. What was it like? Right now in that palace, what hearts were being torn to pieces?

"Peaceful," I said. "Yes."

I moved down the stairway alone, back out into the snowy night and to the cottage, where Mathena sat on the couch, waiting.

She looked at me, an intense, impassioned expression on her face.

Something was happening, I realized. Something new.

"What did you give her?" I asked.

"Medicine for the queen."

"But what? Is it the forgetting potion?"

"No."

"What, then?" I asked more loudly then, my heart hammering in my chest.

Still staring at me intently, she said, "It's time, Rapunzel. We have been waiting a long time for this."

"For what?"

I backed away, toward the door. She was scaring me.

"Your chance to have what you always wanted."

"How? What do you mean?"

"Clareta will give the packet I gave her to the queen. The girl is desperate, Rapunzel," she said calmly. "She will do anything to secure her place at court, to protect herself from the queen's wrath. She will serve this tea to the queen because she believes it will save her."

She was so warm, Mathena, her voice rasping, soothing. She could have been talking to a sick child.

"And then, my dear," she said, placing her hands over my own with such tenderness I wanted to weep, "you can have him. You can be queen in her place."

"But . . ." Nothing she was saying made sense to me. "The queen . . . I don't understand . . . ?"

"This is your destiny, Rapunzel."

"What is?"

"To be queen."

The words were horrible, strange, exhilarating as she said them. I looked at her, beginning to understand. "What is in the package you gave her?"

"Dried juniper, nettle, wild cherry, nightshade."

"Nightshade?"

"Just a touch," she said. "A few leaves and berries, ground up."

"But that's . . ."

"Yes. Enough to kill her."

I sat back. In front of us, the fire roared. Outside, snow was just beginning to fall, lit up by the faint, silvery moonlight.

"But, even if . . ." I grasped for words, not believing what we were saying. "He hasn't returned to me, Mathena, in all this time."

"He did come back," she said. "He could not find you."

"Of course he could have found me. He could have found me whenever he pleased. He came here twice!"

And then I looked at her more closely, as a new realization began to dawn. "Why could he not find me . . . ?" I asked.

Her expression did not change. She might have been telling

me the stew was ready. "Because I hid the cottage and the tower from him."

"You mean, he came back? Looking for me?"

"Yes. He tried to find you, Rapunzel. I did not let him. He's come back several times over the years."

I reeled from her words. The room seemed to spin around me, take on new shapes.

"Why would you do that?" I whispered. A fury and a grief welled up in me. She had betrayed me. She had kept him from me, let me think for years that he did not care whether he ever saw me again. But he had.

He had come back.

"I wanted you to become his queen, Rapunzel. I knew all we had to do was wait. You were not meant to be one of the women he keeps around for his pleasure, like the girl sleeping in the tower right now."

I stared at her, stunned, as it sank into me. What she had done. What I could let happen.

I could be queen.

If what Mathena said was true, I would be queen.

"It's not too late to take the package back from her," she said. "If you do not want this."

"No!" I said too quickly.

She smiled slightly, but did not say a word.

The words rushed out of me: "What happens when the queen dies?" I asked. "Shall we go to the palace, show ourselves to him?"

"We will wait, the way we have all this time."

"For what?"

"For him to come to you."

"How do you know he will do that?"

"He thinks of you, Rapunzel. He's heard stories that your beauty is greater than ever. I have made sure of it. It maddens him that others can see you, but he cannot. He suspects you are under a spell. He will keep looking. Once his queen is dead, nothing will stop him."

I did not sleep that night, lying on the bed next to Mathena and thinking about the girl in the tower with the nightshade tea. Aghast at what Mathena had said to me, what she was suggesting, and yet filled with hope and possibility. Could we change everything, just like that? I thought, too, of the man I'd killed. That had been an accident; this would be deliberate. I would be killing someone on purpose, and not just anyone, the queen. Several times I rose from the mattress and paced about the room while Mathena slept soundly, her face more peaceful than I'd ever seen it.

At one point, I threw back the covers, wrapped myself in furs, and strode outside with every intention of grabbing the package from Clareta and giving her a mild protection tea in its place.

I stopped. I stood under the night sky, shivering in my furs as snow whirled and fell around me. Above me, the girl slept.

My heart was torn. This was what I wanted. All I had ever wanted. I'd suppressed it for all this time, content enough to be a healer in the forest, intent on redeeming myself, devoting myself to the women who sought us out, letting my old dreams slip into long-ago memories that had nothing to do with my life now. Now I thought of Mathena's stories about reading stars for the queen, about the prince climbing my hair and entering the tower,

all those memories that had flowed from him to me. Such riches!
Even now I was breathless thinking of it. I was the same girl
who'd raged in that tower, imagining the ball going on without
her. But between then and now I'd had a son who'd died inside
of me, and if it had not been for the queen, I might have lived in
the palace, away from the herbs and the backbreaking work and
Mathena, and my son might have lived. He might have grown
strong and bright!

He might have lived.

And all this time, Mathena had known that this chance would
come, had been waiting for it.

Already, it felt like something I was destined for.

In the end, I did not go to the tower. I stood there wrapped in
furs, staring up at the night sky with all its stories, and decided
to let fate run its course. I turned around, slipped back into the
bed, and though I did not sleep at all that night, I did not venture
out of bed again.

The next morning, I stood at the door with Mathena and
watched Clareta ride off into the snowy forest, back to the palace, the herbs we'd given her tucked into her bag.

"Godspeed," I said, and I meant it.

The next few weeks passed in a tense state of waiting. I told
myself that I had waited for seven years and I could wait a few
days, or weeks, or months, longer. Whatever it had to be.

It did not take months or even many weeks, however, before
word of the queen's death came to us. The news came as all news
did: first from one woman, and then from every other woman
who visited us.

The queen had taken ill one night and slipped into a violent fever. The next day she died in her bed, with her husband and daughter by her side.

"It was terrible," we heard. "One day she was the vision of health and the next she was gone."

There was talk of poison, just as there had been with Josef's father. The maid who'd actually served the queen her tea had been executed the same day, though she'd denied any wrongdoing. I listened to the reports with horror. I couldn't even imagine it: two lives, extinguished in a day. I moved from guilt and shame to relief, excitement, and then the feeling that none of it could be real. How could it be real? How could all these distant horrors be of our making?

Everyone spoke of the queen's sudden death, in the days that followed. For a while our work became harder, because the spells needed to be stronger to cut through all the pain and sadness that had spread throughout the kingdom. The queen had been beloved. She had brought peace and prosperity to the kingdom, the light of God and all His fortune. Now everyone was bereft, from the king himself down to the lowliest servant. It was a terrible omen, we heard, again and again, that she had died so suddenly, having borne only one child, and a girl at that.

Talk started right away, of what the king would do next. Who would bear him a male heir? What would the fate of the kingdom be, now that the queen, who had aligned our kingdom with the East, our longtime enemy, was gone?

The whole kingdom seemed to have a new energy crackling through it. We could even feel it in the forest. Whenever I could, I escaped to my tower and stared at those glittering spires in the far distance, waiting.

If I had learned anything in the forest, from tending the garden every year, from filling the soil with crushed bones and dead things, from eating the flower that bloomed from the midst of the rapunzel, and from being raised by Mathena, who had bigger plans for me than I could have ever imagined, it was this: that out of death comes life.

Always.

6

Winter turned to spring. The air smelled of perfume, and the plants burst from the earth. I'd worked in the garden all morning, lunched with Mathena on vegetable stew, and taken a nap, and now I was standing in the tower window, looking out over the bountiful forest, the trees full of singing birds and flowering branches. I'd painted my lips with berries, and was wearing the prettiest dress I had. I knew he might appear at any moment.

And then, before I heard the sound of the horse's hooves, I saw him, winding his way underneath the trees, on the forest floor, the silver reins and the jewels on his clothing radiant in the sunlight. It might have been a group of fairies out exploring, the way the vision shimmered.

He looked up at me, leaving me breathless. I wanted to turn and run down to him, but I did not want to stop watching him, afraid he might disappear.

"Rapunzel!" he said, as he pulled those elaborate reins and his horse, black and shining, stopped.

If he had been impressive before, now he was like something that had dropped from the sky, like a god from the stories Mathena had told me, of men who rode chariots that carried the sun. He was covered in jewels, his clothes were even more fine, and though he still had the look of a beautiful boy about him, his face suffused with a sweet impishness, he seemed to take up more space in the world. He was a king now. A widower, a father. There was a regalness to him that had not been there before.

I breathed in.

He dismounted the horse, the sun hitting his boots, the silver looping around them.

"Josef," I said. I loved the way his name felt in my mouth, like a whisper.

"Rapunzel," he repeated, gazing up at me. He smiled with joy, and it washed over his face, illuminating him utterly. "Let down your hair."

I couldn't even think to answer him. Or let him know how easily I could have walked down to him, to the garden.

Instead, with shaking hands, I removed the cloth that covered my head, and let my hair drop to the ground, all of it streaming out the window, catching the light. I steeled myself against the stone as the weight of it threatened to pull me down, too. It was longer than it had been before, and as it hit the ground it formed brilliant heaps. His face turned golden as the light gleamed from my hair and reflected off of him.

He wrapped his hands around the locks in front of him, moved his face into my hair as he watched me with those gray-blue cat's eyes, the rest of his face buried in gold.

I felt it, that touch, those eyes, as if he'd slipped his hand down my spine, tracing the path with his fingertips. I knew, as soon as he touched me, that what Mathena had said was true: He'd never forgotten me. He'd tried to come back for me.

All those days and months and years working in the forest, and this was my fate, right here.

He hoisted himself up and began to climb.

It seemed fitting, though he was king now, for him to climb my hair once again. I laughed out loud, at the absurdity of it, his face as he climbed—he was *enjoying* it, he liked having to climb to his lady, it was the troubadour in him.

His thoughts and memories rushed up to me, through each strand, the way they had before. By now I'd learned to absorb the energy that came to me that way, take it into me and let it pass through me, all that love, that longing for me, the grief he felt over the death of his parents, of his wife, and his great love for his daughter, the kingdom that blazed in his mind and heart. And I could feel his grief. I could see him running to Teresa's room when news came that she was dying. Feel his heartbreak as he took her hand in his, as he watched her writhe in the bed, as he held his daughter afterward and tried to explain to her that her mother was gone. Feel, before then, his anguish at having to marry her when he only dreamed of me, the slow giving over of his heart as he came to know her, love her, see her features in the face of his child.

It was surprising, overwhelming, being in his mind and heart, feeling them roil over me. My own guilt and angst and happiness, all mixed together, were buried in the onslaught of his feelings.

He climbed my hair easily. And then there he was, pulling himself into the tower, standing before me, and once again we were grabbing my hair in bundles through the window as if we were weaving it on a loom.

I wondered if I should curtsy, as Mathena had the day I met

him. I was sure it was mandatory to curtsy in front of the king, or at the very least to kiss his ring. He had several rings now, one circling each finger, studded with gems. Instead, I just stood and stared at him.

He was nearly in tears as he gazed at me.

"You have come," I said, and I smiled to reassure him.

He continued to stare at me, stricken. "I can't believe you're in front of me. I searched for you, and I could never find you. The tower, it disappeared." He reached out and touched my face, cupping my cheek in his warm palm.

"I was right here," I said.

I could feel his awe, his awareness of all the time that had passed. For me it was different—it was as if the last seven years had never happened, as if time had gone backward for us and given us this moment again. Another chance.

"You have not been locked in this tower all this time, have you?"

I laughed. "No."

"Well, now that I've finally found you, I will have to make sure you cannot disappear again."

"How will you do that?"

He smiled, put his hand on his heart, and dropped down to one knee. "I thought I would ask you to marry me," he said.

I looked down at his handsome face, his eyes, which slanted up slightly on the sides like almonds. I glanced up, saw my own face staring back at me in the mirror.

For a moment, the past weighed on me, and I had a terrible urge to tell him that it had been a mistake, to have married someone else at all. I wanted to tell him about his son in the ground. That the result of the time he'd spent with me was a dead, buried child with limbs as twisted as the plant that grew above it.

But I couldn't say any of that. It was not his fault he had been forced to marry another, not his fault she'd been fated to die, not his fault Mathena had hidden me from him until this day.

"Will you marry me?" he asked again.

I did not hesitate. "Yes," I said.

Of course I said yes.

Yes.

7

We ran down the steps together, to Mathena. We did not act like a king and soon-to-be queen, that day and all those first days to follow. We ran down the steps like children, and he pulled me into his arms and swung me around, my dress flying, my hair swirling around us, gathering grass and flowers, and even bits of horsehair as it swiped the waiting animal.

"Mathena!" I called out, and she appeared instantly, from the back of the house, her dark dress stained with mud and earth.

"We are to be married!" I said.

She looked at me and smiled. "What wonderful news." She bowed down in front of us. "It is a great, great day for all of us."

I unlatched myself from him, and rushed over to her, wrapping my arms around her. Brune flew out just then, landing on Mathena's shoulder, and I somehow managed to kiss the bird, too, who looked at me with disgust as she let out a horrified squawk.

It hit me in that moment that I would really be leaving—leaving the forest and Mathena and starting a brand-new life without them.

"Let me have a few days," I said, turning to the king. "I need a few days to prepare myself."

"I will have your chambers prepared for you, ladies ready to serve you. Are you sure you will not disappear again?"

"I promise I will not," I said.

"I'll send my men to get you, and then we'll be married."

"Yes," I said again. "Yes."

He slipped his arms around me, nuzzled my neck.

"We will be so happy," he said. "We will have many children. Among them, a king."

A sliver of pain moved through my happiness, but I did not let him see. I vowed, right then, that he never would.

Mathena and I watched him leave, disappearing into the trees, and then we were alone, as if a storm had passed through the forest, leaving an entirely new world in its wake.

We walked silently into the house, and sat on the couch, before the low fire. She put on a pot of stew to cook and sat next to me. Brune took her place on the mantel, tucking in her head.

"I can't believe it," I said. "I can't believe you knew this would happen!"

"And now you will be queen. This is what I've always wanted for you."

I shook my head. "Madness," I said. "Pure madness to think I could marry a king, and now it is happening."

"Your life will be very different from now on."

"I should think so!" I said, laughing from pure giddiness.

"Just remember that you will not be surrounded by friends there. Even though you will have a husband who loves you, and as his queen you will have great power. You must be careful."

"Be careful of what?"

"Of what happened to me before, when I was at court."

"What do you mean?"

"Things changed when I was there, Rapunzel. I've told you how King Louis changed, how people's hearts changed and it seemed no one believed in magic anymore. At least, not openly. And they began calling me a witch. I've always told you, it's a dangerous word. Especially to priests and those who take the church and its teachings too much to heart. They believe that witches worship the devil. If they get it in their minds and hearts, they can blame everything bad on you."

"But," I said, "we *are* witches."

She shook her head. "We are healers. We are daughters of Artemis."

"Mathena. You changed a man into a stag."

Her face flared. "You must never speak of such things. Not there. Take the spell book, Rapunzel, but hide it! And do not ever say that word around them, and do not practice where they can see. Josef is young like you, and he does not remember. Others will. Even if you are their queen."

"Even if he could remember, he would not care," I said. "I am sure of it."

"He is young and spoiled," she said. "And you may be right. But others have much influence, around him."

I nodded. "I will be careful."

She reached up and brushed the hair out of my face, then traced the length of it as far as she could. "This hair of yours," she said. "Look at it. What a gift you have. It gives you great beauty, and insight into everyone around you. Your beauty is your power, you know. You must watch over it carefully."

I smiled. My hair stretched from the couch and through the open door, where it shone from the grass. Loup was curled up and sleeping in it, faint images of mice and birds streaming up to me from her warm body.

"I will miss it here," I said. "I will miss you."

"This is what you've always wanted," she said, "to marry Josef. And what I've always wanted for you, to be queen. Use your power well, Rapunzel. Protect it."

An emotion passed over her face that I couldn't quite understand. I knew there was more, maybe much more that she was not telling. But I was used to her being full of secrets.

"I will," I said.

"And remember, he has a daughter now, and she is his heir."

I flinched. "I will give him more children," I said, ignoring the familiar ache inside me. "I had a son before. I will have one again."

The next day, we performed a ceremony at dusk, in the river, cleansing me of all my past sorrows. We were naked, the trees all around us. My hair streamed down the river like a golden raft. Mathena raised her arms and called to the four winds to ask for their protection and their power, sprinkled water onto my face and shoulders. We held hands, facing each other, and gave thanks for the earth's bounty.

After, once we'd dried ourselves and dressed, we had our supper outside by the garden, in the warm evening. The moon was rising. Earlier Mathena had prepared a whole roast pheasant that Brune had killed just for the occasion, and we ate it alongside cakes filled with figs and mint.

The food was delicious, and I savored each bite. Brune stood on my shoulder and I fed her whole hunks of pheasant, while Mathena fed Loup, who sat on the grass next to her, her little body rumbling with pleasure. My hair blanketed the ground. We drank wine Mathena had made herself. This was all the family I had ever known, this woman, these creatures.

"I have something for you," Mathena said. "For your new life."

I did not know what to say. I was not used to gifts.

She went into the house for a moment. Brune, as usual, followed after her. I reached out to pet Loup, and the moon bathed us in light.

I looked up at the tower, the stones sparkling in the moonlight. From the ground, it looked endless, as if you could climb it straight to the heavens. The sky was filled with thousands of stars, and trees swayed overhead, filled with sleeping beasts.

She reappeared from the house, with a long, flat package in her arms.

Stepping back in the circle, she sat down, cross-legged, and handed it to me.

"This will help you," she said. "It's my wedding gift to you."

"You will not come to my wedding and give it to me then?"

"No, Rapunzel. You know I cannot leave the garden, but my heart will be with you."

I nodded, trying to conceal my disappointment, and took the package. I pushed back the cloth. Inside was the mirror that had been hanging from the wall in my tower. I looked up at her, confused.

"It's a gift to protect your power and beauty, to ensure the king's love," she said. "It will show you things. You can ask it any question you like."

Was she mocking me? Awkwardly, I held it up with both hands, saw my own face staring back.

"Help me how?"

"Ask it something."

I looked into it again, and, very faintly, my own face rippled back at me. The glass was heavy in my arms. I set it flat on the earth and it swirled under us like a river.

"Like what?"

"Here," she said. "Try this." She seemed to think carefully about what she was about to ask, and then leaned in to it. "Mirror, mirror," she said. "Who's the fairest of them all?"

We stared down into the surface, both our faces reflected back to us.

It rippled then, more strongly than before, as if I'd thrown a pebble into water. And then a voice seemed to come out of it, like smoke. "Rapunzel is fairest of all," it said, low and deep.

I gasped. My head snapped up and I looked at Mathena. "Did you do that?" I asked.

She shook her head, smiling. "There's always been magic in this glass. It's enchanted. Haven't you felt it before?"

I shook my head but, as I did so, realized that there had always been something odd about the glass, that I'd always felt it was watching over me.

"You just need to ask it a question, and it will answer and show you the thing you've been seeking."

"You enchanted it?" I asked.

"No. There was already magic in this ancient castle when we

came here. This glass is very old, from a time when this kingdom was filled with magic. Do you remember how it was waiting in the tower for you?"

I had a memory then, of the glass propped up on the floor, the laughing girl with bright yellow hair dancing about the room, imitating everything I did.

I nodded.

"I knew right away what it could do. That's why I brought us to this place."

"You brought us here? You said we walked and walked and came upon the castle ruins by chance."

She shook her head. "I knew it was here. A powerful sorcerer lived here once. Hundreds and hundreds of years ago. Back then, this kingdom was very great. Many hope that it might become that way again."

I looked down again, at the moving silver.

"Who is the fairest of them all?" I asked again.

"Rapunzel is fairest of all," it said, and it was as if it were whispering in my ear.

I laughed and looked up at her. She sat watching me, the doorway to the house dark and empty behind her.

My last day with Mathena, I stared out of my tower at the forest surrounding me—at the slinking river, the massive garden, the trees on all sides, everything teeming with life and sound and scent. The chirping and whirring of insects and birds, the howling of wolves, the patter of squirrels and rabbits, the soft whoosh of deer running over the grass and soil. The smell of earth and growing things, breezes carrying the scent of river and rotting animals, the fear of travelers surprised on dark pathways.

I took the cloth from my hair, let it stream down around me.

I could sense the horses and carriages as they left the inn, as they entered the forest and wound their way to us. I watched from the tower as they appeared in flashes through the trees, closing in, and then I ran down to the garden, to her.

"They're coming!" I said.

She was bent over the cabbages, which squatted heavy and blue-green, like creatures from under the sea. She looked up at me, lifting a dirt-covered hand and wiping it across her fore-head. The sun shining down on her.

And then they arrived, in a flash of horse and silver and more people than I'd ever seen all together at the same time, up close. A host of guards and servants came to get me. At my direction, they swept up the curving stairs to my tower. It was all move-ment and chaos but before I knew it, my life was packed up and stowed away in carriages and on horseback.

"He has not come himself?" I asked one of the ladies who seemed to be in charge of the servants.

"Oh, no," she said. "The king is very busy. But he is waiting for you."

I tried not to feel disappointed that he hadn't come. Of course he had better things to do, as the king, but now I would be all alone.

I turned to Mathena, who stood by the garden watching ev-erything, a curious look on her face.

"What is it?" I asked, walking up to her. Brune stood on her shoulder.

"I'm just remembering when I was young," she said. "Young and full of dreams. Madly in love with a young magician."

I winced, but knew she was thinking only of the past, when she and Marcus had been lovers and everything had been possible.

I leaned in and kissed her cheek, taking in her faint smell of spices. "You are still young, Mathena," I said. "You can still dream."

"I dream all the time," she said strangely, and just as I was about to respond, one of the soldiers stepped forward.

"We are ready, my lady," he said.

And then it seemed as if I had had no time at all to say goodbye to her.

I looked at her standing there by the garden, soil-covered yet as majestic as any member of royalty. She could change men into stags, make a garden burst with vegetables when everyone else's crops failed. I looked at our little stone house built from ruins, the tower that reached into the sky, the garden. It was all so lovely—it had been the whole universe to me for so long, and now I was leaving. And I was aware, painfully so, that if and when I returned, it would not be the same to me. I would be a queen, accustomed to living in a palace. What would this all look like to me then?

What a strange feeling, suddenly seeing everything from the future, as if I were able to travel through time and this were a moment buried deep in my memory. Like a jewel I could pull out of my pocket at any time and hold up to the light.

"Thank you," I said to her, "for all you've done for me." I wrapped my arms around her, buried my face in her neck. I tried, one last time, to feel her through my hair, to feel her heart pulsing into my own, but it was as hidden from me as it had always been. All I wanted to know was that she'd be all right here alone, without me.

She pulled back first. I let go of her and turned to the soldier, afraid to look at her any longer.

He led me to the carriage and helped me step up into it. I was conscious, then, of the plain shift I was wearing—we'd long since used the last of Mathena's old gowns to insulate and decorate the house—and could feel myself redden with shame. There were more people around me than I'd ever seen, and even the maidservants were better dressed than I. A few soldiers held my hair in their hands and carefully arranged it next to me, on the seat. Their thoughts flowed up to me: their wonder at the king's choice of bride, their unease at the regal, beautiful witch who stood there, covered in dirt, and watched us go.

As the guard closed the carriage door, I was grateful to be sitting alone, out of sight, with furs to wrap myself in. And then the horses began moving through the forest, and we pushed into the trees and brambles. Quickly, I muttered a protection spell, though I knew Mathena had already done so. Soldiers moved ahead of us with swords, slashing through so that the path was clear.

I leaned back against the silk. There was a sense of unreality to everything—the way the forest looked like a place I'd never seen before, from such an extravagant seat, the way the light sifted down through the leaves and silk curtains, how it played across my face. The horses clomped on the packed forest floor. I pushed back the curtain and looked out at the trees and leaves, all soaked in summer sunlight, the patches of mushrooms scattered across the ground. I could smell the earth, the leaves overhead, and I felt like I was in a wonderful, fantastical dream as we moved through the forest, out into the kingdom, to him.

It must seem strange, that I lived for so long in the forest and did not see the world at large until I was twenty-five years old, when I became queen. After all, we were a two-day horse ride away from the palace, a seven-day walk on foot.

I would only understand later why Mathena had never taken me.

We rode for hours that first day, until day passed into night and only the moon overhead guided our path. I slipped in and out of sleep, lulled by the beating of the horses' hooves. Occasionally we stopped to relieve ourselves, servants leading me off the path and shielding me with their voluminous skirts and then doing the same for each other. We ate bread and cheese. They dipped chalices into streams and gave them to me to drink from. We did not stop to rest, however, until the next evening, after we left the forest and rode into the world outside. Even though I had anticipated it, I could not believe how vast that world was. To my memory, I had never stood under a blank sky without branches crisscrossing overhead, and when we finally stopped at an inn at the edge of the woods I could not help but feel like I was drowning. All that night sky, scattered with stars, pulled me in until I could barely breathe.

On the one side, I could see the castle in the distance, its turrets reaching up into the sky. I looked to the other, for a glimpse of the tower, but the forest was a dark mass, and Mathena would have hidden it from outside eyes, anyway.

At first I felt more comfortable inside the inn, where the best room was reserved for me. The innkeeper greeted me, his wife standing beside him and curtsying. I was surprised to recognize her from the forest—in a flash, I remembered her tears, her story of her husband's endless infidelities. She met my eyes and then looked away quickly, her face reddening. I did not betray her, nor she me.

They led me to my room. Again I was tended by soldiers, who walked in front of me and followed after me, carrying my hair up the stairs and arranging it in the room beside me. They were getting adept at this chore: when I turned around, I saw that they'd arranged my hair into a giant spiral.

How strange, to have left one life behind but to not yet have entered the other. Suspended between worlds. Despite the exhaustion of travel, I was restless, ready for adventure. I examined the room—the plump bed, the chest, the tapestry on the wall, the shutters that opened and looked out at scattered houses and shops. I stood in the window and imagined what it would be like to live in one of those houses, what my life might have been if Mathena had not taken me away.

There was a knock on the door and two servants brought in food and drink for me, setting up my supper on a little table, and then left me alone. Below, I could hear laughter and shouting, even stomping on the floor as music started up. For a while I listened. It was all so exciting, knowing that soon I, too, would laugh and dance.

I thought of all the joy that had flowed into me from Josef's body, and fell asleep feeling as if—almost, but not quite—it had been my own.

It was the next day that I first saw, really saw in the daylight, the world outside the forest. Servants invaded my room early in the morning, dressing me and bringing me meat and bread and tea to dine on.

I could hear the clinking of dishes downstairs, the men readying the horses.

And then I stepped outside: in front of me was a seemingly endless landscape with houses and shops and animals, and there in the distance was the palace, which seemed more massive than I had ever imagined. Like the way my tower, when you stood under it, seemed as if it ended above the clouds. Again I felt that strange vertigo, as if I were standing at some great height or sinking in the deep water, with nothing to clutch onto. The sky massive, unending and unbroken, above me.

"Here, my lady," one of the soldiers said, as he led me to my carriage and helped me inside.

Just as I sat down an old woman passed, glaring. She made a strange gesture and pointed two fingers. It took me a moment to realize she was pointing at me.

I blinked, surprised. "What does that mean?" I asked the soldier, just as he was arranging the last bit of my hair on the seat next to me. "Did you see what that woman did?"

"I did not, my lady," he said. He refused to meet my eye, but I felt, through the strands of my hair, that he knew these people did not approve of me, of witches, though so many of them had left their homes in secret, rushing through the dangerous woods to seek our help.

He stepped away. I looked around and caught a servant's eye. She, too, looked quickly away.

It was an unsettling thing, that gesture, the look the woman had given me, the reaction of the soldier and the servant. I sat back in the carriage as we moved through the kingdom, praying the rest of the journey would go quickly and without incident.

We had not ridden more than an hour when I heard a loud thump on the side of the carriage, followed by a general commotion, voices and cries as the carriage came to an abrupt halt.

"Witch!" I heard, through the ruckus.

The word sliced through everything else, the sounds of the soldiers barking out commands, cries and screams from the crowd. I peeked out, through my hair, and saw faces contorted with anger, people gathered on a road lined with small houses.

"Back!" the soldiers were yelling. I saw them push one man onto the ground. Others caught my eye and cried out, making that same sign the old woman had made before. Among the faces I recognized other women who'd come to see us, through the years.

They could come to me in the forest, I realized, in secret, but they did not want me to be their queen.

I shrank into my seat.

The door to the carriage swung open, and a soldier slipped inside, pushed past my hair, and sat across from me. He was a young man with dark hair and a face like a girl, and shining green eyes with long lashes. He was dressed in the livery of the king: a red and black uniform, a sword at his side.

"Do not worry," he said.

"What is happening?" I asked.

"These people, they're animals." His voice dripped with disgust.

I looked down and realized my hands were shaking.

The soldier pulled the curtains down, and the carriage began moving again. We sat in the hushed dark.

I closed my eyes and concentrated, trying to weave a quick protection spell around us.

"How far are we from the palace?" I asked, after an hour or so.

"It will not be so long now, my lady," he said.

I cracked open the curtain some time after that, and looked out on a row of cottages, nicer than the ones we'd seen before, where the crowds had been gathering. Faces peered out of windows, mothers with children in their arms stood in doorways as we passed.

Did my parents live here? Were they still alive? I wondered if there was still a garden filled with rapunzel somewhere, still a woman staring out at it with longing and an inexpressible hunger.

Later in the day, we passed through a great gate, and then there were crowds all around, and stalls of food and bread, and I even saw a man throwing balls in the air and catching them in the most marvelous way. I heard a song that seemed to press right into the carriage, come into the window to where I was sitting, and wrap around me like a quilt.

"It's the new queen!" I heard, and I swear I wondered where she was, this queen. I almost peered out to look for her before I remembered that it was me.

8

The castle loomed in front of us. The spires reached up into the sky, thinner and taller than they'd seemed from the forest, and I craned my neck to see the way they shone in the sunlight.

Everywhere people stood watching as we made our way to the lowering drawbridge. Merchants, entertainers, beggars. It was suffocating, having them all right there, so close I could have reached out and touched their faces.

"Stay back," the soldier across from me said, when I stuck my head out of the window and prompted a frenzied cheer from the crowd. "You must be careful."

"I don't understand," I said, as he pulled the curtain back to hide me. "What are you afraid will happen? Do you think they will try to attack us again?"

"It's possible."

"Why do you think those people were so upset?"

He hesitated. "The former queen has only recently passed," he said after a moment, "and was beloved by the people."

"They do not want the king to remarry so quickly?"

He averted his eyes. "Some may feel that way, yes."

"Do you?"

He looked back at me. "I follow the will of my king, madame. I do not question his desires."

"Ah," I said, assessing him. "Good."

It reassured me to know that Josef inspired such loyalty in those around him.

The drama of our entrance distracted me slightly from my terrible nerves, which were increasing at an alarming rate as we neared the end of our journey. I had thought my proper place was here, in the palace, but as we rattled over the drawbridge and came to a stop, everything seemed foreign and imposing and not like home at all.

A guard outside pulled the carriage door open and helped me down. My hair remained in the carriage, and gradually unraveled and trailed after me as I stepped forward. Looking around, I saw how luxurious the palace was, far more extravagant than I'd known anything could be. The ground was covered in marble and the doors to the castle were giant, with golden men on horseback flying across them as if they could leap off onto the stone of the palace exterior, or into the shining water of the moat surrounding us.

A large group of ladies and servants stood inside, ready to greet me. I craned my neck, looking for Josef, but he was not there.

I could feel the people's eyes passing over me, examining me, and that sense of shame came back, more acutely now, that I didn't have anything finer than the plain shift I was wearing. I forced myself to stand tall and meet their gazes, defiant. But they were not paying attention to my clothes, it seemed.

I heard gasps and exclamations from all around.

"Her hair!" "Beautiful . . ." "Like pure gold . . ."

I stared at the group, in all their finery. Ladies curtsied, men bowed, and I smiled as I stepped into the palace.

"My lady," a woman said, stepping forward. "I am ordered to take you to your chambers. My name is Yolande."

"Thank you," I said.

She was lovely, with a cloud of rich brown hair about her face. I felt instantly comfortable with her, as she led me through the crowd of people and toward a grand stairway, her green and white dress full and swishing as she moved.

My hair dragged behind me. I felt a strange energy, the presence of invisible spirits all around. Maybe it was a memory of my own past in this kingdom, maybe it was the portraits and sculptures all over, or maybe it was the generations of royalty who'd lived here, pressing in. But I could feel it.

The other women rushed to follow, walking on either side behind me. I was not sure yet who they were, whether they were members of the royal family or servants, and was surprised that no one introduced themselves to me, though the men, I noted, all watched me with a combination of what seemed like admiration and suspicion, as we passed. Was it men like these who'd caused the tears I'd witnessed in the forest? I wondered. Were men the same everywhere?

I was too stunned, though, to give too much thought to my reception and the possible foibles of those around me. After years of watching the palace from my tower window, dreaming of what was happening inside, I was here, and everywhere I looked was some new marvel.

It was as if a mountain had opened and I'd walked into it, all marble and flashing stone. Gems studded the walls, glinting when the light hit them. We moved through hallways and long rectangular rooms with massive paintings and all manner of wild beasts hanging from the walls. Great hearths yawned open from each floor, alongside grand, richly colored furniture with intricate designs carved into it and over plush, sumptuous rugs. I wanted to run my fingers over each new thing.

We walked past rooms where painters were at work on entire walls, where lords and ladies played instruments and hunched over games of chess, and across a great courtyard with a pond in the middle of it, at the center of the palace.

A group of swans floated on the water. The sun shone down above us. I thought of Zeus and his swan, and thought that this place, this palace, was fit for the gods.

As we walked, my hair dragged across marble and stone and grass, dipped into the pond, brushed against these ladies who'd attached themselves to me. Amid my wonder at my surroundings, I was able to feel the women's distrust, feel the general sense that the king was doing something wrong, betraying the beloved, newly deceased queen by marrying a strange woman from the forest.

I let myself absorb everything—it was only natural, wasn't it, that they would feel that way?—as we stepped back inside, and as Yolande led me up a set of stairs and down a hallway. I stopped short in front of a large portrait on the wall, the last in a line of portraits, all of stern-faced women in queens' clothing.

It was a woman in an extravagant gown. Her hair was long and black, her eyes bright blue, her lips red as fresh blood. Her expression was warm and lovely and strange, and I felt mesmerized, suddenly, by her beauty. Around her neck hung a gold, gem-studded cross.

"Is that . . . ?" I turned to Yolande. "Was that her?"

"Yes, that was our queen," she said, stepping quickly forward and leading me through a large set of doors and into a series of rooms.

I shivered, convinced that my predecessor was still there, watching me. Knowing what I'd done.

"And these are the queen's chambers," she said.

The room that greeted us was lavish, with tapestries covering the walls and silk curtains hanging in the windows. Had these been her rooms, too? I wondered. They must have been. Suddenly I did not feel at all well.

"Here is your bedroom," she said, pushing open another set of doors, into a sweeping room. There was a massive soft bed, high off the floor, with sheer fabrics hanging down all around it, rugs covering the stone floor, and an immense hearth, and a window, with wide wooden doors I could press open.

"This is my . . . room?" I asked.

I noticed that my things were already scattered about, that the soldiers carrying them had arrived earlier. The sight of my few items of clothing reassured me.

"Yes. And I sleep nearby, as do most of us. We are your ladies-in-waiting."

I turned around and faced the five ladies who'd been following us. All of them were prettily outfitted, with swept-up hair and graceful smiles on their faces—except for one, a plain woman dressed in yellow, staring at the floor, who seemed vaguely familiar.

"When will I see the king?" I asked.

"You are to be married in the morning," Yolande said. "We will wash you and prepare you for the wedding."

"Wedding?"

"Have you not come to be queen, my lady?" she said, amused. "You must not have expected it to happen so quickly . . . ?"

"No, I did not," I said. "I thought surely I would see him first."

"We are following his wishes. It seems he is anxious to make you his queen. We will serve you dinner here, and bring you whatever you may need."

"I would like something to drink," I said, "and to rest for a while."

She nodded, and they left me alone in the vast room.

I wandered through it, mesmerized by all that space, gloomy and beautiful and strange. Everything was so quiet, without the sounds of the forest. I walked to the window, which looked out onto the palace gardens; they were so much larger and more manicured than our garden in the forest, but just as lush.

I had a sudden, intense wave of longing to see Mathena, to be with her right now, in the forest, where I was loved. No one here wanted me, it seemed, other than the king himself.

The mirror she'd given me was hanging on the wall between the window and a large bureau. I caught a flash of my face, and walked over to it.

My hair glowed in the mirror, my face looked flushed, my eyes ablaze.

"Who is the fairest of them all?" I asked it, repeating Mathena's question.

"Rapunzel is the fairest," it said, without hesitation, as the glass rippled.

I clapped with delight. It was almost as if Mathena were right there with me, sitting by my side on the forest floor. There was a

movement in the mirror. I whirled around, thinking a maidservant had sneaked in behind me, but I was alone. I peered back
into the mirror. My own face stared back.

"Hmm," I said. "Mirror, mirror, on the wall. What else
should I ask of you?"

The glass rippled again, as if I'd thrown a pebble into it.

"Will I have a magnificent wedding?" I asked.

"You will have a wedding fit for one so fair," the mirror said.

"And . . . will my ladies, the court, come to love me?" I asked.

I stood waiting for my answer, but the mirror remained still.
I let a full minute pass.

"Do you weary of speaking with me?" I asked leaning in,
watching my own face looming in the glass.

I decided to try something else. "Is Mathena all right without
me?"

I expected the mirror to stay silent, suspecting there was a
limit to what it would say at a given moment, but to my surprise
it began to swirl about. My face disappeared, and an image of
Mathena appeared. She was bent over the garden, dirt smudging
her face.

"Oh! Is that you right now?" I whispered.

She raised her head sharply and peered into the sky. Then
she looked all around, until her eyes fell on mine. I gasped. The
image vanished and again there was a normal mirror in front of
me. My own face staring back.

I exhaled.

It was a very charming gift, I told myself. That's all. Still, I
felt a vague anxiety that I tried to ignore as I continued exploring.

I opened a carved door, stepped into a small chamber, a closet.
Perfect for a workroom. I would miss having the garden, the

root cellar, and Mathena there to guide me, but I had Mathena's book and could have my own little space for working spells as long as I was not too obvious about it.

I walked to the bed and sat down, marveling at the soft mattress, the fur strewn across it. I lay on my back and stared up at the ceiling and closed my eyes.

I will make this my home, I thought as I drifted to sleep, *and be happy here.*

I'm not sure how long I was resting before someone knocked on my door and woke me.

"Come in," I said, quickly sitting up as if I'd been caught doing something wrong. For a moment I was disoriented and wondered if I was still in the tower.

The door opened and one of the ladies walked in, the plain one in the yellow dress I'd noticed before. There was an air of tiredness and melancholy to her. She seemed older than the others, as if she'd suffered a great hardship.

"I have brought you some wine, my lady." She stepped slowly toward me, holding a goblet in her hand. She watched me carefully, as if I might lunge at her at any moment. I thought of the stag, its quiet, stricken face as I stood there and loaded the arrow into my bow. "Do you recognize me?"

"Should I?"

"I am . . . my name is Clareta. I visited you. In the winter."

At first I just stared at her, uncomprehending, and then I slowly realized who she was. The mark on her face was the same, but all the beauty that had been there before had vanished.

I blushed deeply, felt a stab of guilt as I understood that I had done this to her.

"Of course," I said, standing from the bed, keeping my back

straight. "I did not recognize you in . . ." I tried to choose my words carefully.

"I am much changed," she said. "I know. God has punished me for my unfaithfulness."

She handed me the goblet. I saw then that her hands were trembling. Of course she was terrified, I realized—I knew her darkest secret. I wondered if she suspected my own.

I took the wine gently from her hands. "Please sit," I said, gesturing to one of the chairs before the fire. She obeyed, and I sat next to her.

"It is you," she said. "Isn't it? I've been wondering if I was dreaming." She was quick to check herself. "Of course you will be a great queen."

"Do not worry," I said. "I did not expect the king to come make me his wife, either. You must have been surprised to hear the news?"

"Well, I . . ." Her face was scarlet, and she seemed uncertain where to look. "I am so ashamed. What I admitted to you . . ."

There was nothing accusing in her voice. Even without magic, I understood that she thought I would send her back to her family, knowing she had slept with the king and betrayed her mistress. I could use her fear, I realized, and her guilt. It was better than facing my own guilt, over what I'd done to get here.

"Do not worry, Clareta," I said gently. "That was another time."

"Will you . . . keep me? You will not send me from court?"

"I will keep you," I said. "I understand that not everyone here is a believer in magic. It will be nice to know someone close to me is."

I'd meant this as a compliment, something to draw her closer to me. Instead, she breathed in sharply, as if I'd slapped her across her red cheeks.

"I do not . . ." she began, clearly confused about what to say.

"Shh," I said, placing my hand on her shoulder. "It will be our secret."

"Yes, Your Highness."

She looked up at me and for a moment I held her gaze, studying her. Surely she must have had some suspicion about what we'd given her to offer the queen, and about the queen's sudden death, but if she did, she was too concerned with her own position to betray it.

She nodded, and then stood with some formality to leave the room. I watched her go, then drank down the glass of wine to calm my nerves, letting it burn in my throat.

The next morning was my wedding day. I was still half asleep when my room filled with servants and ladies who roused me from the bed and began preparing me for the occasion. Such attention was foreign to me and I sat, stunned, quietly following their directions as they led me into another room where a bath had been brought in. They removed my clothing and held my arms, led me into a deep tub full of warm water with flowers and leaves floating on the surface. It was disconcerting, all those hands on my body, my hair being unloosed and falling all around me in waves, swirling in the water.

All those hands, in my hair . . . I could feel the women's jealousy and curiosity, anger and love and fear, all of it emanating from their bodies, into me. I could feel the rumors swirling in their minds—that I was a witch, that I had bewitched the king, that I would lead the kingdom to ruins. I closed my eyes, steeled myself. There were too many of them and they were all strangers to me still, and so I could not separate out the feelings running through me. All I could do was bear it, wait for this to pass. I would prove them all wrong, I thought. I would force them to love me. But from now on, for my own peace of mind, I would request that Clareta wash and style my hair.

I left the bath and they dried me with soft towels, then covered my body with ointments and powders until I smelled like a garden at the height of summer. Lavender calmed me, lemon freshened and enlivened. They laced me into a long pale dress. They dried my hair and brushed it and wove flowers and jewels through it, and then wrapped it around my head and draped it down my back.

The whole time, their thoughts needled into me: wondering how I'd managed to attract a king from the middle of the forest, and so quickly; comparing me unfavorably to the queen they'd lost so recently, who'd been so much more pious and refined.

Finally, they led me to the glass hanging on my wall, which rippled like a storm-ridden river with anticipation.

I was astonished at what I saw. Even though I was no stranger to my own beauty and the effect it could have on others, I had never seen myself like this. My hair surrounded me, in golden avalanches. My lips were more red than they'd ever been, my hair shone and shimmered, my eyes were wide and bright and lined by long dark lashes. I was wearing a radiant ivory dress that made my skin look like cream.

Was this me?

Flickering behind my reflection, I saw myself with my hair dragging on the ground, full of leaves and twigs and blood, before the regal queen I was about to become came back into focus.

The wedding took place in the palace gardens. Flowers of every kind, every color, burst from the ground, and trees coated in white blossoms swayed above us. There were armed soldiers everywhere, standing at attention.

When it was time for me to walk down the aisle, my ladies followed me, carrying my train. I clutched a bouquet of orange blossoms, wildflowers, and myrtle, grateful that no one would see my hands trembling. The moment I saw Josef standing at the end of the aisle, dressed in elaborate robes and waiting for me, I relaxed. He wanted me here. He wanted me to be his queen, even if others in the court were not as sure.

He smiled as he saw me. I could feel that smile like a hand sweeping down my back.

And then, as I approached, I saw her for the first time, the same woman from the portrait . . . but she was a child, swathed in lavender silk. Standing near Josef at the altar, her hands filled with flowers. My heart stopped for a moment, and I faltered. It was as if I'd seen a ghost, haunting me. The queen come back to punish me for what I'd done. For what Mathena had done, wasn't it? What Clareta had done.

Her hair was as black as ebony, her skin pale and smooth, like a first snow covering the forest floor. And her lips were a brilliant red, like cherries full and hanging from their stems.

But she was just a child, seven years old, a little girl. Snow White. Not a ghost come to haunt me.

She was the same age my own child should have been, had

he lived. The same age I'd been when Mathena took me to the forest. She was standing stiff and straight, and did not seem to carry herself like a child. As I neared her, she stared at me with her huge round eyes, expressionless. A sick feeling came over me as I looked at her, and then a terrible longing. I nearly stopped in place and crumpled to the floor. It was as if my own son had appeared, grown into this exquisite creature.

I breathed in and focused again on Josef, his warm face always ready to break into a smile.

And then I reached him, and it was as if I were opening the cottage door and seeing him for the first time, dazzling, right in front of me, the first man I'd ever seen up close.

He loved me, had searched for me.

"You're here," he whispered, the way he had before, as if I were an apparition and might float away. I took his hand and squeezed it, to reassure him.

Later I would hear reports of the commoners protesting outside the castle gates. The number of subjects arrested for going against the king. I would hear, too, about how much larger the previous wedding had been, how it had gone on for days and days. But his wife had just died, and now he was marrying a woman rumored to be a witch. Small wonder this one was more intimate.

But I did not know those things then, and I was happy. The priest stood before us and spoke of God and heaven and country and I promised to honor the kingdom and my king, my husband, until I died, and then I was married to him, and I became his queen, and a ring was placed on my finger, and a crown on my head.

After, there was a great feast, and he took me in his arms

and danced with me. I, who had never danced before and did not know all the intricate dances they did at court, just held on to him, laughing, as he swept me over the floor, and as my dress whirled around my ankles and I tripped over my own feet, trying to keep up with him. The music was wonderful. I felt every note vibrate over my body as, around us, the most beautiful dancers glided across the floor.

He led me back to the great high table. Snow White and her nurse were seated next to us. Just below sat my ladies-in-waiting and all kinds of splendid nobles who stood and bowed as we approached. The king introduced several of them to me, including the head of his army, Lord Aubert, who kissed my hand and bowed. They all seemed friendly enough, but by now I did not need my hair, or my magic mirror, or any manner of tea leaves or tarot to know that these people did not trust or welcome me into this court, despite their deep bows, the smiles on their faces, and their kind, empty words. I tightened my grip on Josef's hand and he slipped an arm around my waist.

"This is the Princess Snow White," he said, as a servant rushed to pull my chair back for me. "And this is your new queen, Rapunzel."

Snow White stood and curtsied while staring up at me, her expression serious, almost worried.

"I am so pleased and honored to meet you," I said.

A small, shy smile took over her face. I was utterly charmed, despite myself.

I sat down. Courtiers came up to offer the king and me their love and fidelity. Musicians wandered through the hall, singing songs about love. There was more food on the tables than I'd ever seen, and Josef wanted me to try everything. He lifted his arms and swept them through the air. "That is what life is for. To try everything. You will never miss the forest, now that you're here."

The revelries lasted until very late in the night, until I could barely keep my eyes open for exhaustion.

Finally, the king announced we would retire. He stood, extending his hand to me, and I took it and stood next to him. I was woozy with wine and food, all the twirling over the dance floor, the cut flowers scattered across the tables, the feeling of being madly, madly in love—not only with Josef but with this palace, this life—but also the subject of so much ill will, which Josef himself seemed not to notice but I could feel in the air like cold rain. Instead, he was happy, he was drunk, and he lifted me into his arms and carried me out the door, down the hall, and to his chambers.

A group of guards stood waiting and opened the great gold doors to let us pass. Inside, there were candles and torches, and the bed was covered with furs and flowers.

He set me down on the bed and I tumbled out of his arms, lay on my belly with my arms stretched out on either side of me. He unlaced my dress, and I was like an oyster being removed from its shell, especially with my hair piled on my head and not hanging down to protect me. Suddenly I felt naked and raw there, in front of him. I was sober, and everything became less like a dream.

He removed his robes, his shirt and pants, watching me, and then he climbed in bed and pulled me into his arms.

He pressed his palm to my cheek, and I leaned into it.

"Josef," I whispered, loving the sound of his name in my mouth.

It was not at all like the frenzied coupling of all those years before. The fire crackled, throwing shadows on the walls. The feel of his skin on my skin seemed more sumptuous than any velvet.

"My queen," he said, smiling down at me. I could not help but smile back. Naked, with his arms wrapped around me, he looked so boyish and sweet, happy. It was hard to imagine that he was a king, that he could lead our kingdom into war and battle.

His palms moved up and down my body, caressed my face and hair. He removed the clips from my hair, one by one, and smiled as my hair fell down around us. His joy and desire vibrated up into me, through the strands.

I was grateful to Mathena then. She had known that I needed to be his wife, his queen, not the girl in the forest whose hair he climbed while his true queen prepared for their wedding day.

He wrapped himself in my hair, luxuriated against it.

All those years she had waited, knowing this day would come.

9

I woke slowly. Sunlight was filtering through the room. Josef slept next to me, his palm resting on my belly. I moved my hand over his.

I stretched like a cat, twisting on the soft sheets. "Queen Rapunzel," I whispered. Right now in the forest, Mathena would be bent over the garden or out hunting with Brune. Lying here next to the king, his hands still imprinted on my skin, seemed so wanton and decadent.

I stood and slowly made my way off the high bed, to explore. Here was where he'd been, all this time. All the days I stared at the palace from the tower, he'd been right here.

Outside the window, the castle grounds lay before me, the gardens and several small buildings in the distance. Beyond them, houses with thatched roofs and the wall surrounding all of it.

I ran my fingers across the large bureau, the desk on which several manuscripts lay. I picked one up, marveling at the exquisitely penned letters. I began reading, carrying the manuscript back to bed with me.

It was a long poem, in a complicated rhyme. I read lines here and there, about a dark wood, a poet who'd lost his way. There were beautiful illustrations beside the text, brightened by gold leaf.

"Are you partaking in some morning study?" he asked, causing me to start.

I smiled. "You have interesting taste in literature," I said.

"This comes from far away at great cost." He sat up and took the manuscript from me. "It's about a sinner who journeys through hell and sees the punishments of the damned."

"How delightful."

He laughed. "It's fascinating. And the words the poet uses are so precise and beautiful. It's like he's captured the sound of a rainstorm."

"I've not had much opportunity to admire the beauty of words," I said.

"You will now. There's a magnificent library here, and you'll find much to amuse you in it. I'm having books brought in from distant lands, dozens every week, the rarest manuscripts."

"That's wonderful," I said. I reached up to kiss him, full of admiration for him. He was so learned, so filled with passion. I could feel it pulsing from him, in a heartbeat.

"Today you might spend time with your ladies," he said, "or exploring the castle. I have much business to attend to."

"Oh," I said, surprised. Of course, he was a king and had important things to do.

"You will be all right, will you not? This is your home now. You are well loved here."

"Of course," I said.

We dressed, and I called for Clareta to put up my hair. We went to Mass, as was the custom, past the handsome young men in sharp uniforms and into the hallway. We walked down the curving stairway and across the courtyard to the chapel. It was a wonderful room; walking into it was like entering a gemstone. Light shone in through multicolored glass windows. When I looked more closely, there were whole scenes inside them, showing saints pierced through with arrows or hanging over flames. Snow White was sitting with her nurse in a raised seat to the side of the priest, staring intently at a small book in her hand, her brow furrowed.

The priest, whom I would come to know as Father Martin, stood at the front of the room. He was startlingly handsome, and had a charisma about him that explained why all the ladies in the chapel were dressed as if they were attending a palace ball. When he began speaking of sin and punishment and hellfire with a vividness that shocked me, I felt compelled by it, despite myself. It was all so different from anything I'd heard before.

He spoke of God's wrath. The sinfulness of worshipping false gods, consulting medicine doctors and witches. I stiffened but made sure to look at him without wincing, though I could feel the eyes of the court on me.

Throughout the service, the court stood and sang, and then sat down again. Their voices melded together, expressing every kind of emotion all at once. Tenderness, love, and yet the most dramatic fear, anger, wrath. Even though I loved to sing, I knew I could not sing these songs the way they did here. It was completely alien to me, all of it as extravagant and strange as the jewels they all wore, wrapped around their fingers and wrists and necks.

I felt embarrassed that the courtly manners were all so foreign to me. I felt tricked by Mathena, who'd talked to me of Artemis and Apollo, Hera and Zeus, and taught me about herbs and stars rather than God. It was infuriating, even. Why hadn't

she taught me how to behave properly? Why hadn't she taught
me about God?

After, Josef leaned in to kiss me. "I will see you this evening,"
he said, and almost before I could answer, he was surrounded by
his advisors and being led away.

My heart sank as I watched him leave. Snow White and her
nurse left after them. My own ladies surrounded me.

"Where are they taking the princess?" I asked Yolande, who
had positioned herself to lead me back to my chambers.

"To her lessons."

"I suppose we can relax this afternoon, can't we?" I said,
smiling, with more enthusiasm than I felt.

We retreated to my chambers, and it occurred to me for the
first time that they might become a new tower for me, in a way.
I sat on the couch while my ladies arranged themselves around
me. Clareta and the youngest girl, Cicely, started playing cards
together. Yolande offered me my choice of fabric from a basket,
and I selected a piece of pale silk as well as some gold thread,
thinking I might embroider something sweet for the young princess. Yolande placed herself on the floor next to the couch, and
began embroidering a kerchief with a wonderful smattering of
tiny flowers, while next to her Lilace worked on a silk pillow,
using colored thread to create a scene of lords and ladies in revelry. Stella, the redhead, crocheted a bit of lace for her sister's
upcoming wedding.

I watched and studied them. They still seemed more like a
mass of painted faces, dangling ribbons, and twirling skirts, and
less like distinct people to me, but they were there to attend me,
entertain me, comfort me.

I found myself thinking of the princess more than anything else.

"Why do they call her Snow White?" I asked. "Is that not an odd name?"

"Oh," Yolande said, smiling. "She was such a beautiful infant. None of us had ever seen a baby with skin that pale and lips that red, and that black hair already covering her head. She was an astonishing child. One of the ladies even thought she might be a changeling."

"A changeling?"

"Yes, a faerie exchanged for a human child. She was that unnatural-seeming."

"I know what a changeling is," I said. "I just did not think people spoke of such things here."

"It's true; the priest was not happy about the rumor, Your Highness," she said. "There was quite a controversy."

The other ladies were nodding now. "People started giving her tests meant to detect a faerie imposter," Stella said.

"What did Queen Teresa do?" I asked.

"She was furious. She was very devout, you know."

"The priest even gave a sermon about it," Clareta said. "Telling us that faeries were false gods. It didn't stop all the talk, though."

"She was just too perfect," Yolande said. "We couldn't believe she was real."

I laughed. "That's so silly. Changelings have withered, dry skin and deformed limbs. They're not beautiful at all."

They all seemed to gasp at once, and then burst into giggles, at my words.

"You must not let Father Martin hear you speak of such things," Yolande said.

"The king does not care what Father Martin says," Clareta said, turning to Yolande.

"It's true. He ignored Father Martin's advice about his marriage," Lilace added.

"His marriage?" I asked, turning to the girl sharply.

She shrank back, her face going red. "I didn't mean—"

"The king's marriage to me, you mean?"

Yolande rushed in to answer for her. "Lilace does not mean to offend, my queen. But it is true that the palace priest urged the king to marry a devout woman. And to do so less . . . quickly. But Father Martin disapproves of many things the king does."

"Ah, I see," I said, nodding gravely. "And what about you, Yolande?"

"Your Grace?"

"Do you . . . believe in faeries?" I smiled at the surprise on her face. She had expected me to reprimand her.

A blush drifted over her pale cheeks. "Of course, my queen. But I would not talk about it openly at supper."

As the hours passed, we sewed and embroidered, and the ladies spoke softly among themselves. I started noticing how precious their handiwork was, these women who'd spent so much time at court. My own design was simple, a trellis of plump fruits and gourds lining the silk.

My fingers longed for the earth. Outside, the garden would be overflowing with spinach and cabbage, radishes and beets. I let the pang pass by me, and after a while excused myself alone to my room.

I arranged the herbs I'd brought from the forest into baskets.

I moved a small table from my bedside into the closet, and placed a cloth over it. I cast a protection spell around this little workroom, to prevent unfriendly eyes from seeing it, and sent up a quick prayer to Artemis.

I walked back into the bedroom and stared into the mirror Mathena had given me, at this new self draped in fine fabrics and jewels.

I laughed, leaned in and whispered, "Mirror, mirror, on the wall. Who is the fairest of them all?"

"Rapunzel is the fairest," it whispered.

It calmed me, that voice.

"What is Mathena doing now?"

The glass rippled and swirled, and an image appeared before me, of Mathena stalking through the forest with Brune on her wrist. My heart clenched. I closed my eyes, imagining the rattling of leaves around me, the scent of dirt and leaves.

I opened my eyes and asked one more question: "Will I survive here?"

I stared into the mirror, waiting, a sense of unease creeping over me as it refused to answer.

"Will I survive here?" I repeated, tapping the glass, but the mirror remained silent.

Later in the day, the king called for me. I was happy to set down my thread and little kerchief. My ladies seemed to share my excitement, immediately surrounding me and freshening the powder and paint on my face. Clareta combed violet-scented oil through my hair and then helped me put it up again. I was already getting used to the guilt and anxiety that marked her, that moved from her into me through the strands. It was much better than the barrage of judgment I felt from the others.

He was waiting for me in the great hall, surrounded by his advisors, who were drinking ale and relaxing after the long afternoon session.

"My queen," he said, standing and rushing out to me.

Immediately I felt at ease, despite the gazes of the council. Father Martin was present, too, alongside Lord Aubert. I nodded to them, and then turned to my husband, who took me in his arms.

He was wearing a rich robe with a gleaming gem latching it together at his neck. It made him even more imposing, hanging down from his shoulders as if he were some magnificent beast.

"My king," I said.

"You are a vision," he said, stepping back to admire me. He ran his fingers along the neckline of my dress. "This finery suits you. I will send my jeweler and the head seamstress to you. It will give you much pleasure, I think, after all the time you've spent in less . . . civilized surroundings." He laughed, and I saw he was not mocking me, that he took joy in my transformation.

"I'm glad you still like me as a civilized lady," I said.

He took my hand. "Come, let's walk a bit. I want to show you some things."

He led me from the great hall, as if we were going on an adventure. Everything with him was like that. It was infectious, and I followed him happily.

"So how do you find my daughter?" he asked, as we stepped into one of the palace's many hallways. His love for her was evident, even when he mentioned her casually as he did now.

I glanced back. Behind us, several guards and servants were following.

"She's a charming child," I said, turning back to him. "And so striking."

He sighed. "Yes. She looks just like her mother."

A flash of pain moved through me, and I tried to ignore it. Of course the child looked like her mother.

He stopped before a large window that looked out over the courtyard and pulled me in next to him. The glass bathed his face in a red light. On either side of the window, portraits lined the walls; they seemed to be everywhere, those faces from the past. "Her mother's death is still so recent, and she has become more and more solitary of late. They were very close. Now she seems to have forgotten how to laugh, how to be a child. It's one reason I wanted to marry right away, rather than wait. Everyone thought I should wait."

"I'm glad you did not," I said, and noticed an edge in my voice, a hint of desperation I did not like.

"As am I," he said, turning to kiss me. I raised myself up on my toes to reach his mouth. Already I could feel the heat in my body. Conscious of the guards behind us, I lowered myself and cleared my throat.

We walked slowly down the hallway, with him occasionally pointing out one of the portraits and telling me who the subject was. "My father's great-uncle Edvard," he'd say, or something similar. It was spooky, being surrounded by the dead.

"Perhaps you and Snow White could take a walk together," he said. "I think she would like that."

"I would like that, too," I said. "Very much."

"You will be a good mother to her," he said. He turned to me and stroked my cheek with his long fingers. Unlike me, he took no notice of all the eyes around us.

"I hope to be," I said.

"And you, are you happy?" he asked.

"Yes," I said, growing weak and wobbly on my feet. My hair pulsed with his touch, his passion was a physical thing moving through it. Below it, I could feel his love for his daughter, how much he wanted me to love her, make her better. It moved me, that he thought I had that power. "I love being here, being your wife. And I've never heard such music as there is here. Or seen such dances. It's all so wonderful." My eyes started to mist, as I tried to express how grateful I was, how full and happy. I didn't care if anyone else in the court loved me, as long as he continued to love me as he did. I would love Snow White, I decided, as he did. For him.

"I want this to be the most dazzling court in the world," he said. "Which is why I have the most dazzling queen."

I smiled. "Is it not?"

He took my hand again, and we kept walking. Above us, chandeliers swayed and glittered. "Well," he said. "This was once the greatest court in the world and the most powerful kingdom. We had land that stretched from ocean to ocean, a ferocious army, loyal allies. This court once produced the most magnificent poetry and art and theater. My family's line, the Chauvins, we have fallen very far from what we once were."

His voice shook as we spoke, his passion evident. It was impossible not to be swept up in it, and suddenly I, too, longed for a lost past, one greater than my own, with its ravenous mothers and magical plants.

"I think that's what Mathena spoke about, when she said

that many in the kingdom hope for that kind of greatness again."

"Yes," he said. "Many of us hope for that. I was raised hearing stories of that time. My tutors taught me all the history, made me read the great epics recounting the most famous battles. Did you not study these things?"

I shrugged. "Mathena told me many great stories and myths, but not often ones about the kingdom."

"That's all right. You can leave the past to me. I want you to think only of right now. Forget everything that came before."

I studied him, wondering if he knew about the rapunzel, or anything else from my past, and then realized he was talking about a different one: the past in which he'd left me in the tower and married Teresa instead.

"All right," I said. "There is a plant for that, you know. One that will make you forget everything."

He laughed. "Well, then I will have to procure it for you."

"It's all so exciting," I said, after a moment. "You have such ambition!"

"You will learn the truth of that statement," he said. "This kingdom will be great again. Already I'm filling the palace with riches. By the time we die we'll have surpassed anything that came before us."

"I hope that will not be for a long time yet," I said.

We stepped into a massive room filled with workers. The smell of plaster and pigment was overwhelming.

"Look," he said, pointing up.

There was a scaffold, and on top of it, a man applying pigment to the ceiling. Sketched across it was a massive work, with full figures and animals and clouds and fields. Only part of it had been painted.

"What is it?" I asked.

"A unicorn hunt," he said, "designed and painted by one of the world's masters."

"That's him?" I asked.

"Yes, the great Bernard Morel. And these are his helpers and apprentices. I've set up a studio for them here."

I walked farther in and focused more closely on the ceiling. The flank of the unicorn was already a glowing white, and slowly the scene came to life before me—the hunters lying in wait, the unicorn's horn stretched out in front of it. The scent of paint fell away and instead I felt as if I'd been transported back into the woods, tracking the magical beast glowing above us. I'd never imagined such wonders that could be made at the hand of a man. This was its own kind of magic, I realized.

"It's fantastic," I said.

Josef called to the artist and asked him to step down and meet me. I trembled with the import of that moment, seeing that someone as talented and blessed as the small, weathered man would bow down before me and call me his queen.

"It is an honor," I said, "to meet you and see you work."

"The honor is mine, Your Grace," the artist said. "I feel I'm in the presence of a creature even more rare than the mythical unicorn."

Josef smiled, looking from Bernard to me.

"Thank you," I said.

"Perhaps you will paint her portrait when you have finished this room," Josef said.

"It would be my pleasure."

I was thrilled, but at the same time hated to think of myself as one of the faces on those walls, to think of future men and women standing in front of the canvas and staring at my face, imagining what I'd been like once.

"I have many plans," Josef said, as we walked back into the hallway. "This is why an heir is so important, to secure the kingdom and the Chauvin line, and to continue to make us great after I'm gone."

"I do not think that will be a problem, my king," I said, smiling up at him.

We continued walking down the hallway, and I discovered that the unicorn ceiling was not the only masterwork in progress. In another room, a man was sculpting a large statue from a block of marble, the figure of a centaur emerging from it. In another, a group of painters was at work on a large altarpiece for the chapel, with winged angels dropping from the heavens.

"It will do Snow White good," he said, "to have a brother."

I thought it was doubtful that she would want a brother surpassing her to the throne, but I kept quiet. "I am sure it will," I said. "But in the meantime, I will try to be a good mother to her."

My voice caught, as I said those words. It surprised me, how much I liked the idea.

10

A few days later, I arranged a meeting between myself and Snow White in the gardens. It was a glorious afternoon as I waited for her, after a morning of heavy rain. The gardens were in full bloom. Tall hedges created a labyrinth structure, and paths stretched from every side, lined by herbs and flowers and wonderful trees that looked like hats, draped in bell-shaped white and purple blossoms. My hair was loose and falling on the ground around me, collecting wet grass and petals, the thrum of life vibrating along the strands. In the distance, mountains rose into the sky. The air smelled of honeysuckle and wet earth.

Snow White appeared at the castle door and I studied her as she approached. She was dressed in a red cloak the same color as her lips. She seemed oddly formal, as usual, a worried look on her face.

"Hello," I said.

"Your Highness," she replied, curtsying shyly.

I nodded to her nurse, who stepped back. Two guards appeared behind her.

"Shall we walk together?" I asked.

She nodded, and we set out side by side. Her back was perfectly straight, her hair braided about her head.

"How old are you?"

"I am seven," she said.

"And you study a great many things?" I asked.

She looked at me, seeming to find the question confusing. "Yes."

"What's your favorite subject?"

There was a long pause before she answered. "I like to study poetry," she said.

"Oh, like your father."

"My mother loved poetry," she said, and she turned her head to look straight at me.

I felt awkward, trying to talk with her. Behind us, her nurse and two guards followed. In front of us, the world opened into a series of manicured gardens.

"Did she?" I asked. "And you? You are a lover of poetry?"

"Yes. And I sing, and can dance. I would like to write poetry, like my mother."

"Your mother was a very talented woman."

"I know. Is it true you are a witch?"

I stopped, and was unable to hide my surprise. "What did you say?"

She stared right up at me, unafraid, her eyes so blue they were nearly lavender. "Is it true you are a witch?"

"Who told you that?"

She shrugged. "I have heard people speak of it. They say my father has gone mad."

"Do you think he's gone mad?"

She seemed to seriously consider the question. "He was very upset when my mother died."

"Of course he was. I'm sure everyone was. It must have been very devastating for you."

She nodded, and suddenly looked as if she were about to cry. Her sadness already weighed on me too heavily, so strong it was already latching itself onto my hair, moving into me. I desperately did not want her to cry.

"Look, some elderberries," I said quickly, pointing to bunches of the dark berries. "Do you know what these can be used for?"

"No." She stepped closer to me, looked down at them intently. She plucked a berry from the plant and rolled it between her fingers. "I think the cooks make jam with them."

"They can also help cure someone sick from influenza, when they're mashed and used in a tea. That's what people mean, when they say witch. I know how plants can help us."

She stared up at me with a wondering expression. "What about this?" she asked, pointing to a thick plant with yellow blossoms nearby.

I made sure no one was looking, and pulled off a leaf.

"Close your eyes," I said.

She did, her eyelashes like brushes against her pale cheeks.

"When I rub this leaf against your eyelid, you'll see the face of the man you're meant to marry."

I swept the leaf over her eyelids, and she gasped, blinked her eyes open.

"And who did you see?" I asked.

"My cousin!" she said.

"Oh?"

She furrowed her brow. "I do not think I would like to marry him."

I laughed. "Perhaps not," I said. "Where does he live?"

"In the East." A shadow moved over her face, and I was determined to remove it.

"It's not always accurate," I said. "Sometimes the plant likes to play tricks on people, especially young girls."

"Really?"

"Yes!" I said. I put a finger over my lips. "But don't tell anyone."

"I want to do it again," she said, excited, and for the first time a genuine smile lit up her face, and I was astonished at how wonderful it felt to make her happy.

I plucked off another leaf. She closed her eyes, and I swept the leaf over them.

She frowned and looked up at me. "I still see my cousin!" she said, stamping her feet. "Those plants are mean."

"Hmm," I said. "Maybe your cousin will grow up to be a very dashing man."

"He is already grown!" she said. "He is the age of my father."

I burst out laughing, despite myself. "I'm sure the plants are having fun with you, then. You will marry a very handsome man."

"Maybe I'll never marry. Maybe I'll write poetry in my room."

"Forever?"

"Yes," she said, smiling at me.

I smiled back, delighted at the change in her, and pointed again. "There's poison in this plant."

"There is? Is it dangerous?"

"Only if you eat it, but the most poisonous part is in the ground. They say that slaves used to eat very tiny bits of it so that they'd be too sick to work."

"But is it magic?"

"I don't know. Is that magic?"

She furrowed up her face again. "I don't know."

"I don't know, either," I said. "It's just how things work."

"And that?" she asked, pointing to another plant.

"That will cure eye aches, if you boil it and put it over your lids."

"I will not see my cousin again if I do that, will I?"

I laughed. "I hope not! If you do, I might begin to wonder if you do not love him, despite all your protestations!"

She made a horrified face. "You tease me!" she said, like a child not at all used to being teased. She rushed ahead, full of energy now, practically jumping up and down. "And that one?" She pointed.

"This one is very special," I said. I plucked off a blossom and handed it to her. "This one will make you have very special dreams, when you put it under your pillow."

"What kind of dreams?" Her eyes were large as she stared at me, her face wide open.

"Happy ones, of the most beautiful places."

"I would like that," she said. "Do you think I might dream of my mother in heaven?"

"I . . . I think so," I stammered, taken aback. Her longing was so intense, and it was no different from what I'd felt almost every day in the forest from the women who came to see us. "Put the blossom under your pillow and see."

"All right," she said. My heart nearly broke as she carefully folded the blossom into her palm. "You can also change people into animals, can't you?"

"Is that what people say?"

She nodded. "They say it happened before."

"Well, people like to tell stories, you know. There are many, many wonders in this world."

"Yes," she said, nodding. "Everyone at court likes to talk."

"You do not?"

She squinted up at the sky. "I think it's silly sometimes, the things people talk about. I like to read and play music and dance."

"What about now? Do you like talking with me?"

"Yes. You aren't like other people."

"Neither are you."

For a moment we looked at each other. Had things been different, she might have been my own daughter. I wished, more than anything, at that instant, that she was, that none of the rest of it had ever happened and it had only been me, and her, and him, this whole time. And then, as if it were the most natural thing, she reached up and took my hand. I held on to it carefully, as if it were made of glass.

"It's pretty here," she said. I followed her gaze. Around us stretched the gardens' never-ending pathways. "I like knowing that these plants can do so many things."

"It's important to know what they can do," I said. "You could walk right through this garden and have no idea. And all the while, the plants are scheming and plotting."

"Now I know their secrets," she said.

In the near distance a large structure appeared, like some kind of house. "What's there?" I pointed.

"The falconer is there," she said.

I nodded. "You know, I lost my mother, too," I said.

"Isn't the witch your mother?"

"No," I said, shaking my head. "My mother lived in the kingdom, but she was not a good mother. It was the . . . It was Mathena who saved me, and took care of me."

"She does not sound like a bad witch."

"She's not."

"Someone said that you were the daughter of the witch and a stag."

I stopped short. "Where do you hear such things?"

"Everyone is always talking," she said. "People forget sometimes that I can understand them. I understand everything, you know."

"I know," I said, bending down until we were face-to-face. "People are wrong to forget it. I assure you, I'm not the daughter of a stag. Look at these hands! Look at my face. Don't you think I'd have fur, like a stag, if I were the daughter of one?"

She studied my face and then made a great show of looking over my hands. "That is true," she said thoughtfully. "I'm wondering about my grandmother, though."

"Oh? Why's that?"

A devilish look came over her face as she answered. "She had a mustache!"

At dinner, she sat stiffly at the side of her nurse, occasionally stealing glances at me. I made funny faces at her to make her laugh, and when she did, I felt as if I'd accomplished a significant feat. Josef caught us at one point, and reached under the table to stroke my leg, my hair that was resting on it. His happiness streamed up into me.

That night, as would become his habit, he came to my room but left in the early hours of the morning, leaving me to wake alone.

"Your daughter is lovely," I said, as he slipped into bed beside me. Across the room, the mirror rippled.

He nodded. "I know. I'm glad you've taken to her. She needs someone like you, with your great heart."

I was surprised by his words, flattered that he saw me that way. I did not have a great heart, I knew this. And yet the child had moved me.

"She has changed much, since her mother died, yes?"

"Yes, but she's always been a serious sort," he said. "Even when her mother was alive. Always reading, keeping to herself. As an infant, even, she barely cried, just stared up at you with those blue, knowing eyes. It was a bit unnerving. She seemed like she could understand everything."

"Doesn't she have other children to play with?"

"Some. There are other children at the castle, but I'm told she has not taken to them. I've watched them in the garden at times, and she stands apart while the others play ball."

I watched him, smiling. "You're a good father," I said. "Even with all your kingly duties and your great artistic commissions in every room of this palace."

He laughed, and I could not help but feel a stab of pain as I thought about the boy buried in the forest. Our son. What a good father Josef would have been to him. I thought, for a moment, of telling Josef what had happened. What a comfort it would be, to share that burden with him.

But I could feel him through my hair, his great relief, his

certainty that his daughter would be happier now that I was here, and instead I pulled him to me, unlatched his robe, and pushed it off of him.

"I want to give you a son," I said.

He moved his hands across my belly. They might have been made of fire.

11

The days passed, and with each hour I grew to love Josef and Snow White more, and I became more and more accustomed to life in the palace. Josef's joy became my joy, and I learned from him to immerse myself in extravagant pleasures. I learned to love spice-filled sauces, fine wines, and elaborate desserts full of fruit and cream and nuts. I learned to love damask and silk, the feel of diamonds and emeralds and rubies weighing down my ears and wrists. I learned about art, and music, and poetry.

I had dresses made by the palace seamstresses, and began bedecking myself in the most overstated, ridiculous manner. Beauty, at court, was paramount, with Josef as king. The Troubadour King, they called him, for his love of poetry, art, the kingdom's glorious past, and, above everything else, beauty. And no one was more beautiful than I. Every day I asked my mirror the same question—who's the fairest of them all?—and every day I took comfort in the answer, as if my luck and happiness, my whole future, were bound up in it. Every day, my ladies worked to enhance that beauty. Even when I indulged too much in sweetmeats, they were able to lace me into corsets that shrank my waist to a startling diameter, and apply paint to my cheeks, eyelids, and lips that worked more intensely than any spell Mathena had taught me.

In the time I was without him, I took walks outside through the large castle gardens, which I began to learn in all their variety. Sometimes I walked with Snow White, and told her new stories of what each plant could do, as she told me details of her own studies. Other times, I walked with my ladies, or, on rare occasions, alone, with a guard or two trailing behind me.

One afternoon I was out wandering when I came across a building that reminded me, just slightly, of the cottage where Mathena and I'd lived. A twinge of nostalgia rushed over me. It was the same building I'd noticed before, I remembered, where Snow White said the falconer lived.

I walked up to the door, and realized with surprise that it was made of gold. It was an odd mix of riches and rawness, like our cottage with the cut-up formal gowns hanging as curtains.

I pushed open the door and walked in. The light streamed down through the slats on the sides of the building, illuminating a number of strange shapes positioned throughout the room. The room was wooden, empty except for the posts on which the shapes were sitting. My hair was half in the grass, half in this strange room, and suddenly I was assaulted with images of flight, branches, bodies being broken open.

They were hawks and falcons with chains around their legs. As my eyes adjusted to the light they came into relief. They were the finest birds I had ever seen: magnificent, massive, their claws hooked over the platforms they stood on. Elegant hoods covered their heads, sprouting up from the top, like helmets of great knights. I thought of Brune and her perch on the cottage mantel. These birds were so much more regal. The king's falcons.

It was distressing, too, to see them this way, as if they were in some kind of dungeon. I thought of the bandits in the forest, and shivered.

"Who are you?" a voice said then, making me jump in surprise.

For a moment I thought a hawk had spoken, and as I turned I faced a man standing in the doorway.

"What are you doing here?" he asked. His voice was deep and ragged.

I stared at him. How could he be asking me who I was?

The man was tall and broad, and had a pained look to his face. Like the building itself, something about him was vaguely familiar. He had a hooded bird on his wrist, its wings spread out, and was watching me intently.

I was not used to having to explain myself. I'd always been either Mathena's helper or the queen. People had always known exactly who I was, and had always responded to my beauty—or notoriety—with a kind of awe that he did not seem to feel.

It unnerved me.

"I wanted to see what was here," I said.

I focused all my energy on him, to try to charm him.

The bird on his wrist started flapping its wings suddenly, crying out, and he soothed it, speaking softly and running a finger down its breast until it calmed.

"You're scaring the birds," he said.

"I want to hunt with one of these falcons," I said. The words came out on their own, surprising me.

He laughed. "These are the king's falcons, my lady. If you'd like a kestrel to fly, you might look elsewhere."

His insolence infuriated me. "The king," I said proudly, "is my husband."

I expected some kind of horror to pass over his face, a recognition and a shame, but he seemed unmoved. "Ah," he said. "You are the witch."

"I was raised a healer," I said.

"It's not an insult," he said. "Despite what Father Martin says. Here, let's go outside. The birds are getting restless."

We walked back out into the afternoon light, which seemed glaringly bright after the hushed darkness of the mews, though now the sun was hidden by clouds. The air smelled, suddenly, of approaching rain.

His foot landed on my hair, and he stepped back quickly, apologizing, but not before I took him into me: his love for beast and wood, his respect for all natural things, his distrust of the palace and all inside it.

Now that I could see him better, I was struck by his features. His hair was black and thick, and his eyes were like ink. He was quite handsome, but in a coarse way, as if he'd been carved out of a boulder.

I realized I was staring and looked away. "I was raised with a falcon," I said.

"I know."

"You do?"

He nodded. "I knew Madame Gothel. Well, my father did. She was here when I was a child."

"Your father?"

"He was the king's falconer before I was, just as my grandfather was before him. My father knew Mathena well. She spent a lot of time out here, in the mews."

"She raised me," I said.

"I know this. Everyone talks of it. Even I cannot avoid hearing about it."

"And what do you hear?"

"That the king has gone mad and married a witch."

I bristled. "Do you think he has gone mad?"

There was a small smile hovering on his lips. "I do not judge the actions of my king, Your Grace. And I would never question my new queen." He bowed, with a flourish.

I laughed, and then forced myself to sober. "That is comforting," I said. "Tell me more about Mathena, what you remember. I know barely anything of her life here." I hated the plaintiveness I could hear in my own voice.

"She was the queen's favorite. The queen could barely turn in her bed without consulting Mathena first. They often went hawking with the king. King Louis was an avid hawker."

"So you were just a child when you knew her?"

He nodded. "But I'll never forget her. My father admired her a great deal. Said he'd never seen a more able woman than her. She had a lot of power here at one time. She had the ear of the queen and, through her, the king."

"It is hard to imagine that now."

"Things shifted at a certain point. It seemed like everything changed at once. That happens at court, people gaining power and losing it. Things have changed much since your husband took the throne, too."

His tone suggested that he did not think it was for the better.

I gestured toward the birds in the mews. "Why do you keep them this way, chained up and with hoods over their heads?"

"That's how they're trained to hunt, to work with a human hunter."

"Brune, Mathena's falcon, always flew free, with us."

"I know. The queen gave Brune to Mathena, as a gift. Brune was trained in the same manner as the other birds. My father trained her, the same way I train these birds now. They're ferocious hunters. It's not in their nature to serve men."

"I did not know that," I said. "About Brune, that she's so old."

"I'm happy she's been able to survive these many years. It's not usual, but then she has a very unusual mistress."

"Indeed she does."

He watched me then, making no attempt to fill the space between us. A multitude of questions battered at me about Mathena's past.

Instead I repeated awkwardly, "I would like to go out with the hawks one day. Perhaps you might accompany the princess and me on horseback. I understand she is partial to horses."

"I'm at your service," he said. "The king now has little use for me, though I keep the finest hawks any king could want. My name is Gilles."

"I will call for you."

Just then the sky opened and rain began pouring over the earth. I looked up, letting the rain stream down over my skin and dress.

I had the odd feeling that Mathena herself had caused it, angry at me for trying to uncover her secrets.

I shook the thought away, and went running for shelter from the wet afternoon.

12

It rained nearly every day after that, but I didn't mind, and sometimes preferred this wet world around me. Either way, I loved that unobstructed, treeless sky. I spent afternoons luring Snow White away from her studies and riding through the sodden countryside with her. There were whole swaths of the kingdom I'd never seen to the north of the palace, away from the forest where I'd grown up. The Dark Forest, as people called it in whispers, lay to the south. I came to learn that people not only spoke about the bandits and witches who lived in the forest, but about enchanted swans, mythical centaurs, and fire-breathing dragons. Sometimes, just for fun, I liked to mention my dragon friends and make my ladies shriek with horror.

It was wonderful, riding through the meadows and farmland with Snow White next to me, and the guards following. It helped satisfy my craving for the woods, and made it easier for me to adjust to life at court, with all its formalities. I kept my hair loose and flying in the wind, creating a golden ribbon behind us. On occasion, when I summoned him, the falconer Gilles would join us with one or two of his hawks. His quiet, honest presence was calming, and I came to count on it. I loved looking over and seeing Snow White smiling, leaning into her horse, her hands stroking its sleek neck, her hair streaming out behind her. Above us, the birds would glide and dip and cry out, and I'd spur my horse to go faster, to try to keep up. To fly. Lush green rolled out on all sides of us, and we rode through villages and past sprawling farms and peasant cottages with gardens in front of them.

It was on those rides that I first noticed the failing crops that plagued the kingdom. Though it was nearing harvest time, we passed wheat fields with dirty brown stalks, sticking out from pools of mud. Fields of scraggly, half-dead barley, gardens that were decimated or rotted over.

"Do you see that?" I said to Snow White and Gilles, when they slowed down at my command and pulled up their horses beside mine.

"It's all the rain," Gilles said.

"What is?" Snow White asked.

"The crops," I said. "There's no wheat."

"I don't understand," she said, looking around.

"The crops are failing. These people can't make bread, if there's no wheat. See how the wheat is brown instead of gold? That field should be full of golden wheat, and men harvesting it."

"Will you show me?" she said. "I want to see."

The three of us dismounted, and walked across the wet grass. The field in front of us was empty. A few cows grazed on the grass nearby.

I bent down and pulled up a piece of wet, moldy wheat plant. Where there should have been a bright head of grain sparking from the top, there was nothing. Just a rotten stem.

"Do you know what wheat should look like?" I asked, handing the stalk to her.

Again she made that worried face, and I realized she did not. She was a child of book learning, in the palace of a king obsessed with art and words.

"There should be grain here, all along the top. It should be alive, vibrant."

She stared at it intently, rubbing it through her fingers.

I looked up at Gilles, who was watching me curiously.

Snow White scrunched up her serious face. "Can we do anything for them? Can we make the wheat grow again?"

I thought of all those years of gardening, and working with the earth. All those women whose hunger I felt vibrating through my locks. "We can't make it stop raining," I said, "but I think we might do something."

"Really?" Her face lit up as she turned to me, clutching the plant in her fist.

"Perhaps you can help me gather herbs from the palace garden. We can make a mixture of them that might help these crops, that might help the wheat grow better next year."

"That is a good idea," Gilles said. "A generous one." He caught my eye and I looked down, embarrassed but pleased by his admiration.

Snow White nodded vigorously. "I want to do that," she said.

"Then that is what we'll do."

Over the next days, as Snow White and I—and other ladies of the court we gathered to help us—collected herbs from the garden, the castle was also beginning to prepare for the greatest event of the entire year, the harvest ball. It was the same ball I'd wanted to attend years before, the night Mathena locked me in the tower. All across the kingdom the richest subjects planned which of their daughters could afford to go and made clever uses of fabric to create suitable dresses for them, in hopes of attracting a nobleman for a son-in-law. At court, every servant was tasked with some type of elaborate preparation and the kitchen was busy for days as cooks created herb-scented breads, pastel-colored pastries, sugared-flower sculptures, and any number of other decadent treats.

Father Martin warned the court at Mass about excess and overindulgence, but could not dampen enthusiasm for a ball that everyone loved, and had loved, for centuries.

At Josef's urging, I had seamstresses working night and day on a dress that would be more dazzling than anything anyone had ever seen before. Ten ladies sewed gems onto silk, so that when I moved the dress would gleam like the moon.

"Soon you won't fit into these gowns anymore, will you, Your Highness?" the seamstresses said. "We'll have to make you a whole set of new ones." And they clucked over my flat belly, managing to touch a few stray strands of my swept-up hair, enough that I could feel their longing for an infant prince.

The pressure weighed on me, that I was not yet with child. But instead, I focused on my beauty, which was easier to control. I rarely ate, so that my waist would be more narrow. I used every spell I knew to make my skin smoother and my hair more lustrous, my eyes brighter. I had Clareta brush oils through my hair to make it shine.

I was not unaware of the irony, that I was starving myself and surrounded by riches when people were going hungry because they had no other choice, outside the castle walls.

But I was a queen.

I helped Snow White, too, as she selected a rose-colored silk for her dress, and fur to line the neck and wrists and hem. It was a great pleasure for me, giving myself over to such decadence, having this little girl and all my ladies to do it with.

I called Snow White to my chambers and stood her in front of my own mirror, lifting the silk to her chin. "Look at how pale your skin is, how red your lips."

She beamed with delight. I smoothed my palms over her hair, sprinkling in some rosemary oil to ease her worries. I could feel, through my own hair dangling down and brushing her arm, how much happier she was, but there was still a deep grief in her I wished I could erase completely. Knowing I was responsible for it broke my heart.

The morning of the ball, I gathered Snow White and all my ladies and we spent the day preparing. The princess and I both took long baths in perfume, and Clareta washed my hair and sculpted it into an elaborate, towering pouf, weaving jewels and a large plume right in the center of it. I brushed Snow White's hair myself, her luxurious black locks, as she squirmed with anticipation.

Finally, I stepped into the dress, which seemed to hang from my body like water sliding over rock. I stepped in front of my looking glass. My skin and hair glowed, like rays of the sun. My body shimmered from every angle.

I dismissed my ladies, who left my chambers in a flurry to get into their own dresses, pin up their own hair, leaving Snow White and me alone in the room.

In her rose-colored dress, Snow White was the most beautiful child I'd ever seen, a miniature woman, the silk wrapping around her slender body, her black hair piled on her head. Clareta had even made her lips more red with paint, her skin more pale. I loved watching Snow White's delight as she caught sight of herself in the glass.

Outside, the sun dropped in the sky, and in the distance I could hear carriages, one after another, arriving at the palace.

The ladies all gathered in my chambers. Yolande, in particular, looked wonderful in a dark-gold-and-red-striped gown that displayed her breasts and made a swishing sound as she moved. Paint exaggerated her already pretty features, and her eyes shone and glimmered like stars.

"You might have to leave my service after tonight," I said, "when a handsome nobleman claims you."

"That would be wonderful," she said with a sigh. She, like most of the ladies surrounding me, was wholly dependent on the court, and could only prosper at the side of a high-ranked noble.

On a whim, I grabbed a sachet of lavender and mint from my workroom. "For luck," I said, handing it to her. She smiled gratefully.

When we were all ready, we swept to the ballroom.

Snow White walked next to me, her small hand in mine, her little heels clicking on the marble. I was brimming over with pride; I couldn't wait for Josef to see her, for the whole court to see her. The sound of lutes and dulcimers greeted us, as we walked slowly through the hallways. The scents of bread and meat quickly followed. The whole palace was coming under the spell.

When we walked into the ballroom, Josef made a great show of admiring us, presenting us to the court, the kingdom's queen and heir.

We basked in it.

He pulled Snow White onto the dance floor, lifted her in his arms, and twirled her around, her black hair coming undone and flying around them. She was more truly happy than I'd ever seen her and I watched them, my eyes filling with tears, with happiness.

"You will both dance with me!" he cried out.

He pulled me to him, too, grabbing my hand, holding Snow White in one arm, and the three of us danced, ignoring the learned steps and jumping about like fools.

Later, full of drink, after the nurse had led Snow White off to bed, Josef and I stumbled to my chambers. We collapsed onto my bed. He clawed my dress off of me, unclipped my hair, which wrapped around us, taking in all his joyfulness. I could feel some pain there, too, but it was too buried for me to understand and he himself was intent on ignoring it. The moon shone silver through the window as he moved in and out of me, one hand cupping my face and the other tightly clasping my hand. I couldn't get close enough to him. I would have disappeared into him if I could have.

After, we lay there together, in each other's arms. I watched him sleep, his body warming me as the cool early autumn air swept in through the window.

His discontent worried me, cutting through the haze of my own happiness.

I placed my hands over my flat belly. For months now I'd been drinking catnip and mugwort and casting spells to make me more fertile, and yet I was not with child. Josef had not said anything, but I knew he would soon.

As the hours passed and sleep evaded me, old anxieties began to creep in, too. I wondered if I was unable to have a child, if somehow what had happened before had rendered my body unfit, like a stalk of wheat with no grain. I thought of my twisted son, buried in the forest.

The old grief moved into me, and I threw off the covers and walked over to the mirror. My face loomed up in it, a white moon in the black night. I stepped back and looked at my naked body, my belly. My hair was like a storm raging on all sides of me.

"Mirror, mirror, on the wall," I whispered. "Who's the fairest of them all?"

"Rapunzel is the fairest," it responded, in a whisper to match my own.

"Will I have a child?" I asked. "Will I give birth to the king's heir?"

The mirror rippled. I thought I heard a voice, very faint, but it did not seem to be coming from the glass.

I turned back to the bed. "Did you say something?" I asked.

"Hmm?" He opened his eyes.

"I thought you spoke to me. I'm sorry, go back to sleep."

"Come to bed," he mumbled, but was instantly asleep again, his breath loud and heavy.

I looked back at the mirror. For a moment I was sure my hair was wrapped around my throat, and I started with surprise.

13

As the air grew colder, and the rain did not stop falling, Snow White and I rode out into the kingdom nearly every afternoon with baskets of herbs mixed with bones and leaves, throwing handfuls of the mixture onto the gardens and wheat fields. We'd dismount our horses and run through the wet fields, sprinkling the mixture onto the ground, stomping it into the earth with our feet. I kept my hair pinned up, though I longed to let it loose over the soil, let the vibration of earth move into me. But we had a great task before us, and I could not endure the distractions.

It did not take long for the farmers and peasants to take note of our efforts, and they began watching and waiting, coming out of their houses to bow to us, running up to throw flowers or ask for alms.

One day a woman holding a sick child ran out of a rickety cottage with a sparse garden in front of it. My instinct was to shield Snow White from them, but to my surprise the princess stepped around me and walked right up to the infant.

"Oh, your baby is sick!" she said. She laid her hands on the child, took it in her arms. I watched in wonder, surprised that she could even hold him, she was so small herself. The mother watched with her own kind of wonder, clearly believing that the touch of the princess might be enough to heal the child.

"Did you say that yarrow and mint will cure a fever?" she asked, turning to me. "Can we find some?"

"We can," I said, taken aback. "We can bring some tomorrow."

She nodded, and then looked up to the woman. "Do not worry," she said. "We will bring you what you need."

Snow White handed the child back, and then walked purposefully over to her horse to retrieve her basket. Carefully, she sprinkled the mixture over the woman's garden, as tears streamed down the woman's face.

"God bless you, Your Highness and Your Majesty," she said, attempting to kneel down in front of me.

I rushed to take the infant myself, worried she might drop him in her supplication, despite her tight grip.

The baby melted into my chest, looked up at me with glazed eyes. He was burning with fever. I almost couldn't bear it as I held him to my chest, how right it felt to hold that tiny body.

Snow White walked back, rubbing her hands to clean them. "We will take our leave now, and come back tomorrow."

When I handed the child back, I almost felt as if a piece of my own body went with him.

We returned the next day, as she'd promised, and after that we began to do more and more in the villages and countryside. Along with our usual mixture, we brought a variety of plants and oils that could aid with any number of ailments, and we took a larger retinue of guards to carry our supplies. Gilles was often with us, quietly riding his horse and taking care of the hawks. The king trusted Gilles, and insisted he accompany me, especially out in the open countryside with his daughter, the heir to the kingdom. The hawks overhead comforted me, and Gilles did not seem to mind taking them out and training them in the open air. I'd wanted to go hawking myself, when I'd first met him in the mews, but this was more than enough: watching them overhead, these magnificent birds that reminded me so much of my life before. This gorgeous man and child pressing forward on either side of me, atop hooved, gleaming beasts. It satisfied me, that part of me I'd left behind.

One afternoon, after we returned our horses to the stable and said good-bye to Gilles, Snow White asked me to walk with her.

She was holding a bundle of wildflowers I hadn't noticed her gathering. She took my hand and led me through one stretch of the garden to a small graveyard, still blooming with flowers despite the autumn chill in the air. I'd seen it before, but stayed away. The palace portraits were bad enough; I did not like so much unfamiliar death right in front of me, all the time.

The stones were scattered all around us, blackened and covered in moss. A guard stood off to the side, watching us. Other than that, we were alone.

"It's beautiful here," I said, to be kind.

"This is my . . . My mother is here," she said. She stood there, her skirt flapping around her ankles, strands of her hair in her face. "I wanted you to meet her. She was a very good mother."

Suddenly the late afternoon air seemed especially cold. A hawk screeched in the distance, from the mews.

Queen Teresa Chauvin, the stone read. Underneath was a quote in Latin.

I felt like I was going to be sick. I dropped to the ground, holding my stomach.

"Are you all right?" Snow White asked. She was concerned, innocent, as she reached out to touch me. I had killed her mother, yet here she was trying to comfort and steady me. The whole world spun around me. My teeth chattered from the cold.

I nodded, wincing up at her. "Yes," I said. "I'm just tired from the ride."

"Are you sure?"

"Yes." I positioned myself cross-legged on the wet grass, willing the sickness to pass. My skirts flounced into a circle around me. "Thank you for bringing me to meet your mother. That is very kind of you."

Snow White's face relaxed, and she sat beside me. I could see how important this was to her, and was determined to act as calmly as I could, despite my intense, overwhelming discomfort. She was *right there*. Her body, in the ground beneath us.

Snow White placed the flowers delicately over the stone. She leaned against me then, brushing her small body against my arm, a strand of my hair tangling down. I braced myself as her grief pummeled into me, laced with images of her mother's arms wrapping around her, her mother lying sick in her bed, her face thin and pale, her eyes wild.

I breathed out, grabbing a flower from the ground and pinching it in my fingers, twisting the stem, watching the soft petals flaking off in my hands.

Her grief became my grief, and I mourned for her mother— for what I'd done to her—as well as my own. I'd been Snow White's age when Mathena had rescued me, but the mother I'd lost hadn't loved me the way Teresa had loved Snow White. Still,

I could not help but wonder. Was my mother buried somewhere now, too? Was she still alive, perhaps living in one of the cottages we'd passed, that day or another? Were there other children now?

There were tears running down Snow White's face, sparkling like little gems.

I glanced up. There was a woman standing there, at the edge of the graveyard. I started in surprise.

"What is it?" Snow White asked, alarmed.

I turned back and the woman was gone. But her black hair and her red lips seared into me.

"Nothing," I said. Of course it was nothing. I smiled at her reassuringly.

"You saw her, didn't you?"

"Saw who?" I asked. My heart was racing.

"My mother," she said.

There was an intense expression on her face. Her brows furrowed, her eyes shining.

I didn't know what to say. It was a trick of the light, I was sure of it. A trick of my own mind, riddled with guilt.

"I see her," she said. "Father Martin says it is wrong to speak of such things. He says my mother is in heaven. But I see her. Do you believe me?"

So many feelings coursed through me. Guilt and love and despair and loss and a kind of terror I'd never felt before. I focused on that lovely, worried little face and tried to smile.

"Yes," I said. "Of course I do."

Over the next days, as autumn began to strip the trees, Snow White and I continued distributing herbs until we were too cold, even with heavy furs draped around us. I found it soothing to ride through the kingdom, my hair unspooling behind me, letting all thoughts of Teresa fade into the blur of the countryside, until I convinced myself that I'd imagined her standing there.

It did not take long for rumors to start up at court. In Mass, Father Martin spoke more adamantly about the sin of witchery, and I could feel the thoughts and suspicions swimming around the minds of everyone around me.

One evening the king himself asked me about it.

"It's wonderful, to see my daughter flourishing," he said, leaning over to speak in my ear, in the great hall. "But I'm worried about what I hear. There's talk that the queen and princess are practicing magic openly in the kingdom."

"She's only helping me feed the people, my lord."

"People?"

"Your royal subjects," I said, "in the countryside and villages."

He looked at me blankly.

"Have you not seen the failed crops?" I whispered.

"No."

"The wheat is all blighted," I said. "I fear that people will starve come winter, with no bread. Half the fields I pass are filled with dead plants. It's all the rain."

"What have you and Snow White to do with this?"

"We've made herb mixtures to help the soil, that's all. Your daughter has a kind heart, you know. She wanted to help."

He waved his hand, as if to dismiss any discussion of rain and soil. "There's talk of unrest."

"In the villages? The people are grateful, my lord."

"No," he said. "In the East. Some estates near the border are threatening to rebel."

"Oh, but that's a different thing, is it not?"

"There are rumors of the sinfulness of this court," he said. "That we practice magic here."

"But that's ridiculous," I said, trying to sound convincing. Of course there would be such talk. Mathena had warned me about all of this.

"They're looking for a reason to go to war with us," he said. "Ever since Teresa died. They whisper that I killed her to marry you."

"But you did no such thing!"

"This does not prevent them from saying it."

"Will they start a war with us?" I was trying not to sound anxious, but had made my voice too loud. Lord Aubert was watching us closely. On the other side of the hall, a group of dancers entered, draped in diaphanous veils.

It would be my fault if we went to war. The thought came at me like a hand around the throat.

"I don't think so," he said. "But we should not want to give them more cause than they already have."

"How can you be sure they won't?"

"Because of Snow White," he said.

"What do you mean?"

"They hate us. They've always hated us. But they love Snow White, and they won't start a war when she's a child in my palace, the heir to the kingdom." He softened, leaning in closer to me. "It's why I had to marry Teresa. We might have gone to war then if I had not."

It was a painful thing to hear, even with his sweet, handsome face right next to mine, his warm breath on my skin. Suddenly I was back in the tower, my heart sinking and the room going cold as he got up to leave.

I turned away from him, and stood abruptly.

"Rapunzel," he said quietly. "These are old sorrows."

"I'm not feeling so well, my lord," I said, not meeting his eye. Around me, they were all watching—the king's council, my ladies, all the members of the court, even the dancers who were doing handstands now in the center of the room.

I stepped down from the high table with the assistance of a guard and quickly moved past them all, my ever-present ladies and maidservants following behind as I swept through the halls to my own chambers.

Back in my room, Clareta took my hand and led me to bed while Yolande dipped a cloth in hot water and placed it on my forehead. As she did, her hand brushed my hair, and I could feel her thoughts entering me. Her disapproval of a queen and princess who distributed herbs to peasants, her affection for me despite it, her conviction that I would ruin the young princess with my teachings. I slapped her hand away, annoyed.

When they left, I took out the spell book Mathena had given me. I needed to look for new fertility spells, as well as for information on how to protect myself from ghosts.

I filled my days with pleasure, but it was during the nights that my own restlessness overtook me, making me go back and back to the image of Teresa standing in the graveyard, her body in the ground, the moment when Clareta had handed her a cup of steaming tea. The tears on Snow White's face and those sad, sad eyes, the possibility of war—all so that I could be queen. I'd lie next to Josef, unable to sleep, watching the mirror pulse and ripple on the wall, listening to the leaves that rustled outside the window and whispered to me, through the howling wind. *You don't deserve any of this.*

One night, when I managed to finally fall asleep in Josef's arms, I dreamed that I was awake still, lying alone in my high bed, furs and satins strewn around me. My hair stretched out from me like a thousand snakes, spilling from the bed and onto the floor. It kept growing, streaming out, like a river rushing along the forest floor, pressing against the door and slipping through the open window and the whole time taking everything into itself, all the old secrets and heartbreaks, betrayals, longings, the old magic that spread through the palace like dew or fog, almost invisible, always there, and it was choking me now, my hair flowing out, all that feeling flowing back to me until I could barely breathe, until I was gagging for air, and then it was running out in every direction, falling to the ground outside, getting tangled in tree branches, wrapping itself around the palace, while inside it poured through every hallway, filling all the great rooms, stuffing itself into the breathing mouths of everyone who lay sleeping inside, including the king, including Snow White, and I tried to scream but I couldn't make any sound anymore, it was all my fault, all of it, and then it was not just hair but vines and thorns and the palace was wrapped in them, thorns and brambles, the whole kingdom wiped out, every mouth filled with thorns and leaves.

I woke, gasping for air.

The room spun around me. It looked so beautiful and clear and wide open. I relaxed, as relief moved through me. It had just been a dream.

I wrapped my arms around Josef, and tried to go back to sleep. After a while, I gave up, pushed back the covers, and went to the mirror.

It rippled in front of me. "Mirror, mirror, on the wall," I said, keeping my voice low.

I stared at my distorted reflection, my pale face. I could not bring myself to ask the usual question.

Behind me, there was a movement. A figure. I whirled around, but the room was the same as always. Josef lay sleeping calmly on the bed, the moon caressing his handsome features.

I turned back to the mirror, and it was there again, but closer now, a woman. Her eyes big and round, staring right into me.

I screamed.

"What is it?" Josef asked, sitting up in bed.

"There's someone here," I said, turning back to him. Again, the vision had disappeared. "A woman. I saw her in the mirror." I rushed back to bed, into his arms.

"What woman?"

"I don't know. I just got a glimpse of her, but then she was gone."

"A spirit, you mean? That is what you saw?"

"Yes!"

He laughed, shaking his head. He reached out and ran his hand over my hair. I could feel what he was thinking: that I was as silly as his own mother had been, with her face always turned to the stars.

"Josef!" I said. "Do you not believe me?"

"I believe you," he said. "My mother saw spirits all the time."

"She did?"

"Yes. One in particular . . ." He waved his hand dismissively.

"Who?"

He sighed. "My mother *claimed* that the spirit of the old prophetess inhabits the castle. She often attempted to speak with her."

"Prophetess?"

"Yes. Her name was Serena. She lived here a very long time ago, back when this kingdom held its rightful place in the world. There was powerful magic at work here then. Most people have forgotten her, but my mother put great stock in Serena's predictions.

"What did she predict?"

"Many things, over the years. She knew that priests were coming, and that the old ways would die. She knew there would be war between the West and East. She saw all of it. They used to say she was crazy when the visions came over her. She predicted the end of the Chauvin line. She said that the kingdom would fall when a . . ." He stopped himself.

"When what?"

"It's all madness, Rapunzel," he said, shaking his head. "Serena was a young girl taken from her home and forced to give prophecies for the king and queen, almost a thousand years ago. The stories of her in the old epics are wonderful. But for a woman like my mother to sit in the dark and try to make her appear, to have so much faith in those old stories . . . it was madness."

"But maybe I saw her," I said.

He smiled. "Maybe you're half dreaming. Maybe it's the hour when dreams are more real than rocks or rivers."

"Perhaps," I said, pressing up against him, trying to feel safe.

14

That year, the snow and ice came quickly. One day the ground was covered in dead leaves, and the next we were submerged in snow, which piled up in great, gleaming mounds under a silver sky. Inside, everyone massed together. The great hall was constantly full of courtiers, who came in from their estates all over the kingdom to gather around the king and eat from his table. There was little else to do at the estates, when at court there was endless entertainment and wonderful gossip to pass the time. I knew I myself was a favorite subject, but I made sure to focus on Josef and Snow White, both of whom I loved more than I could have ever imagined loving anyone. I would not let petty talk and petty jealousies distract me from those pleasures, and kept my hair tightly wrapped.

I did appreciate being surrounded by all that life. I spent less time in my chambers and more time in the great hall or one of the galleries, playing chess or cards with Snow White, or Clareta or Yolande. It was the best way to soothe myself in a palace full of ghosts and secrets, reminders of my past wrongs.

Outside, the wind howled. Snow piled up so high I could barely see outside. I often asked the mirror to show Mathena to me, and watched as she sat every day in front of that fire with only Loup and Brune for company, and the occasional desperate soul. I was sorry for her, that her ambition for me had left her so alone.

My main focus that winter was on giving the king an heir. I'd been at the palace since the previous spring, and many had expected me to be pregnant by the time the first snow fell. I continued to study my spell book and use every spell I could find to help me conceive. I used every trick I could to seduce my husband, keeping him enchanted, and we spent whole nights and the occasional afternoon blissfully tangled up in each other's arms. But as my belly stayed flat and my cycle kept returning, I began to despair, wondering if my magic was leaving me.

The painter, Monsieur Morel, finally finished the unicorn ceiling and we all admired it, danced under it, and the master was free to paint my portrait, which he did in the same room, the unicorn and hunters rushing overhead. I spent many hours that winter frozen in place in front of the small man as he captured me on his canvas. I wore my most elaborate silk damask gown with the Chauvin family crest woven into it, along with my crown and the heaviest and largest of the royal jewels, which hung from my ears and neck and wrists.

When I took breaks from posing, Snow White came to visit me. She'd sit at my feet and I'd brush mashed-up horsetail and aloe pulp through her thick black hair. As black as can be. I liked to brush it up and let it fall, in waves, along her back. Once in a while she'd shiver, and look up at me.

"This will make your hair very strong," I said once. "Impossible to break. And then it will grow and grow. Did you know that my hair is so strong your father was able to climb it?"

"What?"

"He climbed my hair," I said.

"Why would he do that?"

"I was in a tower when he came to me," I said, "to make me his wife."

"So you let down your hair?" She whipped around to face me, her hair flicking to the side and hurling pulp across the room.

"Careful," I said, gently turning her back around, "and yes. It fell right out the window, streamed down like a waterfall. He grabbed it with his hands and hoisted himself up."

"That is so silly," she said.

"You can't imagine your father doing such a thing?"

I leaned down to see her scrunch up her face, the way she always did when she was considering something. "I suppose I can," she said. "But that doesn't make it any less silly."

"Are you calling your father silly?" I asked, smiling.

"Well, he paid a lot of gold for this unicorn painting," she said. "That seems pretty silly to me."

"It's very important to him," I said, "to fill this palace with treasures. And it's a stunning work of art, don't you agree?"

She looked up and my hands slid to her forehead. I leaned down and kissed her there, making her laugh. "It is," she said. "Even if unicorns aren't real." She leaned her head back even more so that she could see me. "They're not real, right?"

"Not as far as I know," I said. "But the world is strange. It's impossible to predict what new miracle you'll run into, from one moment to the next."

"That's true," she said, nodding. "I did not know I would meet you."

I winced. "I suppose it was unexpected for you, wasn't it?"

"Yes," she said. "But you make my father so happy. And me, too."

It continued to snow every day, and soon it was the winter solstice. The palace was swept up in preparations for Christmas, as hundreds of geese and swans were cooked in butter and saffron. On Christmas I woke up sick and spent the morning bent over a chamber pot, while the rest of the court was at Mass. Immediately there was talk that I was with child. I took to my bed while the rest of the court feasted and rejoiced. When I was strong enough, I rubbed yarrow oil on my belly, willing a child into existence.

Later, I sent the maidservant away for a moment and shuffled over to the mirror. My own wan face stared back at me.

"Mirror, mirror on the wall," I said, as the glass began to ripple. "Who's the fairest of them all?"

For a moment it was silent. And then: "Rapunzel is the fairest," it said.

I laughed. "That is very kind of you."

The glass continued to ripple. I almost felt I could put my hand in it, that it'd feel like plunging into water.

I tilted my head, continued to watch myself.

"Am I carrying the king's heir?" I whispered then.

For a moment the glass did not change. Then it stopped, became flat and still, and my face came into sharp relief. I waited a few seconds longer, and was turning back to my bed when I heard that one word, "No."

I swung around. "What?"

My own panicked face stared back at me, and the mirror was silent once more.

᜵᜶᜷

I spent the next few days lying in bed, while Josef visited me every hour or so and Snow White spent afternoons reading in bed beside me. She spread out, stretching her legs, holding a manuscript to her face, sometimes reading stories out loud to me from the Bible or the old epics.

When my cycle came after the New Year celebration, the disappointment everyone felt was palpable. Josef took me in his arms and there was no way for me to avoid feeling his grief, as well as the beginning of his suspicion that there was something wrong with me. I felt his heart pulsing up to my hair and forced myself to smile, to kiss him, as anxiety twisted inside me.

"Don't worry, my love," he said, stroking my hair, my face. "It will happen in the spring."

When the snow finally started to melt, Snow White and I rode out into the kingdom, our skirts and hair flying. And slowly, beautifully, the world turned green again. Because Gilles was out training a new peregrine, we brought guards with us instead—a host of them, at Josef's insistence—and watched with delight as the people came out of their houses and bent over their gardens, which were lush and full, or came out into the wheat fields to marvel at the brilliant green stalks, far thicker and healthier than they'd ever seen before. We stopped and talked to the people we'd helped in the fall, including the young mother whose baby boy was crawling now, who stared up at us through long lashes.

One afternoon we went farther out, and when we reached a perfect, open meadow, we hitched our horses to a tree and began wandering through the grass and wildflowers.

I signaled the guards to stay back, as Snow White ran about, plucking up batches of yellow cowslips and purple sweet violets, letting the grass stain the pale hem of her dress. I watched, amazed that this was the same gloomy girl I'd met a year before. I ran after her.

Suddenly I heard the sound of bells. I looked up, saw a great bird in flight, with bells strapped to her legs by leather fastenings. The sky was a rich perfect blue and the falcon's wings spread so beautifully, spanning across the heavens. For a moment I was lost in the vision of it, as if I myself were in the air like that, strong and ferocious. The open sky, endless, and that massive bird soaring through it.

And then I saw another, smaller bird, gliding through the air. "Look," I said, pointing up. Snow White and I stood side by side watching as the two birds circled and swooped. The falcon was hunting the smaller bird—a blackbird, I realized—and they danced, up and down through the air, around each other . . . and then, in a flash, the falcon struck the blackbird, taking it to the ground.

Before we could approach, a horse burst out of the trees, and Gilles rode out into the meadow.

"Gilles!" Snow White called out.

I stepped forward.

"Your Highness," he said, clearly taken aback. "And Your Majesty. Are you alone?"

"Our guards are back there," Snow White said, pointing.

"Good. There are bandits who wander these parts."

She laughed, unconcerned, and handed a bunch of cowslips up to him. "We've missed you on our adventures," she said.

"And I, you," he said, taking the flowers and dismounting the horse. He bowed to her. "Thank you for your kindness, Princess. I've seen the crops shooting up all around, healthier than I've ever seen. There's abundance everywhere. I even heard that some farmers were able to harvest wheat before the first snow came."

"Yes," she said. "Isn't it wonderful?"

He glanced up to me, smiling, before turning back to her. "Indeed. Did you see my new falcon, Princess?"

"She's beautiful!" she said, as we all walked to where the falcon stood over the blackbird.

Gilles walked up to the falcon, speaking words of praise, as the bird ripped her prey apart. We all watched the falcon eat as if she were starving, a bloody mess on the ground. After a while, Gilles signaled for her to leap back onto his wrist. She squawked, annoyed, but obeyed. He laughed, a wide, open laugh from somewhere deep inside of him, and stroked her breast with his fingers.

"I want to touch her, too!" Snow White said.

"I don't know if that's wise . . . She's a bit wild still. We're in the middle of our—"

"It's all right," she said, interrupting him, putting her hand on the bird's head. "She wants me to touch her."

I held my breath, but the bird just looked at the child. Gilles looked from the bird to Snow White and back again, and then stood still, waiting to see what would happen.

"Beautiful creature," Snow White whispered. "Lovely beast." She raked her fingers through its soft feathers. The falcon tilted her head.

"How can the bird let her do that?" I asked. Brune would never have let a stranger touch her like that.

"I don't know," Gilles said, careful to keep his voice low so as not to upset the bird. "I've never seen anything like this."

Snow White just looked up at him, laughing with delight. "She likes me petting her."

"Well," he said, clearly charmed, "how could any creature resist such a sweet princess?"

We watched, transfixed, as Snow White continued to stroke the bird, her pretty hands smoothing down the white feathers.

"So you're training this falcon?" I asked after a moment, pulling my eyes from Snow White to Gilles.

"Yes. Tomorrow I'm training her to hunt cranes."

"How do you do that?" Snow White asked, looking up at him.

"Teach her not to fear them, first."

"I thought falcons were fearless," I said. "Brune was."

"No creature is without fear, my queen," he said. "You have to work it out of them. Teach them to be brave. Brune had to be taught once, too."

"How do you do that?" I asked, fascinated.

"Come to the mews tomorrow, and I'll show you."

"I would like that," Snow White said, pulling back from the bird. "You will be very brave tomorrow, won't you?" she asked her.

The falcon tilted her head in response.

The three of us rode back together to the palace, the falcon high in the air above. I was exhilarated, completely alive as we flew on horseback through the wide-open world. I was happy, despite everything.

❧

The next day, Snow White and I went to see the falcon, walking hand in hand to the mews, with several guards trailing behind us. She glowed with excitement.

As we walked past a hedge, I thought I saw a pale figure behind the leaves, but when I looked more closely, there was nothing there. I turned my head, tightened my grip on Snow White's hand.

Gilles was standing outside with the falcon on his wrist, the hood covering her face.

As we approached, two assistants walked out of the mews, carrying a crane, which was flapping its wings and calling out. The men carried the crane to a stake, held its wings down to subdue it, and began binding it to the wood.

"Oh," Snow White breathed.

"It's all right," I said. I looked at her. Her face was serious, her eyes wide.

She nodded.

"Do you want to turn back? We could read together, or walk through the gardens."

"No!" she said.

Gilles' eyes lit up when he saw us. My own heart quickened for a moment, too, and I ascribed it to my surprise—at the tied crane, at Snow White's insistence—rather than to him. "Ah, you've come. This is her biggest test yet."

"Welcome, Your Highness," the other men said, bowing to me.

"You must tie it like that?" Snow White asked, pointing.

"She has to know that she can kill the crane," Gilles said, "that she's strong enough."

"But the crane doesn't have a chance to fight for its life," she said. "It's not fair."

"You're right, it's not. But the falcon needs to learn what she can do. We must keep the crane very still and quiet, so it doesn't scare her. That's why we tie it up. It happens very quickly."

Snow White looked up at me for reassurance. I became conscious of how fascinated and excited I was by what was about to happen. I wanted the falcon to kill the crane, without a trace of fear.

I squeezed Snow White's hand. "It will not feel a thing," I said.

When the crane was in place, Gilles removed the hood and released the falcon.

"Look at her," I said, as the falcon swooped in the air and then down to the crane. She struck the crane with her clenched foot, killing it instantly. The next moment, she was ripping at the crane's breast.

After a few minutes, one of the assistants lifted the falcon from the crane and perched her on his wrist.

Gilles placed his hands against the crane's breast. Then he reached inside and pulled something out, bright red and dripping.

"What are you doing?" I asked.

"We feed her its heart."

"Why?" Snow White asked, stepping forward. She was no longer horrified, I realized. She knew the falcon had done well.

"She eats her prey, becomes master of it by taking it into herself. This gives her the crane's power, its beauty."

"Her reward," I said.

I thought of Mathena and me eating the red petals in the forest, the eyes of the stag as it turned into a beautiful naked man.

The falcon stretched her wings, stamped her feet with excitement. The ringing of bells filled the air.

Gilles held the heart in his hand and stretched out his arm.
And then the falcon ate.

After that, I started visiting the mews regularly. Often I went
alone in the mornings, when Snow White was busy with her
studies. I came to love the birds, all their majesty and power. I
became a falconer, the way I'd been in the forest. I hadn't realized how much I missed it: the freedom I'd felt racing over dirt
and leaves and pine needles, Brune in the air above me, all manner of creatures crouching in the trees. I loved the feel of a bird
on my wrist again, the moment when it first came back to me,
after I'd released it. The way the falcon and falconer became one,
my heart in the air soaring above me. It distracted me, too, from
life in the palace.

Though spring had come and the earth burst open all around
us, my womb remained barren. Each night I could feel the king's
frustration, which he tried to hide from me. I could always feel
it—when he lay next to me, when he stroked my hair—those
cracks in his heart. Clareta's hands betrayed even more: that my
ladies had begun whispering among themselves, wondering why
I could not carry the kingdom's heir. As Clareta strung pearls
through my hair and sculpted it into ships and castles, I could
feel her own doubt, the way her mind stretched back to that win-
try day when she'd come to the forest, leaving the next morning
with a package in her grip.

By the time summer came again, and the wheat fields turned
the countryside golden, healthy grain sparking up like fire, I
started to feel like there was only one thing for me to do. If my
own spells did not work, maybe Mathena's would.

Plus, I missed her. I missed the forest and the life I'd had before, and I knew she would never visit me in the palace.

I told the king that I wanted to visit Mathena, and he agreed to let me go if I brought Gilles along, as well as a retinue of guards. When he wanted me to go in the carriage, I insisted that I'd be more comfortable riding my own horse, dressed in the simple clothes I'd worn before coming to the palace. No one needed to know that I was queen.

He agreed, of course, for my safety.

"My lady of the forest," he said. "Don't stay away too long. I'm instructing my guards to keep close watch on Mathena, so that she doesn't lock you away from me again."

"I promise I'll return, my king." I smiled and curtsied to him.

It was my first ride back into the forest after over a year of being away. My ladies packed a few satchels for me and helped make preparations. As the stablemen led out the horses, Gilles seemed uncharacteristically excited, greeting me with a warm smile.

"I haven't seen Mathena since I was a boy," he said.

"I wonder if you'll find her changed."

"Perhaps I'll find that I myself have changed and don't see her as I did then."

"I wonder that, too. About myself."

"I imagine your life there was quite different from the one you have now."

I smiled. "A bit."

We mounted our horses and set off slowly away from the castle, through the gates and into the kingdom at large, and then we began to fly. My hair streamed out behind me. The guards rode in front and behind, while Gilles stayed by my side. Occasionally,

I looked over to him and caught his eye, and we both laughed, and I could see that he loved, as much as I did, being wild, out in the open air. That he understood.

We rode hard, back through my past, through the kingdom. We stopped the first night in the inn at the edge of the forest, to rest, and the next day we entered the woods. I breathed in deeply, the scent of forest and life and rot. I remembered the girl I'd been, a bow strapped to her arm, and felt more alive than I had in months.

Once we entered the woods, one of the guards let me use his bow and I hunted alongside the men for fresh venison, though we had plenty of dried meat packed in our bags. I enjoyed the hunt so much that day turned to evening and we set up camp a second night, sleeping on the earth, more peacefully than I could remember ever having slept in the castle, with all its ghosts and secrets. Finally, on the third day, I saw the tower in the distance, and knew I'd come home.

She was in the garden, bent over the earth. As we approached, she looked up at us, her eyes like copper in the sunlight. She looked years younger than she was.

"You've come to visit," she said, as if she'd been expecting me.

Above us, the tower loomed. The trees crisscrossed each other, cutting the light into sections.

I slipped off my horse. Suddenly I was years younger.

She stood and made her way over to me, stretching out her arms. I let her hold me, and took in her scent of earth and herbs, the faint smell of smoke. As usual, I could not feel anything of her, though she touched my hair.

"And who are you?" she asked, pulling away from me and gesturing to Gilles. "You look familiar."

He bowed, and I saw him through her eyes: this imposing man, roughly handsome, his eyes black and burning. He looked like he belonged in the forest, like he was already half wild.

"I'm the king's falconer, my lady," he said. "I believe I knew you when I was a boy, when you were a great friend to my father."

She smiled with recognition and disbelief. "Yes!" To my surprise, she rushed over and threw her arms around him, genuinely moved.

He folded her into his arms more gently than I would have expected, given his gruffness.

"It's an honor to see you again," he said, as they broke apart. "My father spoke so highly of you. I remember you clearly."

"Your father was very loyal to me. He was the only one who was loyal to me, at the end."

"You didn't deserve the treatment you were given."

I looked back and forth at the two of them, speechless.

"Let's go inside and get something to eat," she said, "and then you can tell me why you've come." She looked over to the three guards, who were caring for the horses discreetly. "Would you like to join us?"

They seemed taken aback by her offer, and bowed awkwardly. "We are fine here, my lady," one of them said.

I knew they were thinking of bandits; they'd been keeping watch vigilantly ever since we entered the woods, not knowing that we were already protected.

"Very well."

We stepped into the cottage and there was Loup, rubbing against my ankles, meowing up at me. I bent down and picked her up, carried her with me to the couch. Brune stood on the mantel, and looked away from me haughtily.

"Brune!" Gilles said, striding over to the bird. "What a grand lady you've become. You have aged better than any of us, haven't you?"

Brune hopped on Gilles' wrist, letting out a squawk of recognition.

It was disorienting, seeing Gilles standing by the fire in this little house, as Mathena busied herself preparing tea and heating two bowls of stew for us. She served them to us with thick slices of brown bread. Brune stayed on Gilles' shoulder, and occasionally he passed chunks of meat up to her. As I ate, I could feel my strength coming back to me. My heart starting to mend.

She had always been a powerful witch.

"This is where you grew up," he said, shaking his head, sitting across from me now with his bowl in his lap. "And now you're queen. Did you ever think such a thing would happen, when you were a girl?"

"Oh, no," I said, shaking my head. "But she did. She knew."

I gestured to Mathena, smiling, but she pretended not to have heard. Gilles watched her as she stood to refill our mugs.

"Well, it is wonderful, anyway," he said, turning back to me, "the way fate can twist and surprise you."

It was comforting, being with the two of them, and with Brune above us, and Loup, old and nearly blind now, curled next to Mathena on the couch. I had the sudden, fleeting thought that I could stay like that and never return to the palace at all.

When night fell, I led Gilles and the guards to the tower, where they would sleep. It was strange, having men inside the house and tower, the only real sign that things had changed dramatically since the last time I'd been there.

"I hope you'll be comfortable here," I said, turning to him. The guards were already laying out blankets on the stone floor.

"I will," he said. "I love this place you come from."

"You do?" I asked, breathing in.

"Yes."

"You know, you can see the palace from up here. I used to stare at it, when I was a girl, imagining what it would be like to go there one day."

I pointed to the window. A faint twinkle was visible, spires lit by the moon.

But he did not take his dark eyes off of me.

"Well, good night, then," I said.

"Good night," he said.

I was careful, as I turned to go, to keep my hair from touching him. It would be too dangerous to look into his heart right then. Too dangerous to look into my own.

Once I returned, Mathena sat me down on the couch, took my hands into her own.

"What is it that troubles you?" she asked. "Is your life at the palace what you hoped it would be?"

I took a deep breath. "I cannot conceive," I said. "And the king is not pleased with me."

She nodded.

"I need you to help me," I said. "Give me something so I can have a child."

"What can I give you that you haven't already tried yourself?"

"You know so much more than I do, Mathena."

I thought of her with Clareta and all those women who came to see us, the way she'd take their hands in her own and cast spells to heal their gardens, their children, their hearts. Surely she could do the same for me now.

A sadness crept into her face as she watched me. "Rapunzel," she said, shaking her head. "You cannot have a child."

"What do you mean?"

"You cannot have a child. I am sorry."

"But . . . I had his child. I had a child."

She shook her head. "It has never been possible, for you."

I closed my eyes, remembering the teas and my ancient suspicions. "Did you . . . Was it the teas you gave me?"

She sighed. "No. I told you. When you killed the stag, something changed. Your fate changed. I tried to protect you when you were with child, because I knew . . . it was not right."

"What do you mean? Was it . . . the flower we ate? Isn't there something you can do to fix it? I must give him a child, Mathena."

She did not answer my question. Instead she said, "He has a child already. The princess Snow White."

"Yes," I said, shocked at how casually she said it.

"How is she?"

"She's a good girl. I didn't expect to love her the way I do. But I do."

"Ahh." She tilted her head, watching me as if she knew something I didn't.

"What?"

"Nothing," she said. "I'm surprised that you love the child. When her mother took him away from you."

"That was not her fault," I said. And then I looked at her directly, trying to read her. "Mathena, did you do something to me, to make me barren?"

"No," she said, and I was sure, in that moment, that she was lying. She smiled softly, and yet her eyes were hard as diamonds. "But it is true that you will never conceive."

I let the information sink into me, and with it, a whole new sense of the world and what was possible, a new grief that bit into my heart.

"What about Gilles?" she asked.

"What do you mean?" I asked, blinking up at her.

"He's an extremely handsome man, don't you think? You do realize he's in love with you."

"Mathena!" I said incredulously, as if I had not had the same thought myself. "I'm married. I love Josef."

"Josef is a king. You can never be fully married to a man who has everything in the world."

"You don't know what you're saying," I said.

I turned away from her, not wanting to hear anything more.

That night, as Mathena slept, I padded out into the moonlight to visit my son's grave. Red, heart-shaped petals scattered the ground all around it. I focused, tried to send all my feeling down into him as if the ground were my hair in all its magic, as if my own heart—with all its love and grief, as fresh as if it'd just happened—could stream down to him, comfort him in the cold ground.

"I'm sorry," I said, "that I could not give you life."

❧

The next morning, I wandered through the garden with Gilles and Mathena, picking herbs that I thought might help me, the right magical combination that might defy fate and anything Mathena had done. Each plant, herb, and vegetable in Mathena's garden was far superior to anything we grew at the palace. I gathered fresh dandelion, mandrake, burdock root, yarrow, and lady's mantle. For Snow White, I gathered valerian and poppies, and some of the fennel that lined the garden. It felt good, seeing the results of my own efforts over the years. Gilles watched, fascinated, asking us about the properties of certain plants.

I plucked up a bit of caraway and shook some seeds into my hand. "Take these," I said, smiling as I dropped them into his palm. "Carry them with you, and you'll attract a lover."

I laughed out loud when he blushed in response.

I wished I could stop time, but the sun rose bright above us and I knew the king was expecting us in two days' time. When I said good-bye to Mathena, I could barely look at her.

"Good-bye, Rapunzel," she said, pulling me to her, letting her black curls brush against my cheek. "Godspeed."

As we rode back out of the woods, the two guards following behind us, Gilles turned to me.

"Did you find what you wanted, Your Highness?" he asked.

"How do you mean?"

"Whatever it is you came to ask."

Around us, wings and leaves flickered in the air. "Yes," I said, through the pain in my throat. "Though I did not receive the answer I wanted."

15

Over the next several years I was, for the most part, happy. King Josef continued to love me and to fill my life with delights, constantly—new delicacies, otherworldly art and poetry. I loved him and was faithful to him, I loved Snow White, and I grew closer to Gilles, my one great friend and confidant at court. My ladies continued to try to comfort and please me, though I spent more and more time away from them. Most often, I passed my days hawking or riding through the countryside or walking through the palace gardens. Snow White and I continued to ride the gardens and fields and to dispense help where we could, though our kingdom was thriving—thriving everywhere, that is, but in the king's own chambers.

I continued to try every spell I could find, every combination of plants, to conceive. I prayed to Artemis and Zeus and Hera, as well as to the god the priest spoke about. But as the months became years, no one believed that I would ever carry an heir. I became known, throughout the court and no doubt the kingdom, as deeply unlucky. I could feel it, through courtiers who brushed against stray strands of my hair, through Clareta and Josef, who never would have voiced the thoughts they carried inside them. That I was unlucky, a witch queen from the forest.

One day Yolande came up behind me, her hand grazing my hair as she touched my shoulder, and I could feel the thought that was buried in her mind: that she would have made a better wife to Josef than me. Her blood was more royal, her womb more fertile. I wanted to turn and smack the insolence out of her, but there was no use. She was not the only one who had such thoughts.

"Mirror, mirror, on the wall," I began asking every morning, my own ritual, "who's the fairest of them all?"

The mirror comforted me, let me take refuge in my own beauty, though that beauty seemed more and more useless to me as time went by.

Josef's advisors urged him to take another wife, but he refused. Father Martin made clear that he thought God was punishing us. Everyone knew what he meant but was forbidden to say it openly: that God was punishing the kingdom for letting a witch sit on the throne.

Even Snow White began pulling away from me as she grew older. It was only natural, I suppose, that she would become more interested in her peers than in her stepmother, but it stung me nonetheless. I watched her at feasts as she danced and laughed with her friends, the fine-boned children of nobles. It didn't help that by the time she was fourteen, she looked even more like Teresa than she had before. More than once I caught a glimpse of her around a corner and was sure it was the dead queen's ghost returning to me. Mocking me, and punishing me, for what I'd done.

It became clear that Snow White was—and would remain— the sole heir to the kingdom. I tried to tamp down my darkest thoughts, but could not help feeling that it should have been my son. That somehow, she had wrested away what should have been his.

That autumn, I found a new spell in Mathena's book. One that was technically for husbandry but that I thought might work on me. I infused each herb with intent, and whispered over them before downing them all in a tea.

The night of the harvest ball, Clareta prepared my hair and painted my face, and I wore a new dress, a shimmering pale blue, the color of a robin's egg. I was pleased with my reflection, though I missed the laughter of my ladies and Snow White scurrying around me. Now Snow White prepared herself in her own chambers, surrounded by her ladies. My own ladies were silent, giving each other secret looks, and I could feel their disapproval as if it were rain.

I stepped into the ballroom and stood framed by the golden doorway, as my ladies arranged my hair around me. I braced myself for their judgments and dark thoughts. Snow White was there already, sitting with a young nobleman and his sister, both from a prominent family. Her eyes flashed up as I entered, and then she quickly looked away. The king sat at our raised table, dressed in rich, jeweled robes. He was laughing, surrounded by lords and ladies.

When he turned to face me, I could feel the blood rushing to my face, under his gaze. The rest of the court was silent now, watching me, but I cared only for what he thought.

His face lit up when he saw me, as if a torch had been set ablaze within him. He smiled. "Rapunzel," he called.

As I approached the dais, one of the ladies gathered around him met my eye. She was red-haired, someone I'd never seen before, dressed in a pale pink dress that nipped in at the waist and exaggerated the span of her hips. She had hair stuck through with diamond pins and hanging down to her elbows. Her hand, I realized, was on my husband's shoulder.

I glared at her, whispered a quick spell, and she snatched her hand away as if she'd been burned.

"My queen," he said, as affectionately as he ever had.

I forced myself to smile.

He leapt from the table, came around, and swept me out to the marble floor. Everyone moved aside. I looked up, caught sight of the redhead watching us, envy animating all her perfect features.

We moved around and around. I leaned into him, let him guide us both, as above us the chandeliers seemed to drip ice.

"I love you," I said, into his skin, over and over.

That night, I waited for him to come to my room. I lay on my bed with my gown unlaced and pulled down over my shoulders, my hair unfurling to the floor. Around me, the torches flickered along the walls and through the diaphanous curtains that dropped around me. I could feel the magic working. Tonight, I hoped, we would finally make another child.

My skin was warm, soft. I ran my palm down my thigh, pulled up the crisp fabric.

I concentrated, reciting additional spells under my breath. For fertility, for love, to make him come to me.

I rose from the bed and looked out of the window, up at the

star-strewn sky. Surely he had left the ballroom and prepared himself for me by now.

I went back to bed and struggled not to fall asleep, though the mattress felt so comfortable, the fire so warm, the wine had made me so relaxed . . .

I wasn't sure how much time had passed when I woke, but the night was quiet now. I listened, but did not hear even the faintest music from the ballroom, or any sound of carriages leaving from the front of the castle.

I left my room and stepped into the outer chambers, where a guard stood staring into the fire. He turned quickly at my approach. "Your Highness?"

"Has the king come to visit?" I asked, trying to keep the desperation out of my voice.

"No, my lady," he said, bowing to me. But he did not seem to want to meet my eye.

"He has not sent for me, either?"

"No, my lady. Not that I have been told."

"Do you need something, Your Highness?" another voice asked. I turned as Clareta entered the room.

"Lace me," I said. "I will go to see the king myself."

Her eyes darted to the guard and then back to me. Then she nodded, and moved quickly behind me to move my hair and lace me into the dress. I'd wanted him to see me lying half in it, with the flames reflecting off the stones, before I slipped out of it.

As she touched me, I could feel her pity moving through me. She believed the king had rejected me. I was furious at him for letting someone like her think such a thing, and gritted my teeth until she finished.

"Shall I accompany you, Your Highness?" the guard asked. "And announce you to the king?"

"Yes," I said, lifting my chin. I knew he would follow me, regardless.

The palace seemed deserted, full of ghosts and secrets. As we passed the portrait of Queen Teresa, I did not look up, afraid to see her face staring down at me in the dark.

Behind me, my hair made a rustling sound as it swept over the floor. A terrible premonition pulsed up through it, from the stone itself.

Torches cast shadows, stretched my body into something monstrous and long on the floors and walls.

"Your Highness!" a guard said, as I approached the king's chambers.

"I am here to see my husband," I said.

"I believe he is sleeping," the guard replied, visibly uncomfortable. I studied him for a moment and then realized, in one sharp flash, that something was wrong.

I walked straight to the door then, before he could stop me.

"Wait!" he said, as I pushed into the king's chambers and made my way to his room. I could hear the guard storming after me. In front of me, I heard muted sounds from the king's bedroom. A cry, a laugh.

I threw open the door.

He looked up.

He was spread out over his massive, fur-covered bed. On top of him the red-haired woman from dinner moved, her sweat-covered body glistening in the firelight, her neck stretched back, face turned to the ceiling. Even more shocking was the second woman—stretched out next to Josef, fully undressed, her hands sliding over his chest and her face buried in his neck. When she lifted her head and looked straight at me, I gasped out loud. It was Yolande.

"Rapunzel!" he said, scrambling now to sit up, pushing the red-haired woman off of him. Yolande jumped up and began searching frantically for her clothes.

I stood there, not believing the scene in front of me. The room smelled like musk, sweat, sex.

Josef rushed up to me, a horrified look on his face, and the two women moved behind him.

"Forgive me, my queen," he said, reaching for me.

"Don't touch me!" I spat.

I forced myself to look at Yolande, who was awkwardly trying to slip her thin body into her complicated, multilayered dress.

"I want her banned from this palace," I said, without even thinking. The words were flames leaving my mouth. "I want both of them gone immediately."

"Rapunzel—" he began.

"Both of them!" I said.

Already there were several guards at the door.

I turned to them. "As your queen, I command you to take these women from the castle."

They looked from me to him, unsure how they should proceed. I turned back to the king and he seemed to recoil from my gaze, my anger like a fist in front of him.

Yolande was suddenly at my feet, on her knees. "Please, my queen, do not send me away!" And then, to him: "I implore you!"

She could have said anything at all to me then. I didn't care. All the pain and worry I'd felt since coming to the palace seven long years before, feeling all their judgments and disapproval every day, every month, every year—all of it gathered together into one tight knot.

Another moment more and I would have used magic to cast her out of that room. With rage like that, I could have done anything, I was sure of it. But then Josef nodded to the guards. "Take them from the palace," he said. "Obey your queen."

They had tears streaming down their faces, the two women, both barely dressed, and never in my life had I felt hatred the way I did then.

"Please, my queen," Yolande said again.

"Take them!" I said, and suddenly I was the wild creature from the mirror, my shadow self. I could feel the reddening of my body, the dirt in my mouth and twigs in my hair. I was so close at that moment to destroying all of them. I could have pointed at each one of them and turned them to flame. "Take them away!"

He stood next to me as the guards took the two women from the room, crying and pleading for mercy. I remained unmoved. I had *killed* for this man, this king.

A moment later they were gone.

"Rapunzel," he said, turning to me, once we were alone. "I love only you. I—"

"Don't speak to me," I hissed.

Shock and fear entered his face. He'd never seen me like this. No one had ever been angry at him like this. He was a spoiled king who could have anything he wanted.

But he couldn't have me. Not now. Not anymore.

"Good night, my king," I snapped.

I stepped away from him and moved toward the door.

"Rapunzel," he said. "It is you that I love. You who are my queen."

I'm surprised I did not turn him to stone when I looked at him. He meant it, I realized. But it didn't matter.

And then I turned and left the room, walking as calmly as I could back to my own chambers.

"Mirror, mirror, on the wall," I whispered, in the faint light of the fire, after I'd calmed down and let my rage melt into sorrow. "Who is the fairest of them all?"

I wiped tears from my face, and peered in to see. In the glass, I saw Yolande and her thin, tall body, the pale freckles sprinkled over her shoulders. Kissing his neck. I blinked and saw my own tear-stained face, my eyes huge and full of pain, fury.

"Rapunzel is the fairest," the voice said.

I focused all my desire, my pain and rage, my humiliation, down into a point of light, but now there was nowhere to go. What else was there, beyond this?

"Then why did he bring them to his bed and not me?" I asked, staring at my own face. "Why, if I'm the fairest in the land? When he knows how much I want to give him a child?"

But the mirror had no answer for me.

Just my own wild face, staring back.

16

After that, Josef pursued me as ardently as he ever had, trying to dance with me at the evening feasts, coming each night to my rooms the way he'd done before, but I refused him each time. It didn't matter how handsome he was, how authentic his love. I'd waited for him, been locked in a tower for him. I'd never lain with anyone but him in all the years I was without him. I'd killed for him. I'd loved his daughter when my own son lay in the earth.

Now my body turned cold when he was near. He was not a bad man, I knew this. He loved me, though that love might not have been as deep as I would have liked. He was a man who loved pleasure and joy and did not mean ill toward anyone. But he was not a faithful man. He was spoiled, as Mathena had said. Used to having whatever he wanted. It was what he'd been bred for.

At times I thought I should be more understanding and forgive him for what he'd done.

But I could not. My heart was cold, my disappointment bitter.

It did not take long for everyone else to see the great divide between Josef and me. It seemed to hurt Snow White more than anyone. She worshipped her father, as any girl would. She overlooked his sins, focused on mine.

One night at dinner, I was seated at the high table next to Josef. We were entertaining a visiting retinue from one of the great estates in the countryside, led by one of the king's most favored knights.

Snow White was laughing, flirting with the young male members. At fifteen, she was the image of her mother, and had suitors in every corner asking for her hand. The king turned to me and asked me to dance.

I refused.

I'd never refused the king so publicly, and an awkward silence came over the table. Snow White stopped laughing, and stared at me with disgust.

"I will dance with you, Father," she said loudly, standing and walking toward him. "If your own queen will not."

"I would be delighted," he said, quickly recovering. He stood and held his arm out to her.

I watched them, unable to move. My hair hung down to the floor, where it whirled around at my feet like a golden lake, stretching out on every side of me, and I could feel, then, the thoughts of those around me as they watched the king and the princess move into each other's arms and start to dance. Their horror that the queen from the forest, unworthy, with a reputation for being a witch, could reject the king.

More than that, I could feel their love for the princess Snow

White. Their wish that she were queen rather than me. I was assaulted by their memories of and love for Teresa, their disbelief that this young princess could mimic her mother so precisely. Most of the retinue had last been at court for Josef and Teresa's wedding, and now they felt as if they were being thrust back through time to that long-ago day. Lord Aubert glanced over at me, his lip curling, his thoughts rushing out at me as if he'd thrown a handful of rocks: that the king had been foolish to marry me rather than just take his pleasure of me, that there would be blood shed because of it.

All I could do was sit and watch them dance. The king was as handsome as ever in his robes, his face lit up with laughter, his joy irrepressible, even now, and she was the vision of grace, twirling out onto the floor and then back into his arms, tilting her head back and smiling up at the young men she'd been talking to just moments before.

Her eyes caught mine, two hooks. Only I would have seen how much hatred there was in them. Hatred, despite all those other moments, all that love. I winced and looked away.

My heart was full of grief, and loss.

Later, Snow White cornered me in the hallway leading back to my chambers. Her eyes flared with anger. "You embarrassed my father! How could you treat him that way, when he married you? When he brought you in from the forest?"

"I don't . . ." I stopped. I did not know how to explain things to a child, how to tell her that the king had been unfaithful to me, humiliated me with my own lady. That it was not my fault.

That she would do and feel the same in my position. How could I explain any of that, about her own father?

"Your father has hurt me," I said simply.

She was furious, shaking with rage. My own ladies stood back, and just watched in shock. "My mother would never treat him that way! You have driven him away from you. You don't deserve to be married to a king! You, the daughter of a stag."

It felt as if she'd punched me. "Snow White! Do not say these things to me. I love you as if I were your mother."

I stepped forward and reached out my hand to touch her face. She swung her arm to push me away and her fingers brushed against my hair as she did. The jolt that went through me stunned me. All her rage and hurt, streaming into me. I could see, feel, her ferocious love for her father, her fierce loyalty, the way her heart had slowly turned against me as she watched me reject him. How betrayed she felt by me, when she'd loved me so much.

There was nothing I could do.

"You are not my mother," she said. "Don't compare yourself to her! She was a princess. Not a witch like you."

I breathed in. "I only mean to love you," I said. "I would never do anything to hurt you."

But she stalked away from me.

It was a terrible winter, being locked in that palace, the hatred as present as marble and stone. It was too cold to hawk, or to ride on horseback, and, just like that, my few solaces were taken away from me.

Josef left me more and more alone, realizing that he could

not sway me. At every meal and every dance, Snow White was surrounded by admirers. When she was forced to be in my presence, she refused to look at me.

It seemed my only friend was my mirror.

"Mirror, mirror, on the wall," I'd ask, "who's the fairest of them all?"

"Rapunzel is the fairest," it would reply, every time.

There came a night, finally, late that winter, when the inevitable happened. The king took another lover. I did not know who it was and did not want to know, but I could feel it every time my hair brushed a person or even the walls, my bed, the rim of the bath. Clareta came and told me herself, begged me to fight for him, but I would not. I could not.

Instead, that night, when everyone was asleep, I ran to the kitchen,

I took a knife and sawed off my hair, letting it drop to the floor. Each cut was like a blade going into skin, but I kept going, I couldn't bear it anymore, this hair that forced me to feel everything everyone was feeling, all the time. Their hatred for me. My husband's betrayal. Snow White's disdain.

I sawed it off in great hunks, let it slither onto the floor, golden and shining. Alive. I took it and tossed it into the fire, setting it all aflame.

I fell into bed, exhausted. My hair hung ragged to my shoulders, and it ached like a wound.

I slept.

When I woke the next morning, it had all grown back.

There was only one person left who loved me. When the snow finally melted, I went to the mews.

"My queen," Gilles said, turning around as I approached, a falcon preening on his wrist.

I saw in his face what had always been there. That burning in his eyes, when he looked at me.

"I want to ride into the woods," I said.

"Now?"

"Now."

"Do you need guards to come with us?"

"No."

We raced to the forest. My hair flying out behind us, snaking through the trees, a flag and a sail. We passed the inn and kept going.

The wildness of the woods was the only thing that could soothe me, finding my shadow self that lived there, that girl with her hair filled with forest. As night fell, I called out to the four winds, the corners of the earth. The falcons soared above us and it was like my spirit, my soul, was careening through the air and ripping into the star-strewn sky.

We entered the woods and I screamed out into the air. We stopped the horses and ran to get water.

I turned to Gilles.

With him, I did not need magic, did not need to enchant him or call him to me.

The next thing I knew, he was pressing me against a tree, his arms around me, his palm on my face, my neck, running down my breast.

I ached all over. From the center of my body. My hair flew

all around us, in the wind. I slid down the tree, the bark scraping through my hair, pulling him with me. My body wrapped
around his, and my hair cradled us. He was so thick, strong,
pushing me down into the leaves.

I was shameless, pressing myself into him.

"Rapunzel," he said into my ear. His mouth was right against
me, so that I could feel his hot breath.

I hadn't realized how trapped I felt in the palace. I sat on
top of him, maneuvered him into me. I couldn't take him deep
enough into me.

It had never felt this way before, with Josef. This felt as natural as the blossoms preparing themselves to come to life once
more. Death moving into life and back again.

My body was strong, open, powerful. I felt like if I concentrated, I, too, could hurl myself into the air the way the birds
could, rip apart whole animals with my teeth and claws.

We lay on the earth, my body loose and warm, and my hair
wrapped around us. His heart pounded underneath my palm,
pulsing up to me. I could see the way he'd dreamt of me every
night after those long days of riding through the countryside.
The way he'd desired me as Snow White petted the falcon on
his wrist, as Mathena hugged him in the garden, as he stood in
the tower and looked down to the house where I myself was
sleeping, watching me slip out into the moonlight to cry over
my son's grave.

I could feel, too, his own heart: his love of wildness, of beast,
of bird. His longing to leave this kingdom one day and make a
home for himself outside its excesses, its privileging of the court
above all things.

He looked at me. He put his hand against my face and it

made me feel warm, protected. I felt safer here than in those castle walls with the moats and ramparts.

He pressed his mouth against mine. His eyes flicked past me. "Look," he said.

I twisted my head and saw, in the moonlight, three silver foxes, sleek and beautiful like something from a dream.

"Are they really foxes?" I imagined three cursed men moving through the woods. For a moment I was sure I knew exactly what it felt like. As if I were a wild thing, cursed to live inside the body of a human woman.

"Yes, they're real," he said, laughing at me.

"It's hard to know."

"Know what?"

"If they're real."

"There are ways to tell," he said.

"I killed a man once," I said. "Because I didn't know." I was surprised at how easily I could tell him this.

"What happened?"

"I thought it was a stag. I was hunting with my bow, and hit it right in the neck. And when it died, it turned into a man. I watched him die."

He moved his hand through my hair, sending shivers throughout my body. "I'm sorry for that," he said. "She should have taught you how to recognize an enchanted human."

"He told me that Mathena had cursed him. As he was dying, he said that."

"I am sure she has cursed more than one man in her time."

I stiffened for a moment. Immediately, he reacted.

"Does that bother you?"

I wasn't used to someone paying close attention to me. "No,"

I said, lying. "But she did not curse him. She wanted to save him, and then change him back."

"Perhaps," he said. "She is a powerful witch, Rapunzel. She was powerful back then. I can only imagine what she's capable of now."

"I owe her my life," I said. "I used to miss her so much, when I first came to the palace."

"I'm sure she'll stay well away."

"What do you mean?"

"Well, she was banished. She cannot return."

"What? What are you talking about?"

"Mathena was banished from the palace."

"But . . . no one has ever told me that."

"No one dares tell you, I expect. You are the queen. She raised you. I thought you knew this."

"But Josef . . . he invited her to come live in the palace when we were married."

He leaned down and kissed my forehead. "Rapunzel," he said. "They would have killed her, had she come."

I shifted, moving my hands over his chest, twisting to push my back against him. He wrapped himself around me, like a lettuce leaf. One hand on my breast, another on my belly.

"She left the kingdom to take care of me," I said, my voice small. "To save me."

He was quiet. "Is that what she told you?"

The trees swayed back and forth, the night wild and open. Above us, I saw a million stars through the branches that laced the sky, like pieces of thread.

I did not answer him. I reached out my hand, traced the ground, the leaves, acorns, pinecones, needles, bits of bark.

His hand moved down, pressed between my legs. I opened them, let his hand move inside me.

My hair glittered in the moonlight, and a swath of starlight spread across the black earth. In the distance, wolves howled, and my heart with them.

17

It was a gorgeous spring day when I asked the mirror the question I'd been asking it for years. I wasn't even paying attention, I was so anxious to get to the mews, to Gilles. I'd thought that it would be difficult to return to the castle, after what had happened, but instead I felt more powerful, more free. Habit, more than anything, was what drove me.

"Mirror, mirror, on the wall. Who is the fairest of them all?"

"She is."

I stopped and wondered if I was hearing things. I peered inside. The mirror like water, like something I could slip into.

"Who is the fairest of them all?" I repeated.

I waited, and for a moment there was nothing, no response. And then two words rumbled out of the mirror, moved into me like arrows.

"Snow White."

"What?"

"You may be the fairest in this room, but Snow White is a thousand times more fair."

I stared at my face in the glass. Didn't I look the same as I always did? My hair golden, the color of wheat and sun and daffodils, my eyes bright blue, like sapphires. I was a bit older, yes, I was over thirty now, but I had been careful. My figure was long and slender, my waist nipped in, my breasts high.

I pressed my face against the glass.

Her face loomed up at me like a reflection in water.

She was so young, lush. Like a piece of fruit hanging from a tree, so full it was about to burst.

Snow White.

I slammed my fist against the glass, waiting to hear the cracking, but nothing happened.

Snow White is a thousand times more fair.

I ran from my room, from my chambers, to find her.

"Where is the princess?" I asked a young maid scurrying past. "Tell me!"

"She is bathing, I believe."

I ran to her chambers, pushed open the doors.

"It is the queen, mademoiselle," I could hear one of her ladies saying, rushing before me.

She stood naked in the bath, her ladies positioned around her.

"Your Highness," she said.

I took her in, the length of her body. She was shorter than I, and more rounded. Her breasts were full, her nipples a perfect pink. Her hips flared out from her waist, her sex a patch of dark. Her skin luminous, as white as milk. Those violet eyes, lined by thick lashes. Her black hair tumbled down to her shoulders, wet and curling.

When had she become a woman? She was only fifteen, wasn't she?

"What's wrong?" she asked. Her voice was cold, hard.

I stood there. Foolish, a witch queen, speechless in front of a bathing child.

But what could I say?

Two of her ladies stood on either side of her, their hands filled with wet cloths. Behind her, another was waiting to plait her hair, the way she always wore it now, braids lining her face.

I turned and left. I started running, desperate to escape, to get as far from her as I could, far away from all of this.

I rushed back to my rooms, and the mirror.

I bent toward it, lowered my voice to a whisper. "Who is the fairest of them all?" I asked.

It was like water after you throw a pebble across the surface.

The voice came, unmistakably: *She is*.

"Who is?" I asked.

The answer came more quickly, with no hesitation.

Snow White.

"You are wrong," I said, as the image of her naked, in the bath, flashed through my mind.

For a moment, I imagined casting a spell around her body and changing her into a stag. I laughed as I thought of it: that perfect beauty metamorphosing, her lovely face growing a long snout, the black wet nose, the big soft eyes, antlers twisting from her head. Her hands dropping to the ground and becoming hooves. The way she would bound through the forest, her eyes glittering, speaking of enchantment. The consciousness she would have, knowing that she was a princess trapped in the body of a beast.

The mirror rippled. The herbs smoked in their jars, with anticipation.

"Mirror, mirror, on the wall," I asked. "Tell me. Will she marry? Will she be loved? Will she have many heirs?"

A terrible pain seared through my chest as I asked the questions.

What I saw in the glass made me cry in frustration, in grief.

That night, I dreamed of the crane and the falcon. I was the falcon, flying above everything, weightless. Faster than any other creature as I moved through the sky, from the castle to that enchanted forest, the old tower, and back again. It was such a feeling of freedom, the way the air rushed toward me and then split in my wake. Below me, the ground was emerald green. I came upon a stake with a crane tied to it, and as I darted down from sky to earth, a hunger moving through me the way it had when his child had been growing inside me, the crane was her, Snow White, tied to the stake with her violet eyes sewn shut.

Gilles walked up to her as she writhed there, her black hair tumbling down to her shoulders, her skin as pale as cream. I was ravenous. I would need two mouths to eat enough to fill me.

Before I could move, he reached in and pulled out her heart. Bright red, like her lips, like the flowers that hung over my son's grave, like the blossom Mathena had plucked from the stag's remains. He held it in his hands and it burst into flames.

And then everything shifted, and I was in the ballroom, perched on the back of a chair, and Snow White was in her father's arms, naked and lush, red blood flowing from her open breast down her pale skin. There was a sickness in me as I watched, and I hated her for lying that way in her father's arms, hated his hands on her skin, though she was dead and I knew I had killed her and all around them the courtiers wept.

"My love," he said, looking up at me, as my wings spanned out on either side. "Open your mouth." He let her fall from his arms and walked toward me, lifting her flaming heart over my face.

I woke, gagging, unable to breathe.

A silver light moved through the room. My breath came in rasps. I clutched my chest. The window was open, and I could smell the faint perfume of flowers. Slowly, the room came into relief. The same bedposts and curtains, the same hulking wardrobe filled with colorful silk dresses.

I sat up. In the clear quiet of night, everything seemed to make sense in a way it didn't in the daylight. I thought of Snow White standing in the bath, staring brazenly at me with her head high, and my heart twisted in my chest. I hated her. In that moment I hated her so purely and fully that I felt it through my whole body, as powerfully as the desire I'd felt once that had brought the prince to the forest, when I was locked in the tower. It was a hatred made of light, of diamonds, shaped like an arrow moving from my heart to hers.

Her heart in flames. I could almost taste it.

And then a sadness and pain broke open inside me, like a physical wound, as if it were my heart that had been pulled from my chest. Everyone loved her. All the court, all the lords and ladies and knights, the cooks and maidservants, the people in the villages and the countryside and even the East—all of them loved the daughter of the dead queen, with her glowing youth and her book learning and the pure love of God that moved through her. I, too, had loved her ferociously, loved watching her laugh in the garden as I showed her the magic hidden in plants, loved watching her ride next to me as we raced through the kingdom. Even now, thinking of those days, her scrunched-up little face, I wanted to cry out with grief and loss.

But everything was different now. I'd felt her rage like a physical thing. I wanted to scream into that quiet night, that castle filled with black hearts. I, too, had been born with gifts beyond measure. I should have been loved, the way she was. I should have been happy and surrounded by heirs, the way she would one day. This was not what my life was supposed to be.

I grabbed my head in my hands, trying to make the thoughts, the pain and rage, go away, but it was flowing through me like an angry river, and I felt suddenly like I wanted to die, I wanted to fall wounded onto the ground, let my body turn to plant, to roses.

I'd killed the stag, I'd killed Teresa. The only child I'd birthed had been twisted and wrong, but I loved him, my twisted, dark heart, the blood-red flowers that grew from his grave.

I *was* a witch. The girl in the mirror, wild and feral, her hair full of leaves. I was never the regal queen, even when I played the part well. I'd never belonged in the palace, only to the forest and wind.

Something in me snapped. I pulled a dressing gown around me, grabbed a torch, and stalked out of my room and through the greeting room, into the hallway. A guard was sleeping outside and I stole past him, tears falling down my face.

I slipped down the hallways and made my way to the west side of the castle, past sleeping guards and servants. I stormed down the hallway, pushed out into the night air. Overhead, the moonlight bathed my skin. I was weeping, my bare feet pressing into grass and earth.

I could see the silhouettes of soldiers stationed at the castle walls and I started running then, without even knowing where my feet were taking me, stumbling over roots. Then I was at the mews, at his door, the one man who cared for me, my one solace.

I walked into the mews, past the birds tied to their perches, and went back to the room where he slept.

"Gilles," I said.

He was awake, hunched over his desk, reading by candle-light. The flame flickered, casting shadows against the wall.

He turned to me as I entered the room. Even in the dim light, I could see his face fall open as he saw me.

"Rapunzel," he said.

I stumbled to him, dropped to my knees.

"My love, what is it?" he asked. His face was full of worry.

"I need you to do something for me," I said. "I want her heart."

"What?"

"Her heart."

"Whose . . . ?"

"Snow White's."

The words hung in the air like a storm about to be unleashed. The thought, niggling in the back of my mind, had burst forth like an arrow to a stag's throat. And once it had a shape and a presence, it became larger and larger, and it was everything I'd ever wanted, all my pain and grief, all the things I should have had in my life and didn't.

If she wouldn't love me, if the people would love her and not me, if the king would lavish her with attention and love while I wilted away in my chambers, growing older and older and less and less beautiful with each passing year, if she would live in-stead of *my son,* then I would have her heart.

He looked at me in horror. "Rapunzel, you are asking me to kill the king's heir?"

"Please, Gilles," I said. "Do this for me."

I could see his horror and love, his fear and confusion, playing out over his face.

"No one loves me but you," I said. "I have nothing but you. Please help me."

I could feel the love coming off of him. I took it inside me as if it were a piece of warm bread he was offering. I focused in, made it into a point of light, used every bit of power I had to sway him, if his love for me was not enough. I leaned in and kissed him, letting it flow back from me to him.

He looked back at me in horror. "How can you ask such a thing?" he said.

I could feel him weakening under me. I slipped my arms around him and I was on top of him, straddling him on the chair, my feet bare and covered in grass and mud. "Bring me the heart of Snow White," I whispered. I took his face in my hands, brought his lips to mine. "Will you do this for your queen?"

His eyes glittered in the dim light. He didn't have a choice.

His voice cracked as he answered.

"Yes."

18

When I woke up the next morning, the sun was falling through the open windows, streaming in like water. I sat up, and all the events from the night before came rushing back to me. My feet were scraped up, my nightgown wet and stained. A maid-servant, who'd been hovering near the doorway waiting for me to wake, entered the room, casting her eyes down when she saw the state I was in.

As soon as I was dressed, I went to Mass and to eat in the great hall, looking for Snow White all the while, wondering if I'd really asked Gilles to bring me her heart and if he was going to do as he'd promised. Snow White was not in her usual place next to the king. A shiver moved through me. Quietly, I ate my bread and meat, forcing myself to swallow.

After, I went to see Gilles. I walked over the castle grounds to the mews, and the light was so strange and different, the sun behind a mass of silver clouds yet with rays of light streaming through them. It seemed a sign of some kind. A sign that things would change, finally, for me.

I walked inside and rapped on the door to his private room. There was no answer. After a moment, I pushed the door. He wasn't there. I stood, letting myself inhale his scents, his presence. I could almost feel his hands moving over me and his mouth on my skin.

I walked over to his bed and spread myself out, letting myself linger though I knew it was dangerous for me to be here. I needed to stay away from Gilles, in case anyone had seen him and the princess and realized what had been done. But for one moment, just this one, I let myself remember the days when the three of us had gone riding in the kingdom, when Snow White petted a falcon as if it were a cat, when her face showed such joy seeing the flourishing crops throughout the countryside.

I shook the memories away. Those days were long past. I concentrated on this moment now, whispering a simple protection spell over him. That he should meet no obstacles in his path and return unharmed.

I forced myself to leave his room and enter the mews. Without him there, it was eerier than it'd ever been before. I thought of my dream then, which flashed before me, and how she'd been tied like the crane. I imagined her, suddenly, with jesses around her ankles, bells tinkling when she moved, her face covered in a black hood.

I looked out the door, into the daylight. The perches outside were empty.

"Who's there?" A voice cut through the empty air. "Your Highness?"

I whirled around, expecting to see Gilles, but it was one of his assistants, who bowed to me.

"Yes," I said, collecting myself. "Hello. Is your master here?"

"He has gone into the woods."

"He has?"

"He said he heard news of a young gyrfalcon, and so he left this morning."

"Ah," I said. "Well, that is wonderful news."

"Perhaps I can assist you?" he asked.

"I wanted to speak to Gilles about a matter involving the king. I suppose he will not be back before nightfall."

"I expect he will be gone a few days," he said.

I nodded. "Very well, then."

He bowed once again before me.

I turned to leave and then thought to ask him one more thing.

"You have not seen the princess today, have you? I was hoping she'd join me for cards."

He shook his head, but I could not help but notice with annoyance the blush that crept into his cheek, thinking of her. "I have not," he said.

I turned away, nearly stumbling out of the mews and onto the soft grass. I hurried back to my chambers, as quickly as I could.

"Your Highness!" a lady called out as I rushed by her, but I did not stop. I wanted to go to my mirror, and see if it was done.

"Queen Rapunzel . . ." one of my ladies began.

I ignored her, pushed into my bedroom just as tears started running down my face. There was so much happening inside me that I could not understand, so many feelings running through me at once.

But my room was not the refuge I had expected. My husband was there waiting for me, standing in his robe and crown. I closed the door and we were alone.

"Josef!"

"Rapunzel," he said, his voice soft. "My queen. What is the matter?"

"I . . ."

He moved forward, took me into his arms. It had been nearly a year since he'd visited my bedchamber. For a moment, my heart froze in my breast. Did he know? Could Gilles have betrayed me? Suddenly I was certain of it: that Gilles had gone straight to him and told him what I'd asked. And now the king was in my bedroom. They would have me hanged for treason.

"How are you, my lord?" I asked, my voice catching. "I did not expect you."

"I was just at a council meeting," he said. "And then I came to see you."

"What is it?" I asked. "Has something happened?" I braced myself, tried to get my wits together and have some control over what would happen next. I had brought Josef to me once and made him love me. Surely I could defend myself against him now.

He brought one hand to my face, the other to my breast. "I've missed you," he said.

I forced my body not to tense up, but to melt into him the way it would have done once, when I loved him. I watched him, as he bent down and kissed my neck, murmuring into my skin.

"And that's why you're here?" I asked.

"Yes," he said, lifting up his face to look at me. I studied him for a moment, expecting to find something angry in his expression. Instead, I saw that same glazed look in his eyes, that mist of longing and desire. He was still enchanted, after all these years, despite all the other women.

The thought hit me: that he had come to say good-bye to me, before they took me away. He leaned down and kissed me, his mouth soft and warm. I forced myself to kiss him back, though my insides were twisting. I was sick with fear.

As he held me, I reached up and unloosed my hair, let it fall around him. Immediately his desire overwhelmed me, as it passed between us. I looked at him, trying to figure out what he knew, what was buried in his heart, but there was so much worry and war there already that I could not see past it, and so, for the first time in almost a year, I lay with him, let him pull off my dress and move inside me, though I could not enjoy this coupling.

I closed my eyes but could not block out the horrible scenarios flashing before me, what they would do if they found out that I'd tried to have the princess killed. I saw myself hanging from the gibbet, my hair extended like snakes on the ground below me, or bent over with an ax at my neck, the iron cold against my skin. I could feel my feet encased in hot iron shoes, forcing me to dance and dance as everyone screamed with laughter and delight.

After, he fell asleep in my bed, with his arms around me. I lay awake beside him. When I could see he was in a deep slumber, I unwrapped him from me, gently, and went to the mirror.

I stared right into it.

"Mirror, mirror, on the wall," I said. "Who's the fairest of them all?"

At first nothing happened. My own face stared back at me.

Just when I was about to ask it again, the answer came: "She is. Snow White."

Her image flashed across the glass but it was different now, darker. I tried to focus, just as it faded out of view, revealing, once again, my own face.

I nearly cried out with pain and frustration. She was alive yet. Perhaps sitting in the great hall this very moment, next to Gilles and the council.

The look on my face with those thoughts took me aback. My

wrinkled forehead and pulled-back lips made me look old, hideous. Quickly I relaxed my face and watched my beauty return.

The sun was beginning to set when the king woke and turned sleepily toward me, grasping me in his arms. He took his leave, as if all were normal, kissing me full on the mouth. I stood and watched the closed door, waiting for them to come for me. Instead, it was my maidservants and ladies who entered to ready me for the night's revelries.

When Snow White did not appear at dinner that evening, a team of guards was sent to find her. Later, they reported that they could not locate her anywhere in the palace or on the palace grounds. All her ladies were questioned. None of them knew where she was, only that she'd been gone since that morning and that they'd assumed she was wandering the gardens or reading in the library.

When I returned to my chambers, I rushed to the mirror, stared in at my own face, wide open now with desire, with hope.

"Mirror, mirror, on the wall," I said. "Who's the fairest of them all?"

"She is the fairest of them all. Snow White."

Her image sparked in the glass.

"Show her to me as she is now," I said.

Instantly her image disappeared. In its place was a tree with tangled, massive branches, a trunk covered in knots. Above, the sky was darkening with gathering clouds. Then there she was again, with a cloak around her now, a heavy hood, her eyes full of terror. The branches seemed to be reaching out for her on all sides. Eyes stared at her, from the dark woods. I watched, breathless. Was she alone?

I peered in, willed the picture to widen, so I could see more of what surrounded her. I did not recognize her location; she might have been near the tower or on the other side of the forest.

And then he came into focus. Gilles. A horse beside him, walking behind her, as she looked on every side of her, afraid of her own shadow, the trees looming on all sides.

My heart quickened again as I watched and saw the blade gleaming from his belt.

"Is this happening now?" I whispered. "Are you showing me what is happening right now?"

The mirror remained silent, and the image faded out, until my own face appeared again. Softer now, though I could not help but notice the lines stretching from my mouth, the way my eyes sagged.

The council met to plan a course of action. The king and his advisors were convinced that Snow White had been taken by his enemies to ignite a full-blown war between the East and West. Some posited that it was Queen Teresa's relatives who had taken her, a dissenting group led by her uncle, who wanted to claim Snow White for the East and sever all ties to our kingdom. Everyone had a theory. I sat back and watched, helping each rumor along when I could. Checking the mirror every hour for some sign of her fate.

❦

One day, nearly a week after Snow White had disappeared, a guard came to the door of my chambers and delivered a message to me from Gilles.

"He wants you to know he has captured a gyrfalcon," the messenger said, "as you asked him to."

A trembling came over me as I let his words sink into me.

"Thank you," I said, forcing my voice to stay calm.

"He asked me to deliver this to you."

And he handed me a small box, with designs forged over the top of it. I took it, with shaking hands. "Thank you."

He bowed.

I retreated to my bedroom and sat down at the desk. I traced the designs on the box with my fingers. Fittingly, there was a falcon in flight, its wings spanning the length of the box. Under it, birds of every other kind, oblivious to the threat above them.

I breathed in.

I opened the box.

And there, lying in the velvet interior, was a bloody heart.

19

The torches flickered in my dark room, casting monstrous shadows on the wall. I locked the door and slipped out of my dress. I took her heart in my hands, and focused until I could feel her life's force emanating from it, into me.

I almost loved her then, the way I had when she was a child.

I took her heart and placed it over the fire. I brought my bloody hands to my face as I watched her heart cook, as the smell of meat drifted through the room. I moved my palms down my face, my neck, my breasts, my torso, whispering a spell to take her youth and fertility inside me, to meld her heart with my own.

I thought of the day he first climbed my hair and created a child with me in the tower. The feel of that child kicking in my womb, the boy who should have been king. "My child, my son," I whispered, with tears running down my face.

I took her heart from the fire, letting it burn my hands as if it really had turned to flame.

And then I ate it.

As the days went by with no sign of Snow White, the whole palace was in turmoil. Josef was beside himself with worry, and met with his council constantly, gathering reports from spies and anyone his guards saw fit to question. Soldiers amassed outside the palace gates, waiting for instructions from the king. Huge numbers of people were brought in for questioning. Some were tortured so thoroughly that they confessed to all kinds of horrible plots. Others spoke about Queen Teresa's murder nearly a decade before, until the old rumors started up about the king himself. Those caught speaking openly about the king's guilt were arrested, and soon the gallows filled with their bodies.

Strangely, the mirror went silent, even when I asked who was the fairest of them all. Day after day, my own face stared back at me in the flat glass. But the mirror had always been fickle, and I thought I knew the answer, anyway.

At first I avoided Gilles and the mews, but no one had mentioned his name except to note that he'd caught an especially fine gyrfalcon in the forest.

I made a great show of how much I missed Snow White, and how I worried for her fate. I dressed in black and wore a black veil. I spent hours in the chapel with Father Martin and all the ladies of the court, praying for her safe return. I made sure to always be seen with a prayer book in my hand.

She was the heir to the kingdom, the fate of us all. Though I had not been able to provide an heir in all this time, I felt that Snow White's heart had changed something in me. My hair was more soft, more shining, my face more lovely, my figure more pleasing. People began commenting on this so much that I took pains to make myself more plain, and answered again and again that I only appeared to look more beautiful because the girl who was the fairest in the land had vanished.

Which was, of course, true.

In the privacy of my chambers, however, I took much pleasure in my increased beauty, the vitality I felt running through my body. I told myself that when I gave birth to the kingdom's heir, it would all be worth it, all this suffering.

One afternoon, when I could no longer stand being apart from him and had relaxed enough to feel safe, I went to the mews to see Gilles. I covered my hair and dressed in a long cloak, so no guards would recognize me and follow.

I found him outside with one of the hooded hawks, which stood on his wrist, not moving.

"Your Highness," he said.

"Gilles," I said, letting his name linger on my tongue. He looked so beautiful and ferocious, standing there. My body reacted immediately, and I was sure it was her blood and youth in my veins.

"You look especially well," he said. "Much healthier than when I saw you last."

"I feel well," I said. "Like I've been reborn."

"You'll see I found a gyrfalcon," he said, gesturing to the bird.

"Yes."

I stared at him. He stared back at me, his expression unreadable.

"Perhaps we might go inside?" I asked, quickly glancing around. The grounds were empty. The court was too tense for revelry.

Still, to be safe, I took a moment to cast a protection spell around us, to blur the sight of anyone who might see.

He nodded. We stepped into the mews, where he replaced the falcon onto its perch. He turned to me then, led me into his room.

Once we were alone, I practically fell into his arms. As we moved onto the bed, I felt a surge of energy in my body that I'd not felt in ages, since we'd been together in the forest. I could not get out of my dress quickly enough, could not take him deeply enough into my body.

He moved on top of me, his hands clasping mine, his mouth devouring my own.

When we broke apart, it occurred to me suddenly that I could not feel Gilles' mind or heart at all, though my hair was loose and our bodies tangled together.

I sat up in alarm. He looked up drowsily.

"Where did you take her?" I asked.

"To the woods."

"That is where you did it?"

"Yes."

"Where did you leave her body?"

"I buried her," he said, so low I could barely hear the words.

My hair lay flat and dead along his chest and arms. It unnerved me, this absence I had never felt from him before.

"Was she . . . Did it happen quickly? Was she afraid?"

"She did not know what was coming," he said. "Let us not speak of this again, my queen. It is too dangerous, even here."

I nodded, but could not rid myself of this new sense of dread.

⌁

That evening, when I went to the great hall to dine, the king was shut in his chambers with his most trusted advisors. To my shock, Father Martin was sitting in Josef's place at the high table, the ladies and lords of the court gathered around him.

I wanted to turn back and run to my chambers, but forced myself to walk regally to the table, nod and cross myself, and sit next to him.

"It is the sins of this court that have led us here," he was saying, waving his hands in the air. "God is punishing all of us for the excesses. The feasts and balls, the extravagant clothing, the indulgences of the flesh." He paused, ever so subtly. "Witchery."

I froze for a moment, as I reached for my wine, and looked at the faces of the court. Some had the decency to drop their eyes, others stared back at me without shame, not bothering to disguise the suspicion on their faces. Slowly, I took hold of the goblet and brought it to my mouth, determined not to let anyone see how shaken I was.

I set my wine back on the table.

"Thank you, Father Martin," I said, in a loud, clear voice. "We must remember our worldly enemies in the East, too, who are always trying to defeat us."

"Amen," they all said.

It was a tremendous relief, arriving back at my chambers. I spread out on the bed, hoping for some relief. A moment later, there was a pounding on my door.

"Enter!" I said, bolting up and rising to my feet. Had they come for me now?

It was Clareta. "My queen," she said, curtsying.

"What is it?" I asked.

"I am . . ." She took a breath. "Do you think that Madame Gothel has taken Snow White?"

"What?"

She looked down and then up again, obviously nervous.

"I love the princess," she said. "Which is why I speak this way. I do not mean any offense to you, Your Highness, and I do not speak . . . I've never spoken about what happened."

"Here, come sit down," I said. I led her to my couch, the way I'd led her to another couch years before, when she'd been similarly shaken and upset.

I took her hands in mine and realized she was trembling. "Did you hear something?" I asked, watching her carefully.

She shook her head. "No. It's the old stories that make me afraid."

"What stories?"

"From when Madame Gothel was at court."

She had my attention now. I tilted my head, watching her.

I made my voice calm, soothing. "Tell me."

She was unable to meet my eyes. She held her hands together in her lap and laced her fingers together and apart, and then together again. I resisted the urge to smack them.

"They say she turned a man into a stag. People do not like us speaking of this time, when magic was practiced so openly. Father Martin does not allow it."

I waved my hand dismissively. "I know this rumor," I said. "The man's name was Marcus." Inexplicably, the grief felt as fresh as a new wound, as if I'd pierced him with the arrow only moments before. "He was condemned to die. Do you know why?"

She took a deep breath and continued. "Madame Gothel was with the queen all the time, they say, and advised her and

performed spells for her. But then things changed. Madame Gothel and Lord Marcus both fell out of favor. Lord Marcus was
sentenced to death. They said he was a . . . wizard. They said he'd
defied the king too many times, that he was to be hung outside,
in front of the castle, and they say that Madame Gothel turned
him into a stag right then in front of everyone and he ran away
to the forest."

I imagined it: Mathena watching him as he was led to his
execution, her stepping forward and changing him into a stag.
Was that when she left the castle and went to the forest with me?
How had she managed to get me, before she left? Was I already
with her then?

"I love Snow White, Your Highness, and I am afraid for her,
afraid that she might have gone to the forest the way I did once."

I shook my head. "You know you are speaking foolishness,
Clareta. An enemy from the East has taken Snow White. She is
probably sitting in the Eastern palace right now, being lavished
with gifts."

"But the herbs Madame Gothel gave me, when I went to the
forest—"

I held my breath. This was the first time Clareta had spoken
about that ancient day, and what we'd done.

"There was something in them," she continued. "Queen Teresa died right after that. I know it was my fault." She burst into
tears then, and buried her face in her hands.

"What are you saying, Clareta?"

She looked up at me. "Madame Gothel despises us. I'm afraid
Snow White went to see her."

I reached out to comfort her, running my hands over her hair.
"You are worried for Snow White, and you are driving yourself

mad with your thoughts. We all are, Clareta. What's happened has nothing to do with these old stories."

But all I could think about was how much Mathena had loved Marcus, how she'd never been able to love again, how she'd disavowed men altogether. She must have hated the kingdom after what happened. And yet, she was the one who'd sent me here, right into its heart.

Clareta pulled away from me then, running her hands down her cheeks. "Perhaps I am being foolish," she said. "Like a child afraid of monsters under his bed. I just . . . What will happen to us all if Snow White is gone?"

"It will be fine," I said. "The worst thing you can do is cause panic in the court at a time like this. You have not spoken of these fears to others, have you?"

She shook her head. "I only came to you."

"Good," I said. I lowered my voice and leaned in. "You must not speak of any of this. Do you understand?" I pressed my palm to her face, willing her to silence.

"Yes," she said.

"Everything will be fine," I said. "I promise."

After Clareta left, I rushed to the mirror, which had been silent and dark for days. "Mirror, mirror, on the wall," I asked, yet again, "who's the fairest of them all?"

My own face stared back at me, and then to my surprise the mirror clouded over, sparkled. It spoke in a whisper: "She is. Snow White."

My heart dropped. I stared at my own shocked face.

"Who?"

"Snow White."

"But Snow White is dead."

"She lives still, in the forest."

"Show me."

The mirror shifted, and slowly, faintly, a scene came into view. A young woman lying on a bed. There was a man next to her.

As she shifted, I realized I was staring at Snow White. Though not Snow White as I knew her, but a strange, hollowed-out version, her black hair loose, her eyes huge and haunted. Though she was still beautiful—the fairest of them all—she looked frail, and unspeakably sad. Like someone entirely new.

Another man entered the room as I watched. She did not even react as he came over to her and placed his hands on her thin limbs.

The scene shifted, and I was staring at a large house, a river twisting beside it, trees crisscrossing in the sky.

I recognized it, I knew that house, that river: the house of bandits.

Suddenly it was impossible to breathe. Why was she there?

I had held her heart in my hands!

Whatever I had eaten had not been her heart. I started gagging, uncontrollably, and I rushed to a finger bowl and heaved my insides into it. The memory was visceral: the way I'd bitten into it as if it were an apple, how hard and tough it was, nearly impossible to chew and get down my throat. It had taken at least an hour, maybe two. The blood covering my hands and body, the overpowering scent of metal. I had *felt* myself taking in her beauty and power and youth.

What had he brought me?

I cried out with fury.

He had not killed Snow White.

I slammed my fist down on the table. I started screaming and I could not stop. A maidservant rushed in, and I was crying, feverish, the room spinning around me, and the next thing I knew, the room was full of people and I was being carried to my bed.

Later, I awoke, clutching my throat. I was still half dreaming, swimming in a river of blood, dancing as the iron burned my feet.

I stumbled to my mirror and I looked ancient, my face lined with wrinkles, my hair in scraggles. I looked away and back and I seemed myself again.

I slipped in and out of consciousness. Every time I woke, blinked my eyes open against the light of the sun or torches, I thought again of that heart, could feel the toughness of it between my teeth.

He must have saved her. He must have killed an animal and brought its heart to me instead.

And now she was in the forest, lost. Had he brought her to the bandits? Had they found her, scared and alone? Surely the king and his men would find her eventually, if they hadn't already. And then what would happen—to him, to me?

It was torturous, as I moved from sleep to dream to the waking world, and back again. Several times I woke and saw spirits standing over me, watching me, come to punish me—the prophetess, Teresa, Snow White herself, though she was *alive* and Gilles had betrayed me—and when I tried to scream, they put their hands over my mouth and pushed me back into a dream.

The next morning, my husband entered the room. Even in my weakened state I could feel every muscle in my body tense.

He did not look like the king I knew anymore.

He came to me, sat down on the bed beside me. His face was haggard. His eyes, usually so alert, were red, watery, showing his lack of sleep. A beard had partly grown in, making him look years older. But more than that, it was the way he carried himself, the heaviness with which he came to me, sat on the bed, sighed, and laid a hand on my face.

"Did you find her?" I asked, trembling.

He shook his head.

"I'm sorry," I said, placing my own hand on his.

What a sight we must have been, me too ill to move, lying on my bed of sweat-soaked hair. Him, beaten and ragged, next to me.

"I'm sure now that it is the work of our enemies," he said. "Her mother's family, tired of peace."

"Oh." I just stared at him. "You think they . . . took her? Would they hurt her?"

He shook his head. "They won't harm her. But they want to go to war with us, and they could not do that with her here. They hate our kingdom. They blame me for her mother's death. They think I killed her, just as they say I killed my father before that . . . Though I would never have hurt either of them."

"I know you wouldn't," I said. "I know it too well." And then, though I knew I should keep silent, I asked, "Are you sorry you married me?"

He looked at me. "No," he said. "I've always been enchanted by you. I would have married you instead of Teresa, had I had the choice." I felt tears prick at my eyes as he spoke. "But I have suffered for it."

I clasped his hand, realized that he was trembling. What a

terrible thing it is, to feel your king trembling, even if you know he is only a man, and your husband. "How do you mean?"

"Because you are a witch." The word made me flinch, but I saw that he did not mean it unkindly. "They are saying that Snow White disappearing is my punishment."

I nodded. "So now," I asked, "what will you do?"

He sighed as he ran his palm over my face, wiping away my tears. "We will go to war."

When I was feeling strong enough to stand, I wrapped myself in a fur and went out to the mews to confront Gilles.

He was inside, feeding the hawks.

"What did you do?" I asked.

"What do you mean?"

I lowered my voice to a whisper. "Where is she?"

His face registered the barest surprise, but the expression quickly disappeared. "I killed her in the forest, as you asked."

I stepped toward him. "That was not her heart. It was something else."

"You doubt my loyalty, my queen?"

I wanted to slap him across the face. "How dare you lie to me!" I said, spitting the words. "What was in that box? Tell me what it was!"

"A heart."

"What heart? She lives! I know that Snow White still lives."

He looked around, then strode over to me, placed his hand over my mouth. "Be careful, my queen," he said into my ear. "You must not let anyone hear you speak of this."

I struggled in his arms.

He continued. "You would have our kingdom go to war over your petty jealousies. She is the heir to the throne! She's just a child! How could you have asked such a thing, and of me?"

My hair was tangling around my neck, pulling at my skin. He tightened his arms around me. I continued to struggle against him, furious to feel his love and worry pulsing through.

"Let me go!" I screamed, biting into his palm, and he released me suddenly, causing me to fall to the floor.

I stood up, my whole body alive with anger. I might have been a bolt of lightning, a storm.

"I could not kill her," he said. "Not even for you."

"Then where did you take her? Where is she?"

"I took her to where she would be safe from you."

"In a house full of criminals?" I yelled. As I accused him, I realized how much it pained me, how much I hated the image of her being abused. I had loved Snow White like a mother once and I loved her still, despite everything. "I wanted her dead. I did not want her to be tortured."

"What are you talking about?"

"She is in the forest, in a house of bandits."

He did not seem to understand me. His confusion seemed genuine. "I did not kill her," he said. "I took her into the forest, but I did not take her to a house of bandits. I made sure she was safe."

"Then where is she?"

The room seemed to be spinning. The falcons and hawks became terrifying in their hoods.

He paused. "I took her to Mathena. She has promised to protect her."

20

I stared at him in disbelief. And then I knew, suddenly, that I had to find her and fix what I'd done. I felt it, down to my blood and bones, the terrible mistake I'd made. I turned and ran to the stables and demanded a horse, and then I spurred my heels into its side and raced through the palace gates, past the soldiers' encampments, the streets lined with houses.

"Go!" I cried, digging my spurs into the horse, and we flew through the kingdom.

Guards rushed to follow, but I was driven by passion, by magic, and soon I was out of their sight altogether.

Nothing made sense anymore. All I knew was that Snow White was in the house of bandits, and that Mathena had taken her there. I knew I had been the one to send Snow White to the forest, to ask for her heart, but I'd never meant to make her suffer the way she was suffering now.

When I was exhausted, I stopped, and made a camp for myself in the leaves. After feeding and watering my horse, I let down my hair and wrapped it around me like a blanket.

As I began to drift to sleep, I could see Mathena up in the tower, staring at the castle, imagining me as queen within it. She had known how much I would suffer, not being able to give the king an heir. Knew how much I would come to hate the child Snow White.

Seven years I'd spent in the kingdom, before she saved me. Seven years after my child died, I went back and became a queen. Now eight more years had passed.

The world was hazy around me.

I was half sleeping, half awake.

Suddenly I understood something. She had been lying in wait, hadn't she, all these years? She'd been a favorite at the court for all that time, and then she was cast out. Her beloved, condemned to death. She'd tried to save him, but ended up giving him a fate that was worse than dying.

I knew then why she'd taken me into the forest all those years before, and why she'd spent all that time training me to be a witch.

I sat up, my heart hammering in my chest. All around me the forest moved, shifted, hiding its secrets.

I was her revenge. The one who would avenge her. I had already done it, hadn't I? I had managed to marry the king and become his queen. I had tried to kill the kingdom's sole heir. I had not been able to produce an heir of my own.

She had foreseen all of it, set all of it into motion.

At dawn, I rode through the forest, past the ancient trees and the twisted river until I saw the tower stretching through the trees, and soon afterward I reached the cottage.

The garden was spilling over with rotting vegetables. She

had more bounty than she knew what to do with and could not tend to it all alone.

I pushed open the front door and walked in. My hair seemed to crackle around me as it swept over the dirt floor.

She sat on the couch by the fireplace, a pile of dried sage in front of her. Brune was perched on the mantel, spreading her wings. Loup lay curled in a ball in front of the fire. Stew heated over the embers, and I recognized the smell of cooking carrots, gravy, herbs, meat—a concoction I'd eaten countless times in my youth.

"Rapunzel," she said, looking up at me, as if she'd been expecting me.

It was years earlier, suddenly, and nothing else had happened. I might have dreamed everything. She watched me, and I blinked, looked away. She was still a more powerful witch than I'd ever be.

"Come sit with me," she said, making her voice warm, inviting.

I walked over to the chair across from her and sat down like any number of heartbroken souls had before. I had grown more powerful over the years. I could feel those souls, the clamor of their pain, their furtiveness as they entered the dark woods to consult with witches.

"You look wonderful," she said.

"Thank you," I said. "You look just the same." It was true. Her hair was still deep black, and her face was as I remembered. She had always been a stunning woman. "I could have been gone for one minute."

"Perhaps you were," she said, smiling.

I had a woozy feeling, wondering if I'd imagined everything. "Stop it."

She went back to her sage, sorting it into bundles. "You've turned out just as I hoped you would."

There was a pain in my gut, a sick feeling taking hold. "You did hope things would happen this way, didn't you?"

"What do you mean, child?"

"You hate the kingdom. You hate everything about it."

She looked at me, and her eyes were hard in a way I'd never noticed before. Had they always been that way? "I never pretended to feel otherwise."

"But you wanted me to be queen. Why?"

"You loved a king."

"Don't lie to me," I said. "You know he wasn't my true love, that I was just a foolish girl. You did not want me to see him, to go to a ball, to have his child. You only wanted me to be queen."

"I wanted a good life for you."

I leaned forward. "You sent me to the palace for revenge, didn't you?"

She looked at me. Her brown eyes seared into me. "You are queen," she said, "and you are with the man you wanted. And you are the most beautiful woman in all the kingdom."

"Other than her."

"Who is to say?"

"The mirror you gave me," I said.

She shook her head. "You cannot blame me for your own thoughts, my child. For the fears that come over you, when you look at yourself in the glass."

"Where is she, Mathena?"

"Who?"

"Snow White. I know Gilles brought her to you. Why would he do that?"

"He wanted to save her. He is a good man, Rapunzel. A better man than that ridiculous king."

"You took her to the house of the bandits," I said. "Why would you do that?"

"Why does it matter? You wanted to eat her heart."

"But I . . ."

"Stop it!" she said, sharp and bitter. "Do not be weak. Gilles only brought her here because of you."

"Why do you hate the kingdom so much?"

"Because they cast me out," she spat. "After all I'd done for them."

She was shaking with anger. From the mantel, Brune let out a long squawk. The whole room turned black with her rage.

"Because the king and queen betrayed you?"

"They all betrayed me. I loved the king and queen, and he forced himself on me, and I was innocent. No one defended me."

"King Louis? He forced himself on you?"

She nodded to me as it sank in.

"He raped you," I said. "That is why you sent her to the bandits. So they would do the same to her."

"Yes," she said, through gritted teeth.

"What happened?"

I reached over and took her hand. A lock of my hair was caught on my arm. I felt a spark of energy when I touched her, and then all her agony and rage moved into me, in a rush of darkness that nearly knocked me unconscious. She had always been hidden to me, before this moment. Now I understood why.

"One night, he sent for me. I thought the queen needed me, I rushed to his room. He had had much to drink. I resisted, but it did not matter. He was accustomed to taking whatever he wanted." Her speech had all the fever of words long held back and being released for the first time. "He was a king. He did not care that I loved another, or that I loved his wife the queen. He took me as if I were a common whore."

"And then?" I asked, choking through the blackness of her heart. I had to twist my hand away, for some relief. She barely seemed to notice.

"Marcus found me that night. I told him what had happened. When he confronted the king, Louis named him a heretic and sentenced him to death. I told the queen what had happened and begged her to intercede, but she blamed me for all of it."

I was speechless, watching her.

"No one interceded. None of my friends at court dared to stand up to the king. When they were leading Marcus to the gibbet, to hang him . . . That is when I turned him into a stag. It was the only way to save him. As they were leading him from his cell to the platform."

"And then you couldn't change him back."

"No. I tried but I never could. I tried for nearly twenty years."

"Is that when you left the kingdom? After you changed Marcus?"

"They banished me. I had to leave after performing that kind of magic. That's when I came here, into the forest."

Something seemed off in what she was saying. "To . . . You mean that's when you came here, to this cottage, this tower?"

She nodded slowly, watching me intently.

"But I thought you went with me," I said. "You lived next

door to my parents, my mother who longed for the rapunzel in your garden."

"No," she said. "I came straight here. To leave the kingdom, and be closer to Marcus. I realized I was pregnant with you shortly after that."

"But . . ." I stopped. It was too unthinkable to say out loud.

She nodded. "I am your mother, Rapunzel."

"No. That does not make sense. My mother . . ." I realized, then, that everything I thought I knew about myself, she had told me. The abusive parents, the rapunzel my father had stolen, the mother wasting away from hunger and need. I looked at her again. "You . . . ?"

"Yes," she said. Her eyes grew wet as she watched me. "I thought it was better that you not know."

"Is . . . Marcus was my father?" I lowered my voice as a realization of horror descended on me. "Am I the daughter of a stag, as the gossips at court say? Is that why you did not want to tell me?"

She shook her head sadly. "My daughter," she said, reaching out to take my hand in her own. "Marcus is not your father."

"But then . . ." The momentary relief was replaced by something worse. A dawning notion that was more horrible. Unthinkable.

"Not . . . the king?"

Her eyes did not leave my face. Her hand gripped my own. Slowly, almost imperceptibly, she nodded.

A dizzy unreality made me numb. It took many moments for me to really understand what she was saying, and what it meant.

"That would mean . . ."

I looked to her, waiting for her to tell me this was all a

mistake, but she just sat watching me with those wet, sad eyes.

"Josef," I said, finally, verbalizing the terrible thought. "He is my half-brother."

"Yes."

"I am married to my brother?"

"Yes. As Hera was to Zeus."

I snatched my hands out of hers, and put them on my belly. I was sick. The same sick I'd felt realizing that I'd eaten the heart of an animal. All those years, all that time. Him climbing my hair, coming back for me, making me his wife. My brother. And she had known. My mother.

I shook my head. "Why would you— You wanted me to marry him. You killed Teresa so that I could marry him. How could you do that, when you knew?"

"The prophecy," she said.

"What?"

"The prophecy. An old prophecy, made centuries ago by a very great sorceress. She said that the kingdom will end when a brother and sister lie together on the throne. Now, finally, the prophecy is fulfilled. This kingdom will end with you. Even now the armies are gathering outside the castle gates. The Chauvin pendants are falling. The one heir, Snow White, is gone."

"Is this all . . . because of what they did to you? You would destroy the whole kingdom for it?"

"I loved my king, I loved my queen, I loved the court, more than anything," she said, with a fury and grief I'd never heard from her before.

"Is it because of what I did to Marcus?" I asked quietly. "Is that what made you do this?"

She shook her head. "No. It was done before then, Rapunzel.

I hoped you were the child of Marcus and me, that I had something left of him. And then you were born, and I knew you were the child of the king."

"How?"

She reached down and picked up a lock of my hair, which had pooled onto the couch before falling to the floor below. I braced myself for the onslaught of feeling, which came forth with such vehemence I nearly lost my breath. "You had this blond hair, his blue eyes, his pale skin. You were the most uncommonly beautiful child, and I knew it was your royal blood."

"You must have hated me," I said.

"No," she said. "I have always loved you. I do love you. I *gave* you this kingdom. I gave you a spectacular life."

"I slept with my own brother. My own brother is my husband. It's an abomination! My child—" I pictured his twisted little body.

"We are daughters of Artemis, I've always told you that. Zeus and Hera were brother and sister, husband and wife, and they ruled over all the other gods. You're a queen, Rapunzel. The most powerful woman in the kingdom. You were right to ask for the heart of Snow White, to claim what is yours."

"What about the rapunzel?" I asked. "Is that . . ."

"The forgetting potion," she said.

"That's what the forgetting potion is made of? The one you gave me when I was a child?"

"Yes. I mashed it up, coated an apple with it, fed it to you. That is all true."

"But why?" I asked. "Why did you do that? There was never a garden in the kingdom, never a starving mother. What did you need to make me forget?"

She shook her head. "That I was your mother. All the things you knew, through your hair. By the time I realized what your hair could do, what it told you, you already knew all my secrets. You were only a child, and yet you knew. It took a powerful spell to protect myself from you."

"And now you have destroyed me, and you've destroyed the kingdom. Has it brought you any relief?"

When she did not answer, I stood.

"What are you doing?" she said.

"I'm going to the house of bandits, to bring Snow White home."

"No," she said. She stood, a fierce energy claiming her. "Leave her be. Stay with me, daughter. I have waited so long for this. They made me do this!"

She reached out for me then, and I wanted to cry from the pain of it, that she was my mother after all, and that she loved me despite everything else.

My mother. Finally.

I took her in my arms, and I held her. My hair wrapping around us. All of her darkness moved inside of me, roiling like an ocean, and I knew it would never lessen, that she would always be out here, intent on destruction, that no vengeance could heal her. There was no relief, nothing in the world that could heal the great wound she carried. I knew what I had to do, knew that I could do it.

I thought of all those moments I'd spent with her, growing up. All those days bent over the garden or sitting at her side as we handed out spells and potions, the way she'd carefully taught me how to work the earth. All those moments. And then, for a flash, I saw far, far into the future, when she was very old and bitter, when the little house was full of candy, when children, lost in the forest, would enter it and never come out. I might have imagined it, but she seemed grateful to me now as I watched her, as I focused all of that dark energy, and all of that love, down into a point of light. I took all those memories and fashioned from them a wing, a new life, and turned it from me to her.

I don't know if she knew what was coming. It seemed, from her face right then, like she might.

"I'm sorry," I said.

And then, slowly, her body began to shrink. Her nose lengthened and jutted out, ending in a point. Her face narrowed, with its shocked, hurt expression, which broke my heart even then, and seemed to vanish altogether. Her hair turned bit by bit to feather, her long curls now short and sleek, erupting over her skin, erasing every bit of what she'd been. Her body folded in, over, and dropped to the floor. She looked up at me, her eyes small and wet and glittering, the same soft brown—grateful? I thought I saw it, I hoped I had given her some relief—and her great wings spread out on either side of her body.

I opened the door and after one try, two tries, she started to lift herself into the air.

"Go on," I said softly.

Something clicked, and her falcon's body soared into the air, above me, and I was sure there was some joy, some new freedom in that flight as she flew up the side of the tower, past the window I'd looked out of, up into the sky, and disappeared beyond the canopy of trees.

21

At night the forest filled with shadows. The moon was bright and full overhead, streaking down through the tree branches, illuminating the path in front of me. Behind me, the cottage burned.

I could hear the flapping of wings, looked up and saw Brune with another falcon flying beside her. I smiled, despite myself. Two cat's eyes glimmered down at me from a tree branch before me, and turned away.

I passed the spot where I shot the stag and followed the path he'd taken until he fell. I passed the split oak tree, and I walked along the river, which reflected the moon and stars. I let the horse drink. I glanced down at my own reflection, my streaming hair. I remembered Mathena and me swimming here, the cleansing ceremonies we'd performed here, hand in hand. I petted the horse's long black mane, pulled a few apples from a tree nearby and fed one to him, and put the others in my bag.

Finally, we came upon the clearing, and before I saw the rapunzel, I could make out its rich, strange scent, which even then made the world seem asleep. It was all around now, grown wild, and I wondered how many beasts had come upon it and forgotten their way.

I stepped over and through it, knelt down with it all around me. My hair covered the rapunzel like a blanket, hopefully providing some comfort to him, the man that Mathena had loved. I thought of it, her grief and rage as she cast the spell that changed man to beast, the rage that had colored everything that came after.

It was not Snow White's place to pay for what others had done, just as it was not mine.

I pulled fistfuls of the rapunzel from the ground. I took the rapunzel and crushed it in my palms, releasing its sweet seductive scent, and then took an apple from my bag and rubbed the poison into its skin. When I was finished, I placed the apple carefully back into the satchel.

I kept moving, navigating the dark woods. Finally, I saw the house that stood across the river. From the outside, it looked cozy, lovely, with golden, lit-up windows that would beckon to any traveler.

I left my horse a good distance away. "Stay," I said. "Don't make a sound." I placed my palm on his flank, felt his heart slow down, calm. I cast a protection spell around him and a glittery haze spread through the air; he was gone.

I piled my hair on my head so that it would not weigh me down. I waded into the water, then pushed off the rock bottom and swam across.

When I reached the other side, I crouched down and watched the house. Behind the glowing windows, I saw their shadows moving back and forth, hulking and large, smoke rising from the chimney into the air. I watched for any sign of her.

After a while, I could hear music, rough tones coming from inside, drunken voices. In my blood and bones, I could feel the savagery of these men, alone in this house, liquor erasing any civility they might have had left in them from wherever they came from and whatever women had raised them.

The next thing I knew, a door was slamming and a ragged, bearded man was standing outside, adjusting a knife in his belt. He turned in my direction. Instinctively, I held my breath.

A moment later the door opened again and several other men left the house, one after another, until there were seven in all. One was as short as a child, another tall and thin like stretched candy. Their voices were low and I could barely hear them above the sound of my own heart, but it was clear they had some kind of plan for the night. All those years I'd lived in the forest, and only now did I realize how powerful Mathena's protections had to have been to keep us safe.

They headed around the corner of the house and I could hear the sounds of horses, the clomping of hooves, and then they appeared again, all of them racing forward, on horseback, into the woods.

I sat still, silent, and caught my breath.

There was no sign of her.

I stood, wiping grass and debris from my clothing, and walked as quietly as I could to the house, looking over my shoulders to make sure no one was watching me. Fear made me lose my senses, become afraid of ghosts and other imaginary creatures.

When I reached a front window, I crept up and peeked inside. All I could make out were chairs and a long table, the gaping cavern of a huge hearth.

I went to the front door and put my ear against it, but I could hear only the forest and my own breath. What if she wasn't here?

The thought seized me with a sudden awfulness: What if they'd killed her already? I cursed myself for not bringing the mirror to help me see.

I turned the knob, and the door was locked. I concentrated. Focusing my thoughts, I said a quick spell and tried again. To my relief, the door swung open and I was inside, inhaling the smell of the still-smoking hearth, a fire smoldering down.

I looked around. I'd never been in such a small, masculine space. There were coins and papers and items of clothing scattered about, along with dishes and mugs that held remnants of that night's drink. A staircase led to another floor. I ascended to another large room that contained a number of beds. Seven, lined up against a wall.

She was not there.

"Snow White," I whispered. "Please."

I ran through the house, looking for any sign of her at all.

"Snow White," I said more loudly. "Are you here? Snow White!"

I ran out of the house and back to the stable, to the well, and to the back of the house, where I saw a door on the ground, an entrance to what seemed to be a cellar. Crouching down, I opened the door and yelled into the dark space: "Snow White!"

And just as I was about to cry out in frustration, I heard a faint sound, a voice, in the dark.

I froze, and listened. I heard it again then, more clearly. My name. "Rapunzel?"

"Where are you?" I cried, as relief flooded through me.

"Down here."

My eyes adjusted to the dark and I began to make out shapes

in the cellar. I could not make out stairs. It was a hollowed-out room under the main house, filled with bulging sacks and buckets.

"I've come to take you back to the palace," I said.

There was no response.

"Snow White?"

I looked around frantically for some way to get down to her. Surely they used a ladder, but there wasn't anything in sight. I ran back to the front door and into the house, looking for something I could use.

Nothing.

But I had my hair.

Back at the cellar opening, I lay on my belly and stuck my head inside, trying to find her. "Where are you?" I said. "Are you all right?"

A moment later her answer came. "I don't know," she said. "I don't think so." Something was wrong with her. Her voice was flat, strange.

"Can you stand up?" I said. "Are you hurt?"

"I don't know."

"I need to get you home, Snow White. Before those men come back."

"No," she said. "I don't want to leave."

"What?"

"Go home, Rapunzel. Please."

"What are you talking about?"

"Don't tell anyone you found me."

And then I heard a faint shuffling, and she appeared under me, her pale skin glowing in the dark, illuminated by the small

bit of moonlight coming down. She was even deeper under-
ground than I'd thought.

"Snow White," I whispered. I was shocked at her appearance
even from so far above her, a flatness I'd never seen before in her,
the wide, empty eyes.

And then she was me, locked in the tower, and I was Mathena. But I realized that she could not leave the tower she was in.

"Please, leave me here to die," she said. "I can't go home
again. Not now."

Her despair hung in the air between us, in the damp darkness.

"You must come," I said, my voice rising in desperation.
"They will keep hurting you if you stay."

I could see circles under her eyes, bruises on her skin. What
had they done to her? I thought of that sad little girl I'd first
met, walking next to me in the garden with her back straight,
her dress swishing around her. How happy I'd been to make her
smile and laugh.

When she didn't respond, I continued, "The king is devas-
tated, he can't sleep, he thinks of you every moment. Even now
he is planning to go to war with your mother's family."

"They cannot know me, the way I am now!" she said.

"You will heal," I said. "Be happy again. Let me take you home."

"You don't understand," she said. "I'm ruined."

"People do not get ruined!" I said, though even as I said it I
did not believe it.

She laughed a dull, hollow sound.

"Let me get you out of there and I will prove it to you."

"No!"

"I can give you something so that you will forget all of this."

For a moment she was silent. She was crying now, her tears like diamonds on her cheeks.

"Forget?" she repeated, her voice cracking.

"Yes. You'll be brand-new."

To my relief, she nodded. I knew we had only minutes.

I leaned down into the cellar entrance, and quickly, surely, I started pulling my hair, hand over hand, great chunks of it at a time, piling it in circles until I reached the end. Softer than fur, stronger than an iron chain.

"I need you to climb," I said.

The expression on her face almost made me laugh, despite everything. Here I was a queen and she a princess, and yet the world was as absurd as it'd been that long-ago day when the prince came to the tower to find me.

"It is strong enough," I said. "Believe me."

She just stared up at me as I took the edge of my hair and dropped it through the entrance. The rest of my hair unfurled after it.

She cried out as my hair fell down around her like a blanket. I felt her hands wrapping around it. I braced myself for the rush of feeling moving from her to me.

"Climb!" I said.

I held tight to the doorway as I felt her weight, as she started placing one hand over another.

I felt it then: her pain and anguish, the way they'd taken her body, the horrors they'd enacted on it. I could see their sweating, clenched faces. Their massive hands. I could feel the wound in her body.

In the distance, I could hear the beat of horses' hooves on the forest floor.

"Climb!" I said again.

Older wounds streamed into me; I could feel her shock when Gilles took her to the forest, telling her that there was danger afoot and he was taking her to safety. The constant ache of her mother being lost to her. Her anguish from seeing me turn against her own father, and then betray him with Gilles. She'd known what I'd thought was secret. She felt I had betrayed her. I had to let the images pass, concentrate on what I was doing.

It seemed to take hours for her to lift herself, one arm over the next, my hair gathered together like a giant, thick rope in her hands.

And then I felt something else, beyond the pain and hurt. A strength in her that I hadn't realized was there, that came at me as if the tower itself were smashing into me. She would survive this, I realized. I could see it as clearly as I could see the cellar door, her hand reaching up and folding around my hair.

I could hear them approaching, forced myself to stay calm.

Her hands were bright pink from exertion, her face shining with sweat. As she neared me, I saw that strength, that passion for life, inside of her, past her hollow eyes and thin limbs.

Hurry, I whispered. Willing time to slow down, for her body to be stronger, for Artemis, or the god the priest spoke about, to help us to safety. I whispered a protection spell to the winds, the four directions.

Her hands clasped my neck, and I used all the strength of my body to move back, pressing against the doorframe and pulling her out of the cellar and into the moonlight.

We collapsed together on the grass. I didn't want to let go of her, but I had to. There was no time.

I jumped up, held out my hand. "We must go now," I said. "They're here."

And they were: the horses were wending their way to the stable, which was just in our line of sight. She got to her feet and took my hand and we ran.

"You there! Stop!"

They were calling to us, they'd spotted us, and my horse was waiting on the other side of the river, faintly visible now with the spell wearing off, and there was no time to cast another one, not with the way we were running. I glanced over at her, Snow White, as she raced for her life, toward her future, and I knew then that I did not need to save her, not more than I had already, that I did not need to make her forget anything, and that she would be queen, a great queen like her mother had been, a queen who would bring peace and prosperity to our land, and she would survive and heal and be happy.

I plunged into the river and she threw herself in after me, grabbing onto my hair. We reached the horse and mounted him, me in front and her behind me, the satchel of apples at my side, us riding like men with our legs apart, the queen and the princess, racing through the forest, and the winds helped to speed us along until we were almost flying.

We rode through the forest, her arms around me, until the sound of hooves behind us faded, and then we kept riding, past where the rapunzel grew alongside the river, past Mathena's smoldering cottage and the tower that was just visible through the treetops. Above us, two falcons soared through the air.

I breathed in everything, took all of it in, because the world was wild and open and beautiful and the moment was full and it *existed,* it was happening right then, and for once I did not want to think about anything that had come before or anything that would come after. Here, right now, we were together and we were flying.

EPILOGUE

I sit here now, in my workroom, writing this down as quickly as I can, while outside my chambers the palace rejoices.

I am the true queen, the rightful heir to the throne—though no one will ever know it, and soon enough not even I will remember it. And as the true queen, I have made one decision. It will be my sole decision, but it is the best thing I can do for my kingdom, and it is enough.

It was at the inn at the edge of the forest that Snow White and I learned that King Josef had died in the fighting that had broken out just beyond the castle walls. With no male heir, I was named queen regent, a title I would carry until Snow White turned twenty-one and took the throne. Lord Aubert was acting as regent in my stead. With both me and Snow White gone, the whole kingdom was in disarray

I sent a message to the royal council that Snow White and I were safe, and that in the interest of peace for the West, I would step aside to name her, Snow White, daughter of the West and East, sole ruler of our kingdom.

When I told her what I'd done, she looked at me with that same serious look she'd had as a child, and nodded, and I did not need magic to see the combination of grief and strength and beauty that she will become known for in years to come. There was nothing I could do to console her, except use all my power and everything in my heart to wish her well, so that she might heal herself, and our kingdom.

The next day, we rode to the palace as the people ran from their houses and cheered us along, and in a simple ceremony Snow White took the throne. A new peace treaty was signed, and the fighting ended as quickly as it had begun.

I do not regret my decision.

She will be a good queen. One day, she will be a great one.

The apple sits next to me, gleaming with rapunzel. Behind it, the mirror, reflecting the apple and the room beyond it.

I ask the mirror one last time: *Who is the fairest of them all?*

But I know the answer. Of course I know. It is her time now, and it will be someone else's time after. Her daughter's, her daughter's daughter's. She will have many daughters and sons— I have had portent of it.

In a moment I will put down my quill, and I'll lock these pages away for someone else, someday, to find. Because all of this happened once, and things that happened should not be erased from the earth completely, even when they've been forgotten.

Gilles waits for me outside. He's forgiven me, after everything. I am grateful that he disobeyed me. We will leave this kingdom tonight, and venture out into the world beyond it. He assures me that such a world exists, that he will love me no matter what happens next, and I hope that he is right.

My bags are packed, I have a pouch full of gold, and there is only one thing left for me to do.

The apple could almost be a heart.

I place my hands over it and feel it beating.

ACKNOWLEDGMENTS

I want to express my eternal love and gratitude to my editor, Heather Lazare, who really pushed me with this book, as she did with the last two, and to my agents, Elaine Markson and Gary Johnson, who were always ready to brainstorm and read a new draft and discuss plot twists over takeout in the office. It's such a gift, to have people that smart and generous on your side, and I appreciate them more than I can say.

I also want to thank Jeanine Cummins, Mary McMyne, Jo-Ann Mapson, Jill Gleeson, Joi Brozek, and Morgan Grey, all brilliant authoresses and friends who gave me invaluable feedback throughout the writing of this book. I want to thank Jeanine, too, for dropping everything to read a draft at the last minute while I made monsters out of Play-Doh with her kids.

Thank you to Lance Cheuvront, who told me about hawks and falcons, and to Erika Merklin, who spent a long phone conversation telling me all about her Alaskan garden, and compost teas, and the wonders of bones and feathers and ash. And I want to thank my father, Alfred Turgeon, who let me barrage him over the course of an afternoon with questions about crops and blight. I'm also grateful to him, and to my mother, Jean, and my sister, Catherine, for being so patient and supportive through this and every project.

Finally, I want to thank Steven Berkowitz, who spent hours and hours listening to me talk about this book, and came up with more than a few of the twists and turns inside it. I love you.

THE FAIREST OF THEM ALL

An exploration of what happens when fairy-tale heroines grow up and don't live happily ever after, *The Fairest of Them All* brings new life to the stories of Rapunzel and Snow White.

Living in an enchanted forest, Rapunzel spends her days tending a mystical garden with her adoptive mother, the witch Mathena. When Rapunzel's beautiful voice and golden locks attract a young prince, even Mathena's considerable power cannot stop him from climbing Rapunzel's hair and falling into her arms. But their afternoon of passion is fleeting, and the prince must return to his kingdom betrothed to another. Years later, the prince is now a king, and his wife, the queen, has died under mysterious circumstances, leaving him with a young daughter, Snow White. At last free to marry the woman he has never stopped dreaming of, the king returns for Rapunzel and makes her his queen and a mother to Snow White. But when Mathena's wedding gift of an ancient mirror begins speaking to her, Rapunzel falls under its evil spell, and the king begins to realize that Rapunzel is not the beautiful, kind woman of his dreams.

TOPICS AND QUESTIONS FOR DISCUSSION

1. How is *The Fairest of Them All* different from the fairy tales upon which the novel is based? What are some of the similarities?

2. Many fairy tales have omniscient narrators, yet this novel is told from the point of view of Rapunzel. Why do you think the author made the decision to give us Rapunzel's perspective? How did this influence what you felt about Rapunzel's choices?

3. Many of us dream about living in a world of princes and princesses, where magic is real and a part of life. What aspects of Rapunzel's and Snow White's lives were appealing to you? What are some of the challenges you didn't expect them to face?

4. Talk about what it's like to revisit fairy tales you were familiar with when you were younger. What were some of your favorite fairy tales? What other "updated" fairy tales or myths have you read or watched recently?

5. Princes, kings, princesses, and witches are all common characters in fairy tales, and all exist in *The Fairest of Them All*. How do the characters in this novel compare to the stereotypical princes, kings, princesses, and witches in other fairy tales? When did their actions surprise you?

6. Love of beauty and the complications of aging are important themes in *The Fairest of Them All*; the king and Rapunzel are particularly obsessed with beauty. Discuss some of the pitfalls of a life lived in luxury and the need for everything to be beautiful.

7. At the end of the novel, Rapunzel thinks of Snow White: "She will be a good queen. One day, she will be a great one." Why do you think Snow White would make a good queen? What made her father such a bad king?

8. Describe Snow White's character and the changes she goes through over the course of the story. What did you think of her initial rejection of Rapunzel? How did their relationship evolve?

9. Although Rapunzel and Mathena know a great deal of genuine magic, much of their knowledge is simply an understanding of the earth and of the uses of nature. Why do you think this is associated with witchcraft? Recall some of the magical elements in the novel and their relationship to Mathena (for example: the stag and the magic mirror).

10. Death and rebirth are important themes in the novel. Rapunzel herself says, ". . . out of death comes life. Always." What do you think this means in the context of the novel? Do you think this is also true of the world in which we live?

11. The conflict between religion and magic is one of the central issues of the story. Why do you think the church is so opposed to witches like Mathena? Why is everyone at the palace suspicious of Rapunzel, when (at least at first) she is helpful and kind?

12. Rapunzel's magic mirror is what ultimately pushes her to attempt to have Snow White killed. Is the mirror evil and corrupting, or is it only a scapegoat for Rapunzel's jealousy? Why?

13. Like many fairy tales, *The Fairest of Them All* is largely about love, true love, lust, and infatuation. Unlike most fairy tales, it is also a story about heartbreak, loss, and violence. What do you think about the book's take on love and infatuation? How does the novel's more realistic take on these themes impact the power of the fairy-tale elements?

14. The revelations at the end of the story are foreshadowed early on. Did you catch any of these subtle hints from the stories Mathena told Rapunzel? How did the ending affect the way you viewed the rest of the story? What about how you viewed Mathena?

ENHANCE YOUR BOOK CLUB

1. Do some research on the original Brothers Grimm stories of Snow White and Rapunzel. You can find them here: http://www.worldoftales.com/fairy_tales/Grimm_fairy_tales.html. Are they the same as you remember? How does reading the originals change your interpretation of *The Fairest of Them All*?

2. Write your own fairy tales! Using existing tales as a starting point, or starting completely fresh, come up with a brand-new story to share with your group.

3. Have a movie night with your book club! There are many great movie adaptations of classic fairy tales. If you like animated movies, try the Disney version of Rapunzel, *Tangled*, or go classic with the original *Snow White and the Seven Dwarfs*. If you're in the mood for something different, try *Mirror Mirror* or *Snow White and the Huntsman*, two recent adaptations with a creative take on the story.

A CONVERSATION WITH CAROLYN TURGEON

Have you always been interested in fairy tales, or did you come to them after becoming a writer? How did you come up with the idea to combine Snow White and Rapunzel?

I actually have always loved fairy tales, their combination of light and dark, the glitter and shimmer along with all that hatred and jealousy and eating of hearts! That's kind of my aesthetic generally, beauty and darkness mixed together. My biggest literary influence was magic realism, though; I read *One Hundred Years of Solitude* by Gabriel Garcia Marquez as a teenager and that very much influenced the kind of writing I wanted to do. I came to fairy tales with my second book, *Godmother*, mainly because my first had been so hard to plot and figure out, and I thought it'd be so cool to go into a known story like Cinderella and bring it to life, with all the weird psychology that you know has to accompany things like being a fairy godmother or having a prince come to the rescue when you've been abused and alone for so long. And I've written three more since then! I like how much you can explore through them, using these archetypal female characters.

The Fairest of Them All is the first time I've taken two well-known fairy tales and combined them. I guess I was thinking about all those gorgeous, damaged young women in fairy tales who end up with the dashing prince, and also all those older women who are evil stepmothers or queens or witches. And it occurred to me that these are the same women, grown up. How else are those gorgeous young girls going to turn out, especially in worlds that value them for their youth and beauty above anything else? And when I fit Rapunzel and the evil stepmother from Snow White together, it made sense. They're both beautiful, they're both witches (Rapunzel is raised by a witch, so how could she not be one herself?), and presumably the stepmother was once young and in love and the fairest in all the kingdom. And what we don't see in the original Rapunzel story is what happens later, when she gets older and is a little less dazzling than she was before.

What do you think is so compelling about these stories, that they can be returned to and reworked again and again? Why are they such a rich mine of inspiration for you?

I don't know what it is about them, honestly. I mean, some of the stories we tell and re-tell are awfully strange; look at some of the old versions of Snow White and you'll see what I mean! But these are stories that people have told and retold for centuries, as moral lessons, as escapism, as a way of making sense of the universe. These stories often contain situations that are exaggerated versions of everyday ones so we can escape reality while also shining a light on it, and on our own hearts.

I really like going into these old tales to explore the psychology in them, make these characters flesh and blood and bone. I feel like these stories are part of who I am, stories that helped shaped my view of the world, and so there's something very powerful to me about going in and rethinking them.

What challenges did you face in expanding these fairy tales into a novel?

A novel gives you room to explore all the emotions and thoughts and motivations that inform the extreme behavior you see in these old tales. Like asking for the heart of Snow White. It's shocking, but when you think about and explore the stepmother's motivation, you realize that she's playing out very commonplace emotions and insecurities. She's getting older, she wants to be loved and admired, and attention is shifting from her to this gorgeous young girl. The original tales are all so short, you don't really have time to explore all the complicated emotions you know are at play. And of course, there's all kinds of backstory and setting and detail that you have to figure out and fill in. It's a challenge, but it's also the fun part.

The Fairest of Them All is full of strong, powerful women, and generally has a feminist undercurrent. Was that intentional? Do you feel there's anything like that in the original fairy-tale versions?

I think all my fairy-tale books have a feminist undercurrent. I'm interested in looking at the roles of women in these stories, and especially the relationships these women have with each other. The fairy godmother and Cinderella, for example, the mermaid and her princess rival from the Hans Christian Andersen story, Rapunzel and the witch, Snow White and the evil stepmother ... There's a lot of rivalry and anger and unhappiness in these tales, and I like to explore that and then see if there's some way for these women to transcend their roles a bit and form alliances with each other. Female friendship is important to me, and there's typically not a lot of room for it in the original stories, and certainly not in the Disney movies!

In _The Fairest of Them All_, the main characters are witches, too, so of course they're powerful. How can the castle-bound prince compare with women who understand the earth and its magic?

Mathena is a very unconventional witch—where did your inspiration for her character come from?

I wanted her to be sympathetic and warm and powerful, not the evil hag from the original Rapunzel stories. I don't like that witches, and older women generally in fairy tales, are typically one-dimensional and evil, though of course Mathena is . . . complicated. But I viewed her as deeply haunted and intensely charismatic and stunning and large-hearted, someone I would love to know in real life. She's really a darker version of the sexy ex-circus-star gypsy-like librarian Mary Finn from my first novel, *Rain Village*. In that book, I needed a mentor figure who would help a young misfit girl grow up to become a famous, beloved trapeze star. And so this woman emerged—this black-haired witchy librarian who keeps an herb garden, brews magic teas, counsels the lovelorn (in addition to performing her librarian duties!), and does whatever she pleases. And she's the only one in the town who can look at this misfit girl and see the beauty and magic within her.

Much of the magic that Mathena and Rapunzel practice is actually just an understanding of nature, and the uses of herbs. Do you see a connection between magic and nature?

Oh, yes. I see magic in birth, and in growing things, and in walking into a forest and knowing what each plant is and what it does, and in being deeply connected to your own body and the bodies of others. Knowing what plant someone should bite down on to relieve a toothache, what herb to put under your pillow to affect your dreams . . . I myself do not know the first thing about plants and gardens and very rarely spend time in forests, but it means that the world is even more full of mystery to me, and the natural world full of secrets and hidden attributes.

What led you to work Greek mythology into the story? Do you see a connection between Greek myth and the fairy tales you've rewritten?

I loved Greek myths as much as I loved fairy tales when I was a kid, and they're a bit mixed together in my head. I love the idea of a world filled with gods and mortals, where gods interfered in the lives of humans and changed them into trees or beasts or constellations. I knew that Mathena needed a system of belief different from the Christianity of the kingdom, and it made sense to me that she'd worship Artemis rather than a male deity, and that she'd tell Rapunzel stories about the gods. Both Mathena and her counterpart, Mary Finn, are storytellers, because to me that's a pure kind of magic, using words to make the world appear brand-new. So of course Mathena tells Rapunzel these wonderful tales full of beauty and transformation; it's a part of her character to do so, and it also helps orient the reader to her very different point of view. Probably the main reason I've focused on fairy tales rather than Greek mythology generally is Disney. Fairy tales were just more ingrained in the culture I grew up in because of those films, and so maneuvering within them feels like a more powerful thing to do.

You have a master's degree in comparative literature—did you study fairy tales in your academic career? What do you make of the extensive academic literature on fairy tales such as Snow White? Is it something you find interesting?

I actually didn't study fairy tales while in school. I studied Italian literature (and English literature) as an undergrad and then went on to focus on medieval Italian poetry in graduate school. Part of my Italian studies, though, involved looking at story cycles, these old stories that were in *One Thousand and One Nights* and made their way into Latin and then old Italian story collections like *The Novellino* and *The Decameron*, etc. I started what became my first novel the same week I was writing a paper that traced one of these stories and talked about how it changed over time. I guess that really stuck with me. The power of old stories, the power of refashioning them over and over again into something new, illuminating their hidden parts, giving them meanings and dimensions that weren't there before. All storytelling is really just that—we're telling the same stories over and over again in (hopefully) new ways—but with fairy tales you're doing it more transparently.

In terms of Snow White, I have read multiple versions of the tale, which you can find online. The Disney version is weird enough, but the further back you go, the weirder it all gets. Which I love!

One of the prominent themes of *The Fairest of Them All* is the relationship between infatuation, magic, and love—you describe wonderfully the confusion that surrounds Rapunzel in the evolution of her relationship with Josef. What do you think of the way "love" is used in fairy tales? Do you think there is more "magic" in real love, or infatuation?

Oh, I definitely think that infatuation feels like magic. Imagine being Rapunzel, out in the forest, seeing Josef for the first time with all his riches and glamour and that big gleaming horse. Of course she would imagine that that stricken, dazzled feeling was true love, combined with her excitement, her fantasy about what he represents, the way he could change her life in an instant. I think we often see this kind of instant love in fairy tales, especially in the Disney versions, not to mention in countless romantic comedies and shows like *The Bachelor*. In *Mermaid* and *The Fairest of Them All,* there are moments of instant love like this, but of course this kind of love will probably lead, eventually, to disappointment. We all know the idea that one person can swoop in and save and complete you is a bit flawed, and that the real magic comes with deep, lasting love.

What are you working on next? Do you have more thoughts about reimagining fairy tales?

I'm working on a book about Beatrice Portinari, who's the mysterious woman Dante Alighieri wrote about in *The Divine Comedy* (she's up in heaven and helps initiate his entire journey) and other works. No one really knows anything about her other than that she was an aristocratic girl who was contracted to marry (and did marry) a much older banker and then died at twenty-four. No one knows if Dante actually knew her or if they had any kind of actual relationship, romantic or otherwise. So I've imagined what I think is a really cool and surprising story about her. It's not a fairy tale, but it's a kind of retelling, a looking at something familiar through an unexpected point of view. Plus there will be a medieval setting, a little grittier than the one in *Fairest*, but with a similar overlay of magic and beauty. I think that fans of my fairy tales will like it!

Of course, there are many, many more fairy tales to explore, so you never know . . .